RISE UP

A Novel
About The 1947 Texas City Explosion

Carl Trepagnier

TotalRecall Publications, Inc.
1103 Middlecreek
Friendswood, Texas 77546
281-992-3131 TEX
www.totalrecallpress.com

Copyright © 2022 By: Carl Matthew Trepagnier
Edited By: Chris O'Shea Roper
Book Cover Illustration By: Diane Trepagnier
Title page photo: courtesy of J. P. Blizetec, reprinted with permission
All rights reserved

ISBN: 978-1-64883-1546
UPC: 6-43977-41546-2

Library of Congress Control Number: 2022934269

FIRST EDITION
1   2   3   4   5   6   7   8   9   1   0

Dedication

I respectfully dedicate this story:

> ➤ To all those who died or were injured as a result of this explosion.

> ➤ To all of the magnificent and unselfish professionals and volunteer workers who fought valiantly to curb the extent of this unprecedented disaster.

> ➤ To all those left with sorrow at the loss of family and friends.

About the Author

Carl Trepagnier grew up in Texas City, Texas, and was nine years old (and inside Danforth Elementary School) when the *SS Grandcamp* exploded. After high school, he attended Southern Methodist University on a scholarship, and subsequently graduated from the University of Texas School of Dentistry. He practiced General Dentistry for nine years and, after returning to graduate school, specialized in Endodontics for 27 years. He is a veteran of the U.S. Navy.

After retiring, Carl decided that he would learn to be a better writer and communicator. He took classes at the University of Houston and University of St. Thomas, as well as attended various workshops. RISE UP, his first novel, is the result of these efforts.

Carl has five wonderful daughters and nine beautiful grandchildren. He lives with his loving wife Susie in Houston, Texas.

Acknowledgements

I wish to express heartfelt gratitude to the following:

- To my lovely wife Susie for her constant encouragement and advice and for making my life easy.
- To Chris O'Shea Roper, my editor, for her meticulous professional guidance and for the personal boosts she gave my ego when my confidence faltered.
- To Ann McCutchen who gave me advice in the early stages of development of this narrative.
- To Mary Agnes Neyland, my high school Senior English teacher, my enduring gratitude for sparking an interest in literature that has provided me with so much enjoyment. I remember the exact moment I felt the spark – when she read to the class from Chaucer's *Canterbury Tales.*
- To my entire family for helping me to have a wonderful life.

I also want to recognize the valuable contributions to this story from the following sources:

- Hugh W. Stephens, *The Texas City Disaster of 1947* (1997)
- Allan Peveto, PhD, *Heroes and Survivors* (2008)

Author's Note

The *SS Grandcamp* belonged to a class of ships designated Liberty Ships. Small and speedy, liberty ships distinguished themselves by carrying everything from tanks to biscuits for our troops in WWII. They contributed significantly to the Allied victory. Shipyards churned out these vessels in four weeks (on average) in order to stay ahead of the rate of destruction by German submarines. The *SS Grandcamp* had survived the dangerous Atlantic crossing many times.

After the war, liberty ships became the workhorses that carried peacetime cargoes under the flags of many countries.

On April 16, 1947, the *SS Grandcamp* sat tranquilly moored at the dock in Texas City, Texas, while it was being loaded with a cargo of fertilizer. A fire ignited in its hold and the ship unexpectedly detonated, wreaking immense death and destruction. An anchor that once hung from its side, and which weighed 10,600 pounds, was propelled through the air a mile to the east of the docks and buried itself beside the seawall. The anchor, carried by the astounding force of the explosion, remains where it landed and serves as a memorial to those who died in the disaster.

Texas City rose from its devastation and came to terms with the deaths of 576 people and over 3,000 injured. With determination typical of the post-WWII era, the community put their damaged lives, homes and businesses back together, and looked toward the future. The rebuilt port and repaired industrial complex became one of the nation's busiest. Town administration moved quickly after the explosion to annex the entire area and establish an independent port authority. The public schools desegregated in 1969, 15 years after the Brown vs Board of Education Supreme Court decision. Oil remains king and, along with the port, it still powers the pulse of the city.

Texas City holds a gathering of survivors of the 1947 explosion annually. I am a member of that survivor group, having experienced this cataclysmic event in person. Every year a service takes place at a memorial cemetery north of town, which is dedicated to the unidentified victims. Like those who returned from WWII, survivors seldom talk about the explosion. We have moved on. But we have never forgotten.

Previous accounts of this tragedy have been filled with statistical data, technical information and judicial testimony. This fictionalized account is intended to present the emotional impact on people's lives, to convey some of the pain and suffering they experienced, and how they slowly "rise up" to live again.

The characters in this story are fictions of my mind and any resemblance to real people is coincidental. To the best of my efforts, the depiction of events surrounding the explosions are real and accurate.

Carl Matthew Trepagnier
January 1, 2022

The Ship

Wednesday, April 16, 1947
8:00 am

It was a normal Wednesday morning in Texas City, a small, yet energetic town across the bay from Galveston, Texas. Mothers were starting breakfast and boiling water to make coffee while children were grumbling about going to school. Men began leaving home for work in the nearby oil and chemical refineries, or they were coming off the "graveyard" shift and heading for home.

These workers served the vital industrial complex outside Texas City, which hummed with its diverse activities. Oil storage tanks and chemical processing towers belonging to companies such as Monsanto Chemical, Stone Oil, Humble Oil, Pan American and Carbide Chemical formed a wall-like barrier along Galveston Bay to the west of town.

At the east end of this serpentine body of mechanical behemoths lay the docks and port activities which were owned by the Texas City Terminal Railroad. The "Terminal," as this area was called, connected and unified this diverse system of needs and productivity. Its purpose was to link the Port of Texas City to the adjacent industries. This system of railroad tracks controlled the rail-to-water and water-to-rail transfers of supplies and products at the docks, as well as the all-important links with inland railroads that connected the port to the rest of the country. The Terminal held a powerful and influential position in the intricate life of industry in the area.

This day, April 16, began in spectacularly clear fashion with a cool north wind. Dawn carried the hope of a beautiful spring day as the sun's rays turned the black night sky into cobalt blue over the placid waters of the bay. The town of Texas City itself awoke to the comfortable and familiar rhythm of its blue-collar workforce.

But on the docks of the Terminal Railway, a different air swirled. The *SS Grandcamp*, a Victory-class ship, occupied Slip O. Chromatic circles of oil swirled on the surface of tranquil water near the 456-foot ship's Plimsoll line. The bridge and deckhouse towered above the dockside. She proudly carried the French flag, which flapped quietly in the breeze at the top of her mast. The bags of ammonium nitrate that filled most of her holds were destined to be used as fertilizer to replenish farmlands in Europe that had been devastated by WWII.

The ship's cargo holds were near capacity, and the captain and crew were anxious to return to Marseille or LaHavre after months at sea. The morning's work progressed with both tension and urgency since rain the previous day had put the loading behind schedule.

The foreman who managed the loading of Hold #4 of the *SS Grandcamp* stood on its floor and watched as a pallet was winched through the hatch and temporarily blocked out the sunlight that streamed through the opening. Dust swirled in the air around him, motes playing in the rays of light that crept around the pallet. He ran his tongue over his lower lip, removed his cap and passed a hand through his thinning hair. Thirty-two thousand bags of ammonium nitrate already lay in the hold while another 14,000 waited to be brought aboard. He berated his workers to move faster as they muscled the 100-pound bags into stacks seven high. Some bags, with holes ripped in the six-ply paper, spilled raspberry-colored pellets onto the floor. The workmen muttered to themselves as the foreman shouted, "For God's sake, watch what you are doing!"

It should have been an easy task to complete the loading of the ship's cargo this morning and send her off to her port in France, thus reuniting her captain and crew with lovers, families and friends. But this cargo carried a sucker punch which would devastate the lives of thousands and threaten to kill the soul of a town. The journey of the reliable and solid *SS Grandcamp* neared its end.

SS Grandcamp before the explosion
Courtesy of University of Houston Digital Library

Parking lot 1/4 mile away from the explosion
Courtesy of University of Houston Digital Library

One

For 42 years, except for time in college, Louis Broussard had lived his entire life in Texas City and had barely tolerated it. He effectively hid his frustration, not only from others but also from himself by working long hours and smoking too many cigarettes. He owned Tiger Ship Chandlers, which supplied ships coming into the docks, a business his father Alcid had built from nothing. Everything from food to toilet paper to engine parts came out of a Tiger warehouse the size of half a football field. It stood at the end of a row of warehouses along a gravel pathway named Dock Road. At the other end of the road were the piers where ships berthed in an inlet off Galveston Bay.

Physically, he fit the mold of the successful businessman. A few extra pounds showed around his sides as he entered his early forties. He wore tailored suits and carried his six-foot, broad-shouldered frame well, with an easy manner. But his mind did not share the ease of his physical body.

From his office window, Louis could see the tops of freighters and oil tankers floating in their slips. He loved seeing each of the huge vessels so close. He could take the short walk to the docks and stand next to a great hull with its tall funnel behind the tiers of the deck house. His eyes could follow the curve of the steel hull up to the forecastle and he could imagine himself standing just aft of the prow, salty seawater splashing over the superstructure onto his face.

He had once dreamed of steering his own ship, silently slicing a great ocean with the prow, carving foamy whitecaps that flowed away from its sides. That dream had died abruptly with his Daddy's death when Louis assumed leadership of the business. Sometimes he felt the loss of that dream as a melancholic angst. It continued to visit him, secreted just beneath the surface of his tough-minded exterior despite his resolve to put it aside. Over the years, he had found diversions in food and alcohol. And, of course, there were women. Lots of women.

Years ago, after completing the education his Daddy, Alcid Broussard, had prescribed, he had intended to leave Texas City, go to a maritime school and eventually become a ship's captain. But his Daddy had disrupted that dream by dying suddenly – shortly after Louis graduated from the university. His mother needed Louis to run the shipping supply business that Alcid had built. So being around ships and imagining a life on the oceans constituted all that remained of his plan.

Louis had agreed to be in charge until he could find a buyer. But his mother's dependency, as well as the voice of his Daddy from the grave, kept him tethered to the business. He continued to carry the sense of obligation even after his mother died. As a result of his hard work and commitment, Tiger Ship Chandlers thrived with the industrial boom after the war, and his success made him well known around the small community.

He had eventually suppressed the dream of being captain of his own ship and adapted to the masquerade that was his life now. The desire to have his own life no longer seemed as important.

Louis played the role, often when he was having coffee with the locals at Frenchy's Cafe on Main Street. He took part in their conversations about town gossip, the high school football team or the weather, although he admitted to himself that he did not understand the concern with weather which, for the most part, stayed hot with an occasional hurricane to break the monotony. When the inane chatter exceeded his patience, which was a frequent occurrence, he sought the atmosphere and anonymity of Houston. In his mind, Louis had been leaving Texas City for the past 21 years.

Although Louis hated going to funerals, this cool fall day found him attending one. He hated going to church services even more than attending funerals, but the mother of one of his business associates had died and he felt the obligation. Craving a cigarette the minute he passed through the doors, he chose a side aisle and sat halfway up the rows of pews.

The family and a few friends huddled in the front pews as incense smoke from a censor wafted over the altar toward them. Somber men and women all in black stood up for the start of the funeral mass.

Incense, priests in ornate vestments, and the solemnity that was repeated at every Catholic funeral unfolded as Louis examined the shine on his shoes. He sat casually with one arm resting along the back of the pew and found it amusing that sunlight streamed through the stained-glass oval above the altar directly onto the casket.

God must have directed the lighting, he thought with a wry smile. A pious woman, she probably had a close connection.

Louis' irreverence was interrupted as the priest finished reading the required text. He paused briefly before sharing his eulogy, hands clasped under his chin as he prepared to speak. He spoke thoughtfully and with reverence, using his hands to imply the inevitability of his words.

"We cannot understand the ways of God. We simply must follow...."

Louis heard the words intermittently, distracted by memories of his Daddy's funeral as well as his impatience to be done with this service.

"... The path through grief travels across a threshold in ourselves. Death is a human event and we must cope with it as humans. We should not concern ourselves about Frances being in Heaven with God because her soul never left the mind of God. She is not going somewhere she has never been. Thus, our consolation comes not from Frances residing now in Heaven: That is a given. Rather, it comes from finding meaning for ourselves through our own effort of prayer. We then realize that our spirits will also continue in the mind of God after we leave these mortal bodies."

Louis tilted his head at this idea. As a boy, he had given God the power over everything: football games, algebra exams, his living or dying. His beliefs changed in high school when he learned that the Baptists said God did not want people to dance. But Catholics said He did want people to dance. Someone had to be wrong.

Because religions did not seem very God-like to him, Louis had eventually slipped into indifference about all matters of faith. Belief in unseen and mystical events clashed with his intellect, and he determined to put his fate and faith in hard work – and luck.

This priest, if Louis heard him correctly, implied that there was no Hell, which was a very unusual view considering the dogma of punishment held by the Catholic Church. Hell loomed as a powerful deterrent to sinners. His mother had used it frequently as a fear-filled guide to morality.

Ultimately, Louis did not believe his name would be found on God's census roll.

"Let us temper our grief with joy. The joy that comes with Frances' life of faith in God. She lived a good life and touched many people with her kindness and compassion. We can be happy that she has found her heavenly reward and resides there in peace."

The priest ended with a wry smile. "And I'm pretty sure she is already organizing the ladies' auxiliary to meet her standards."

He moved to surround the casket with smoke from the censor, swinging it over and around, as his piety and attention to the smallest detail brought Louis' mind back to the moment. This priest, reverent yet lighthearted in his remarks to the family, injected a spirit of joy into the proceedings. He acted like a happy man, unlike the dour, overly reverent priests of Louis' boyhood who had caused him so much anxiety about Hell. Curious – and surprising – Louis thought, as he left the church.

Louis loosened his tie on the drive to Frenchy's Cafe, where he started most of his mornings drinking chicory-laced coffee.

"*Comment ca va*, Mr. Broussard?" Frenchy asked as he walked in the door and headed to a booth.

"*Bonjour*, Frenchy."

The cafe owner set a hot mug of coffee in front of Louis, whose mind briefly touched on his Cajun mother as he heard her original language spoken. Louis could speak some in the Cajun dialect and wished he knew more. But his mother had refused to speak anything but English once they had moved to Texas. She had told Louis that the Cajun language sounded ignorant, and she would not allow the dialect to be spoken in her home. Classic French was okay: No bastardized versions allowed.

Louis' mother had held a fascination with everything French. The Louisiana territory and later the state had been named for Louis XIV, who had been called the Sun King because France revolved around him. Thus, Louis' mother had named him after the "Great King." She had told him so many stories about the powerful leader that, he acknowledged, it might have been a major contributor to her son's arrogance.

In the end, Louis had picked up a limited vocabulary in the Cajun patois from his Daddy and had tried to keep it because girls loved its sound. He had dated lots of women but had never married. At some point, he would tire of a woman or just never fully commit to the relationship until she tired of waiting and left. Over time, he had become known as the most eligible bachelor in town.

Sitting alone in the booth, Louis dumped two spoons of sugar into his coffee and looked out the window at Main Street. Frenchy returned to bussing tables that were cluttered from the morning rush. After the first sip of coffee, a pain started in Louis' chest and then radiated into his throat. Sweat formed on his brow and a queasy weakness flashed through his body. He wiped the sweat with a napkin as it formed on his forehead. He pushed the coffee away and began to breathe deeply, trying to calm himself.

"You all right, Mr. Broussard? You look a little pale."

Louis gave a weak smile and waved his hand. He had experienced this on more than one occasion. The episodes worried him, but the symptoms passed each time, so he ignored the problem and identified the pain as indigestion. In a few minutes, the symptoms were gone.

Heading to his office, Louis steered his big Chrysler south on Main Street. Few cars interrupted his drive toward the docks. Waiting for the traffic light to change at Texas Avenue and Main Street, it came to his mind for the first time that the Rice Hotel in Houston also occupied a corner of Texas and Main streets. The Rice Hotel was a symbol of success and wealth in a bustling city. Here, the two streets formed an invisible boundary that segregated Texas City from the Black community locally known as the Hallows on the south side of Texas Avenue. Most houses and businesses in the Hallows bordered the refinery complex, whose baleful sight, smoke and sounds lay a short distance away.

From his car, Louis studied rows of shotgun shacks with peeling paint, many of the yards serving as refuges for broken-down cars and overgrown weeds.

Living under an implied law to stay with their own kind, residents remained in the Hallows and attended their own schools and churches. They knew not to venture north of Texas Avenue after dark. Few overt incidents had occurred, but tensions did exist. A story persisted that a Hallows man who had refused to stay on the south side had been shot and killed by the police chief, but its circumstances had never been confirmed.

Many of the men who lived in the Hallows worked on the docks as stevedores. Lower wages and fewer overtime opportunities like those that were common for white workers encouraged a sullen relationship between the two groups. Rumors of a strike by these crews often passed through men huddled at the docks. In bars and cafes close by, they sat together and vowed to fight for better working conditions, spreading more animosity on the rough waters between the workmen in the segregated communities.

But strikes rarely occurred. In one attempt a few years back, Texas Rangers had stood by as hired thugs using ax handles and two-by-fours had scattered a picket line that sought to create a work stoppage on the docks.

Louis believed that colored crews would find no sympathetic court to gain the traction they needed to make a strike effective. Vincent Russo, president of the Terminal Railway and the most powerful man in the industrial complex, was determined that no strikes or associated violence would be allowed on his docks, even if it necessitated violence to prevent it.

Louis eased through the light as it changed to green. He paid scant attention to colored people. His Daddy had said they were "lazy no-goods" and couldn't be trusted. Louis did not really dislike them. He thought of them as potential trouble that could disrupt his business and his focus on profits. He worked to make money and paid no mind to their plight.

Alcid's stern hand and harsh punishment on Louis as a young boy had laid down a narrow path for him. The burning pain returned to his chest briefly as he recalled how nothing he did had ever been good enough to please his Daddy. Louis often toggled between being confident and arrogant in his success and feeling insecure and unable to be himself. He was aware that he suffered an existential conflict that was created by his Daddy's overbearing demeanor and continuous corrections that still echoed in his mind.

Thus, over time, Louis had slipped into some nervous habits. He fidgeted with his keys or jangled change in his pocket when he had a moment with nothing to do. Restless sleep kept him tired and irritable. Although he continued to refer to the episodes of chest pains and weakness as indigestion, he was beginning to acknowledge that they had become more frequent. He considered making an appointment with his physician, Dr. Morgan, since he had not seen him professionally for ten years. The problem had worried him, but until now Louis had just ignored it and worked harder.

Now as he entered his office, he thought maybe it would be good to see the doctor.

"Coast Guard coming today," his secretary sang out. "Said he would be here at one p.m. sharp."

Louis looked around him. He had just had his office remodeled and had brought in a larger desk and leather couch. Off to one side was a new bar with a small sink and refrigerator. Walnut paneling covered the walls. Behind his desk hung a picture of a Longhorn steer from his Daddy's old ranch in South Texas. And in one corner stood a display case for a collection of antique marlin spikes. It included one that his Daddy had used when he worked on the docks in Galveston moving cotton bales.

Louis' office and warehouse complex sat on a strip of land that was bordered by the docks, the Terminal Railway Company offices and 41 oil storage tanks that stretched almost half a mile to the south. Monsanto Chemical, Stone Oil Company and Republic Oil rose up to the north and west. In addition to providing a fresh coat of paint, the remodeling had included better insulation and paneling that now blocked some of the industrial drone and the squealing sounds of railway cars as they moved to and from the docks on their steel rails.

It was a busy port, with constant movement and cacophony.

Louis was pleased with the office redo and felt that the changes he had made gave him the isolation and singularity that he sought – not only in his work, but in his life.

Louis considered the upcoming Coast Guard visit and concluded it would be a waste of time. He had been on the Safety Regulations Board for a number of years and had heard the rumors of proposed changes in regulations on the docks. Coast Guard representatives, officially in charge of safety rules, routinely rubber-stamped what the Board dictated, and the Board seldom changed the safety regulations. Business leaders on the docks paid scant attention to anything that did not expedite port profits.

Louis invited Mack Hale, his warehouse foreman, to join the Coast Guard meeting. Mack, smart and mature with good judgment at his young age, could provide another point of view for the afternoon meeting.

At one p.m., Louis escorted the Coast Guard representative into his office. He did not know the Captain, who had recently transferred to Galveston. The young officer wasted no time getting into an energetic presentation. He spoke with a deep and confident voice.

"I asked to meet with you, Mr. Broussard, to discuss some changes I think we should consider to strengthen our safety regulations. I want your opinion about the idea of forming a centralized port authority. I am meeting with all members of the Safety Board and other business owners around the docks as a preliminary step to formulating a proposal. I'd like to get your input about modifications that could be made to our safety measures and codes."

Louis and Mack listened while the officer read a list of possible changes and/or additions. Louis had been through these meetings before. He knew that changing rules meant tighter scrutiny and more red tape. More regulations increased the cost of doing business. And in the end, he had little tolerance for governmental intrusion.

"Along with some changes to the existing regulations, we want to establish an independent port authority with a chain of command to authorize actions in emergency situations. We need a plan in case of a major disaster."

The young captain paused. Louis feigned more interest than he felt. He appeared to be listening intently, but his mind had drifted between the presentation and the new contracts piled on his desk.

"Your dock area lacks a central command. What you have here are various safety procedures adhered to by individual companies in the industrial complex. For example, you have several limited response forces that work on their own with no coordination in handling major occurrences such as fires, hurricanes or any kind of real disaster. There is no overall plan for evacuation or treatment of mass casualties."

Louis did not share the captain's concerns. Texas City's oil industry and the port had grown with the massive oil discoveries in Texas. Port business boomed when the war ended, as freedom in the sea lanes allowed more shipments to and from Europe. Huge amounts of money began coming into its businesses; thus, none of Louis' associates wanted more regulations to encumber their activities.

Louis knew for a fact that Vincent Russo and the Terminal Railway did not want more interference. He had heard Vincent loudly protest government intrusion during their gin rummy games at the country club many times. Russo, a small but powerfully built man, always pointed his finger in the air to emphasize his comments. He had held court on the perils of getting into bed with the government.

"We know how to run our businesses," went Russo's mantra. "We have stringent safety rules. We have an excellent long-term record of safety. Anyone can check the hours and days worked without a lost-time accident right there on the billboard at the front gate."

Now addressing the Coast Guard Captain, although not as bellicose as Russo, Louis stood his ground. "We have a good track record. Schedules run smoothly. The system works just fine as far as I am concerned," Louis said.

As the captain tried to respond, Louis aggressively interrupted him. "This port has handled tons of materials without a lost-time accident for a very long time. Check the board at the gate. What do you think, Mack?"

Louis trusted his foreman and often asked his advice on business matters. Mack, quiet and shy, never spoke until he was asked. He possessed a keen intellect and a very disciplined approach.

"Well," Mack drawled. "We have a good safety record, that's true. I believe most of the workers feel safe being in the middle of all the gasoline, oil and chemicals that the port sees every day."

Mack rubbed his hands along the tops of his pant legs before continuing. "However, business at the port is expanding so rapidly that I do wonder about new hazardous materials coming to the docks. We might be a little complacent about the way things are being done. For instance, we could use greater enforcement of 'No Smoking' rules. And it might be a good idea to have double firewalls in the warehouses. So, I do think there is room for improvement."

Mack glanced at Louis. He knew that Louis would not like his suggestions. "A review of safety regulations might not be a bad idea," he concluded, putting his hand to his chin without speaking further.

"If you're looking for a vote," Louis responded firmly, "I'm not in favor of more regulations. I believe you will find that is the general consensus around here. We have a disaster plan. If lightning strikes a storage tank, fire starts, we put out the fire. It doesn't happen frequently, but it is not rare, either. We have procedures for hurricane preparations and for oil spills. We have sprinklers in the warehouses. Business is good! What else is there?"

Louis felt the heat rise in his face as he continued. "Listen, I'm getting tired of you people trying to tell us how to run our businesses. We have contingencies in place. We have a good record. Now why don't you just accept that we are responsible and let us get on with it?"

Mack had never seen Louis so upset. His response to the young officer embarrassed him, but he remained silent.

The officer urged Louis to think about his proposals, thanked him for his time and abruptly left. Louis went to his bar and poured a shot of bourbon. He tipped the glass toward Mack, who shook his head no.

Louis did not like taking the side of Vincent Russo even if he did agree with the little tyrant. An image of his Daddy came to Louis' mind. Alcid would have been Russo's ally in the tug-of-war against more regulations. He would have ranted, cursed, flailed his arms, maybe even thrown the young Coast Guard officer out of his office. Alcid had harbored no patience for those who did not think as he did.

Still, something gnawed at Louis. Had he become too

complacent, too much like his Daddy: stubborn, defiant, self-indulgent? Louis did not want to have the will of that ghost become his own, but lately he found himself unable to control his impatience and anger. He had become more dismissive than ever. He acknowledged that he had become more like his Daddy.

Louis looked at Mack. "Are people really smoking in the 'No Smoking' areas?"

"Every day," Mack replied.

Louis worked late into the evening in his office, shuffling through the papers piled on his desk. He found numbers boring, but meticulously slogged through the tedium of contracts and inventories, while smoking too many cigarettes. Hearing Alcid's stern messages in his mind created a constant edginess. Louis believed that he did many things right in the business, but for the wrong reasons. He lived in the throes of his father's harsh principles and acknowledged that Alcid still directed his life. He had come to realize that the power of Alcid's strict tutoring remained a strong influence that resulted in hubris and a lack of empathy that bordered on narcissism.

At times, Louis felt the dissonance of this influence in his life, but he did not have the maturity to try and change his demeanor. At best, it made him a successful businessman. At worst, it cemented an unconscious anxiety in him.

On his way home, Louis stopped at Aristotle's Cafe near the west gate. He often ate at the cafe, which was located in a larger version of the wood-frame houses on the south side of town. A big rectangular sign hung above the door of its sea-green exterior. Flood lights illuminated the name "Aristotle's." Wooden tables covered by red-and-white checkered cloth filled the dining room. A dance floor occupied space between the tables, and a long saloon bar that Alcid had found in an old cantina in Laredo lined the side of the room. A brass railing gave the bar an authentic western flavor. Large casting nets adorned with seashells and replicas of blue crabs hung from the walls in an eclectic decor.

A waiter brought a bourbon and water as Louis sat down at his usual table. He lit a cigarette and scanned the room. Diners filled most of the tables, including a few loud talkers with raucous laughs. A large group stood at the bar, most of them sailors off of foreign ships. Some spoke passable English; all seemed to be garrulous and animated. The cafe was a boisterous hangout for the merchant seamen. Louis thought it must be the ocean air that infused them with so much energy.

As he watched the other diners, Demetrios Alexander approached his table.

"Ah, Mr. Broussard. So nice of you to grace my humble establishment," he said with a mock bow.

Demetrios owned the cafe and bar. He had emigrated from Greece to New York and lived there for a year before he traveled to South Texas to seek work on a ranch. He had wished to discover the Old West and become a cowboy. He now greeted his guest with a boisterous laugh that echoed throughout the room.

Louis' father had bought a ranch near the Mexican border as a place to hunt doves and he had hired Demetrios, whom he had met in a bar, to be his cook. Thus began a long family friendship. After his father died, Louis sold the ranch, brought Demetrios to Texas City and helped him establish the cafe.

When Louis came to eat, Demetrios sat with him and gave him unsolicited counsel.

"Louis," he began, his words heavy with an old-world accent. "You don't look so good. Life is short, my friend. You need to get out of that office, get a woman, go dancing. Stop living your life like a man blindfolded. Your mother, God rest her soul, would not like who you have become."

He crossed himself and kissed his thumb, then tilted his hand in front of his mouth to signal the barman for a drink.

A waiter brought ouzo. Demetrios raised the glass and toasted, "To life." He drank the liquor in one swallow. "In fact, you look terrible, my friend," he continued. "You have bags under your eyes, you are pale. What's up with you?"

Louis expected such an assessment from the Greek. He admitted to himself that he had not been feeling well. He had not played golf in months and his usual dark tan had now faded.

"It's from eating too much of your food."

Music from the jukebox switched to a single mandolin playing the slow beginning of a Greek song. Several waiters formed a single line in front of the bar, clasping each other's shoulders with their outstretched arms. They began to dance the *Hasapiko*. A few seamen from the bar joined them.

They moved forward in unison, dipped their bodies at the knees, kicked out one foot, and moved backward with another dip. The line moved backward, then forward again. An elderly man from the bar joined them at the end of the line. He stood taller than the rest, with a slight paunch, a droop to his shoulders and a bald spot in the middle of his head. Louis noticed his jaw looked deformed, like part of it had been removed.

He stepped right in on the beat with a big toothy grin on his oval face. He turned his head to the right, dragged his foot across the floor, dipped his body, turned left, dragged the other foot, dipped again, then hopped from one foot to the other, each in its turn and in unison with the other dancers. He moved slowly and confidently, with style and a grace that matched the waiters who performed the dance nightly.

The dancers dropped their hands and held their arms out horizontally like wings. The line dipped and moved right, heads turning to the left. The dancers now spun around gracefully, moving their hands at their wrists in a circle. The beat of the music stepped up and the dancers responded with faster movements, hopping, dipping, moving forward and backward in a frenzy.

Soon, most of the seamen had dropped out, laughing and struggling to catch their breath. The elderly man with the bald spot smiled, kept dancing and matched the waiters step for step. He twirled, threw his head back and yelled "Oppah!" as the dance ended.

Louis watched, amazed at the older man's ability to move so rapidly.

"Looks like you brought in a ringer," Louis said, as the diners applauded.

Demetrios realized that Louis did not recognize the man and smiled broadly. "Who? Him? You don't know him?" Demetrios pointed to the man who was laughing and talking with the waiters at the bar.

"The man with the bald spot? That's the new priest from St. Mary's. He covers the Seamen's Mission at the docks. I like him. He has a little Greek in him."

Demetrios paused and looked straight at Louis. "You have not been to church in a while, have you?"

Louis recalled the recent funeral service at the church but made no response. The dancer, dressed in gray slacks with an open-collared shirt, gave no hint of being clergy. Louis slowly realized the funeral celebrant and this human whirlwind were the same man. Though Louis did not go to church anymore, he thought it inappropriate for a priest to be drinking and dancing in a bar and found the behavior questionable.

"He's the Catholic priest," Demetrios said again. "Father Joseph Irons."

Louis left Demetrios' and drove home thinking about the priest. He certainly had seen two different sides to the man. A dancing priest, Louis thought, shaking his head. What's the world coming to?

The week closed and, without work to distract him, tension closed in on Louis. As was his habit to relieve boredom, on Saturday afternoon he drove to his favorite escape, the Rice Hotel in Houston.

Trees along the way had begun to lose their leaves. The heat of summer had disappeared and fall had begun to show its face. Afternoon recessed into dusk and the sun was flirting with the horizon by the time he passed through Harrisburg.

He had discovered the Rice in 1938 when one of his suppliers had invited him to watch a parade in honor of Howard Hughes from the hotel's canopied roof. Louis had hoped to meet the flamboyant Hughes, who had just set a new speed record for flying around the world.

Louis had enjoyed the ambiance of the hotel, with its reputation as the watering hole of the rich and richer. And the women. They were gathered in the bars and ballrooms, intent on being with the power brokers and the politicians. Howard Hughes was a bonus.

Louis did not get to meet the man, although Hughes' charisma had filled the space like a permanent reminder of his presence. After that weekend, the hotel had become Louis' oasis.

Louis parked the big Chrysler in the hotel garage and strolled through the lobby to the bar.

"Good evening, Mr. Broussard. Or is it still afternoon?" the barman said with a quick look at his watch.

"I believe the evening has begun. How are you, Cletus?"

"Fine. I'm just fine."

"In that case, let me have a Jim Beam and water."

The first swallow of the oaken bourbon broke apart the tension in his body. He glanced down the long mahogany bar at men gathered in small groups, dressed in suits and ties. Some stood tall, others rested one elbow on the scarred wooden bar, enveloped in a smoky haze.

He lit a cigarette, thinking about the power brokers, the deals, the smooth-talking politicians in the Capital Club on the mezzanine, and wondered who he might see in the hotel that night.

After two bourbons, the maître d' of the Flame Room found him a table for dinner. He ordered the filet (rare) and another bourbon (neat). A waiter tossed a Caesar salad table-side for him. As he ate, Louis' gaze wandered to the tables around him and he admired the women in tight dresses and flashy, ornate jewels, including their large diamonds. Accompanied by well-dressed men, some in formal wear, they chatted, confident in their appearance. A prattle of conversation mingling with laughter wafted from tables that were filled by the elite of the city.

After his meal, Louis bought a cigar and sat in the lobby, relaxing while the glittery crowd passed. He knew that there would be dancing later in the Crystal Ballroom on the mezzanine. The last time he had visited the hotel, Tommy Dorsey had commanded the bandstand. This is American royalty, he thought. The women moved casually, slowly, turning slightly from side to side as they talked. They seemed comfortable having Louis inspect them, yet they coyly denied his glance. It was clear that they loved the attention.

The men appeared to have a high regard for themselves, as well. They walked in fluid, measured steps with an air of independence which Louis envied. He wondered who they were and what they did for a living. Did they act this way in their daily lives? Were they this confident under pressure? Did they ever get bored? Would a woman think of them as good lovers? Were they as content as they appeared?

Returning to the bar, he saw an empty stool next to a woman who was sitting alone.

"Do you mind if I sit here?"

She smiled and said, "Not at all."

He studied her face as she turned back to her drink. She also was adorned with jewels, including several strands of pearls and matching earrings. Multiple thin silver bracelets encircled one wrist.

He sat down, close enough now that he could inhale her fragrant perfume and appreciate the shoulder-length blonde hair that encircled her face. She wore a green dress with padded shoulders that wrapped snugly around her thin frame. The green matched her eyes, which were lined with a little too much makeup.

Louis ordered a Jim Beam and toasted her with it. Looking at her, he recalled the time he had seen Lauren Bacall in the hotel lobby. This was not Bacall, but a reasonable copy of her.

"Big crowd tonight," he offered.

She nodded in the affirmative.

They slipped into their own reveries. The room began to fill. Convivial laughter and greetings burst from groups along the length of the crowded bar.

"Do you live in Houston?" Louis asked.

"No. I'm visiting some friends. And you? Looking for a big night on the town?"

"Yeah. I come to get away, find a little excitement and alleviate small town boredom."

"I know what you mean. I hate being bored."

Louis swirled his drink in thought.

"The first time I came here I watched a parade for Howard Hughes on Main Street," he said. "I still see it clearly in my mind. Hughes rode on top of the back seat in an open convertible, waving to the crowd. He had outriders of motorcycle police all around him. He wore a white shirt with long sleeves partially rolled up and a dark tie. He was laughing and having a good time. On top of the world."

The woman smiled, pulled out a cigarette holder and fitted a Camel cigarette in its stem. She waited for Louis to light it for her.

"He was a man with big dreams," Louis said.

"Yes. And the money to go with them." She paused before continuing. "So, you come to the Rice to live out your fantasies?"

Louis grinned. "Maybe. Do you have any fantasies?"

"Well, now. I guess I am always looking for Prince Charming. I'm not much of the housewife and mom type."

She thought for a moment, studied the drink in her glass, took a drag on her cigarette.

He knew her, or many like her. He knew why she sat at the bar alone. Louis caught a glimpse of himself in a mirror behind the bar, his dark Cajun skin contrasted against his white shirt. He smiled, pleased by the way he looked.

"Can I buy you another drink?"

"I would like that…. Yes, I would like that."

They engaged in vacuous chatter for a while. Louis tried to make her laugh with a Cajun joke about a man who sold raffle tickets to win a white mule that, unbeknownst to those purchasing tickets, had died a few weeks before.

She did laugh at the punch line. "Did those people who bought raffle tickets get mad?"

Louis spoke the lines of the story in a thick Cajun dialect. "Jes' one," he said, holding up his index finger. "Jes' one."

Louis excused himself and went to the men's room. He stopped at the Reservations desk.

"Hello Sadie," Louis smiled at the receptionist. "As cute as you look, you should be out dancing yourself."

Sadie smiled, but said nothing, accustomed to Louis' flirtations.

"Could you book me a room for tonight, honey?"

"Of course, Mr. Broussard. Give me a minute."

Louis regarded the opulent marble floor of the lobby. Marble walls coursed up to the mezzanine where music drifted through the arched doorway of the Crystal Ballroom.

Couples stood along the rails above the rococo molding, sipping cocktails and watching others traipse up and down the broad staircase.

Sadie brought Louis the key.

"And Sadie, would you ask Tommy to get the valise out of my car and take it to my room? He'll know where I parked."

Louis returned to the bar. The woman sat on her stool. "Did

you miss me?"

"Terribly," she deadpanned. "I did save your seat from that very large man at the other end of the bar."

"I appreciate that. I'd hate to have to fight him for your company. You know what? It's getting very loud here. We could continue this discussion in my room, if you like."

A coy smile met Louis' offer. "I would appreciate a different view, maybe a bit more intimate," she said.

She took her handbag from the bar. When she stood up, Louis eyed the full extent of her lithe figure. Tall and thin. Graceful. Excited at the prospect of seeing all of her, he extended his arm. They walked arm in arm across the lobby to the elevators.

They continued to talk, trying to get more comfortable with each other. Louis always felt awkward acting as though they knew each other well, as though he really enjoyed being in this hotel with a stranger.

Louis fumbled with her clothes as he undressed her. They slipped into bed. He pretended it was more than what it was, that she was someone special and that she thought the same of him. Soon he thought about nothing but the pleasure of the explosive orgasm that brought his momentary release.

Afterward, Louis stared at the ceiling in the dark, pretending to be asleep to avoid conversation. He heard her get up, go into the bathroom, then quietly leave the room, the door clicking as it latched behind her.

The woman's fragrant perfume remained on his skin as loneliness swallowed him. He turned on the light and looked into the mirror. He did not see the man he was at the bar, dressed in the dapper gray suit and dark blue tie. He didn't see the man full of confidence -- and bourbon.

Instead, he saw puffy eyes with crows' feet around the edges. He saw the depth of sadness, which was usually masked by bravado, in his remarkable blue eyes. He had again tried to make something special out of an arranged drama but had found only a bleached performance.

He thought about his wallet. It remained in his back trouser pocket, minus one of the fifties. He thought about the woman riding in a taxi, traveling in her own world. He wished he had been kinder.

Two

Tuesday, November 5, 1946

Clayton Malveaux dreamed of going to California. He knew he didn't have a snowball's chance in Hell, but something deep inside of him would not let the dream die. So he put his life into boxes to accommodate his reality. He worked as a stevedore on the docks. His compact and muscular body served him well for the difficult physical requirements of loading cargo onto ships. But Clayton wanted more out of life and his mind would not let him rest until he found a way to satisfy that longing.

He awoke this morning in his tiny bedroom to the smell of coffee and frying bacon. His Momma stood in the kitchen in front of a small window over the sink. She could see the flare outside burning off natural gas, the tower and flame rising 100 feet in the air. In the early morning darkness, it showered a bright light over their neighborhood, known locally as the Hallows.

The Hallows segregated Coloreds from the rest of the town. No one knew where the name came from, but some proud soul must have thought the ground was important. There was certainly nothing sacred about its pitiful housing and living conditions. It closely bordered a low levee that separated the area from the Stone Oil Company and parts of other refineries. On the east side of Main Street, Mexicans lived in their own community.

Clayton often sat outside reading his books in the light from the flare to save on their electric bill. He studied textbooks, old magazines, newspapers, whatever he could find. When he was reading, he was able to ignore the continuous drone from the giant refinery next door.

Bare wooden slats on the interior walls of the house covered the studs but provided no insulation from the weather or the noise. Clayton could not get away from the outside world, just as he could not get away from his blackness. Every day he woke up in this bleak room, still a colored man.

The first moments after waking – in the stillness of the dawn when nothing else occupied his mind – ushered in the worst times for Clayton. During that quiet interlude, thoughts of his failure crashed into his consciousness. He wanted to be somebody, but the painful reality of his life overwhelmed him at the first light of day.

He had given up the idea of going to college ten years ago when he had become the sole financial support for his Momma and, shortly thereafter, for a baby sister, Shana. But in his dream world, even at the age of 28, he was living in California and attending college. He left the docks behind with their backbreaking labor. He walked on a Pacific beach or looked up at the large "Hollywoodland" sign that he had seen in a magazine. He longed to be in California where magic happened. He wanted to be in a place where his dream world could come true.

Out there, a Black man could run, jump or even holler if he felt like it, without people thinking that he was stealing something or that he was an idiot child. Out there, he could live where he damn well wanted to live. He deserved to be treated as a man, able to choose what he wanted.

But – always – despair returned and slipped into bed with him. What could he do when he was stuck in this hellhole with the smell of hot oil in his nostrils?

Shana mumbled in her sleep on a cot at the foot of their mother's bed. Soon his Momma would rouse her to dress for her fourth-grade class at Booker T. Washington School a block away.

Clayton slowly rolled out of bed and dressed, put on his stevedore mask and prepared for work. Despite his bookish habits, he did not appear to be studious. Muscles rippled through his stocky 200-pound body. His athletic build and natural strength served him well in his laborer's world.

The aroma of coffee lured him into the kitchen as he continued this internal dialogue. He knew it would be Shana, not him, who got out. He would see that Shana made it to California. This vision for her life pushed him to drag his weary body out of bed every morning, to force his own dream aside and get over to the docks.

Maybe, if he got lucky, they could all end up in California. He smiled to himself as he realized that it would take dynamite to move his Momma, she who was the Rock of Gibraltar. But Shana came first. She would not live her life in the Hallows, even if it killed him to get her out.

As he walked into the kitchen, his Momma stood in front of the narrow white stove and stared at the sizzling bacon, a pot of grits on a burner next to it. Lunches in brown paper bags stood on a rough wooden table.

Clayton poured a cup of coffee from the drip pot. "I'll be late this afternoon. Mowin' day at the church."

His Momma nodded, turning over the bacon. "I saw Father Joe this week. He told me again how much he appreciated you, how smart you wuz. He said you a fine young man."

Ella Mae and Shana Malveaux comprised the entire Black congregation at St. Mary's Catholic Church a few blocks away where Father Joseph Irons was the priest. Every Sunday, dressed in her white linen dress and straw hat, Ella Mae proceeded up the center aisle with her eyes fixed sternly on the cross above the altar. Shana walked close by her side as they entered the front pew. After the first few Sundays, this became Ella Mae's pew since no one else would sit with her. Soon, members of the church came to tolerate her proud, slow march to the first row. Most were polite, but they did not mingle.

She had asked the priest to let Clayton take care of the church grounds and do maintenance work on the sanctuary and rectory for a second job. She took in ironing, including the altar cloths, as well as some church members' clothes. Every bit of income helped.

She also had dreams for Shana. She was a simple woman with simple needs and a simple faith. God would take care of them.

Her husband, Earl, had abandoned her and Clayton, and her unborn child ten years ago. A blessing, she had said, because he spent most of his time and their money in bars up the street, coming home drunk and mean. One summer weekend he had traveled to New Orleans, where he frequently stayed for weeks at a time to gamble and carouse. That time he never returned. Ella Mae, not knowing if he was alive or dead, prayed for his soul, but in her heart, she hoped he would not return. After a year, she believed he was gone forever and, so far, he remained missing. She would not wish anyone ill will but, ultimately, she hoped that Texas City had seen the last of him.

However, she admitted that, over time, he had given her two gifts: This time he left Shana in her womb, and a few years before he vanished for good, he had brought home the saxophone that was now Clayton's prized possession. He had won the horn in a crap game behind a bar in New Orleans. She knew that, for

Clayton, it was the only good thing his absent father had ever done.

Clayton had taught himself to play the instrument. When he was 14 years old, he had sat outside bars close to the house and listened to music coming through the windows, then had come home and tried to copy what he had heard. Playing the instrument became his retreat from the harsh reality of the Hallows. Just the sight of the gleaming gold sax leaning against the wall of his bedroom lifted his spirit. At least he owned something: one thing to call his own. He cherished it and feared that his father would return to pawn the instrument for drinking money. Clayton determined he would never let that happen. He had absorbed enough blows from his father.

Ella Mae rattled around in a cabinet looking for the lid to the pot full of grits as Shana came into the room rubbing her eyes, her mouth turned down in a frown.

"Well, looky here. The princess has arrived," Clayton teased his little sister.

"Ya'll making so much noise in here." She yawned, stretching her arms above her head. "I don't wanna go to school today."

"Well, you can forget that, baby doll. You goin' to school. No sir, we ain't missin' no school." Clayton fixed a stare on her and tilted his head. "You goin' to school. You goin' to be the smartest, prettiest girl in the room. And tonight you gonna tell me what you learned today. So, pay attention."

Shana continued to pout. Clayton reached across the table to tickle her as she quickly spun away and smiled. Clayton continued to look at her, still a child but just a couple of years from adolescence. Her large, round eyes gazed back at him in perpetual wonder. He wished it did not have to be so hard to get a good education, so hard to be a Black person, so hard to be so colored yet so invisible to the world. What would she become if she stayed here, he thought? A woman of servitude bringing more little Black children into the hopeless environment of the Black Hallows?

Taking a deep breath, his determination returned. It was good that she had come along late in their Momma's life – late enough for Clayton to have experienced life in the Hallows and to know it would not be fit for her. He would see to it that she left it behind.

Clayton left for work, the torn screen door slamming behind him. He briskly walked through the Hallows, down Sixth Street toward Dock Road and the west gate of the Terminal. Walking on the shoulder, he stayed close to the paved surface, defying cars as they passed. He weaved slightly at one point and a man in a big black Chrysler blasted the horn, glaring at him with an angry stare. Clayton smiled and waved, enjoying the ruckus he had created.

Once at the docks, he began another day of heavy labor, straining under the weight of cargo crates and bags that were lifted onto pallets and then winched onto waiting ships. Although his lower back pained him this morning and he knew he was moving a little slower than normal, he could still work more swiftly and longer than the other members of his crew.

His foreman knew nothing about Clayton's pain. A foreman's concern remained solely to keep the giant maw of industry rumbling and hissing around him, efficiently moving through another productive day to keep the dollars rolling in.

"Pick it up there, Malveaux. We have no place here for slackers," the foreman complained.

Clayton kept on moving, hardened against the foreman's taunts to put him down because he knew he could outwork anyone else on the docks. He disliked the small man with his bulbous nose and balding head. But he weighed his goals and his desire to get Shana out of the Hallows against any temporary satisfaction he might feel in talking back.

"Yes sir, Mr. Boss. I slowed down a bit, but now I'm ready to go again." Clayton bent his back to load the pallets.

Working in a white man's world required guile and gamesmanship, he thought. Grit your teeth and bite your tongue. You played the game, powerless to do anything except inflict more pain on yourself. Clayton's desire to lift Shana out of the Hallows allowed him no chance for alienation.

Shana and the saxophone had been saviors for him. He filled his spare time with practice and slowly learned to play the instrument. On Saturday mornings, Clayton now had an opportunity to meet with the new priest for lessons. Father Joe, as he encouraged his parishioners to address him, had played the sax in his high school band. He knew he was a poor sub for a real musician, but he wanted to help Clayton any way he could.

"That sounds really good," Father Joe would sing out when he arrived at the music room and heard Clayton's playing. "You've been practicing, haven't you?"

Father Joe knew a Black man's struggle. He tried to see beyond Clayton's impassive brown eyes to the thoughts that churned in that fertile mind. He knew Clayton did all he could to carve out an existence, scratching and clawing at his limited opportunities. He suspected the young man struggled to suppress the anger that seethed in his disenfranchised life.

Father Joe wrestled to find his own place in the racial battle and believed that his church did not do enough to promote equality. It functioned as a spiritual beacon of truth yet, while not overtly racist, ignored the realities of segregation and its evils. It did nothing to help the Hallows, resulting in a silent, yet significant, racism. One of these days, when he was called to another "chat" with the Bishop, he intended to bring up the subject.

During their music lessons, Father Joe did his best to encourage Clayton. "You are doing so well that I think the notes are becoming ingrained. I want you to concentrate more on how the notes sound and less on the mechanics. Practice holding notes longer."

It did worry Clayton, however, at the end of their previous session when Father Joe cautioned that his tutoring might soon be over. "You've caught up with this old second-chair high school sax player. There is not much more that I can teach you. I will need to find you a better teacher."

This day, the work and the industry droned on. Soon enough Clayton would be back in the Hallows seeking a new world through his imagination, his unease burning within him, until time required him to get up and go back to the docks again.

After supper, Clayton worked patiently on the sax. He ran the scales and started over whenever a note did not sound right. He worked to control air flow with his diaphragm. Blowing too hard or too soft caused a distortion of the note; a correct amount of pressure resulted in a clear, crisp sound that was pleasing to the ear. When he finished his practice session, he inspected each felt pad and cork on the sax, loosened the ligatures and removed the reed to allow it to dry, thus preserving its longevity – new reeds were expensive. He dried the horn and polished it with a soft cloth. He returned it to the case, cradling it precisely into its purple felt slots.

He walked to his Momma's bedroom and turned his attention to Shana, who was sitting in front of the radio and listening to music.

"So, tell me, Shana, what'd you learn today in school?"

"Well, we did some arithmetic and worked on the times tables. Some geography. I learned about South America. Hmmm... but I still like recess the best," she finished with a grin.

"I know you get bored with school 'cause you such a smart young girl. But you jes' have to stay with it. Education is too important. It's the only way you got to get out of the Hallows. I ain't gonna let you off easy. Your job is to learn to think, to learn all you can. You gotta listen to them teachers, show respect to 'em."

"I listen," came her indignant reply.

"Okay, okay." Clayton softened his voice. "Jes' keep it up."

She caught him by surprise with her next, quite innocent, question. "Clayton, why don't white people like us?"

Clayton stared at her and felt his own pain in her simple question. He studied her innocent face thoughtfully before responding.

"The way I see it is, they jealous. You see, white people came first. God looked around at all that whiteness, everywhere lookin' faded, pale as white bread. But He always liked color. That's why He made rainbows. So, He made some more people. Red ones, brown ones, black ones, yellow ones. When the white people looked at their own skin all pale and pasty and saw all these other people in their glorious colors…, well, they just got plain jealous."

"Is that true?" Shana asked.

"Jealousy is a mean thing. It causes people to hate. No reason. Jes' this mean thing growlin' inside. Hate is contagious. You can catch it. Can't do nothin' about it if you do catch it. So, be careful. You jes' remember that Black is beautiful. And don't let nobody tell you it ain't."

Clayton spoke to Shana with authority, trying to hide the fact that he did not have the whole answer either for her or for himself.

When not playing the sax, Clayton read books that the school librarian funneled to him, or books loaned to him by crewmen who had access to their ships' libraries. Father Joe loaned him many books, too, on everything from evolution to St. Augustine.

His mother was proud of his diligence, but she discouraged him from reading W.E.B. Du Bois' newsletter that was circulated locally by the school librarian. She feared such ideas would lead him to be defiant and put him on a dangerous path in this violent time of Jim Crow laws. But reading had the opposite effect on him: It kept his anger in check and gave him hope that someday he would be associated with men of such great ideas and vision. He, too, desired to be great.

He tried to explain to his Momma that she need not worry about Du Bois. He was curious about Du Bois because of his prominence as a Black writer. But Du Bois' writing was more political, more about systems than about how it personally felt to be Black. He did not touch the anger inside Clayton, who didn't want to be better than anyone else – just equal.

The South had created state and local statutes after the Civil War to keep Blacks separate. While these laws kept him separated physically, more importantly they reminded Clayton that he was not worthy to sit next to a white man in a movie house, to drink from the same water fountain, or to go to the same bathroom. It implied that Blacks were dirty. Du Bois stated that he thought separate but equal was okay. Clayton, however, dreamed of equal and not separate. He wanted to be a man like any other man.

But Shana came before his own dreams. She wouldn't grow up in this straight-jacket life where Blacks could be accused and punished – sometimes violently – for acts that did not merit harsh punishment. These arbitrary statutes allowed the southern white population to keep their proverbial foot on the throats of Black people. Clayton did not see equality in such perversity, but he complied because of Shana.

Two days a week he would awaken Shana before school and read to her from whatever text he had on hand. She would try to go back to sleep, but he would nudge her, urging her to listen. He might read to her from a magazine salvaged from the church wastebasket, or an editorial gleaned from a newspaper he had found. While the restrictive world of the Hallows kept narrow boundaries on her physical life, Clayton read to her to expand her mind beyond her current knowledge. "Listen to me, Shana," he would say to her, knowing that someday she would recognize the importance of these sessions that she kept trying to resist.

He carried the weight of white heroes on his back as he tried to bring the outside world to Shana so she would know that Black people had a place in it other than what she knew here. If he could only do one thing, he would teach her that she was not an inferior being, that she deserved more from life than what Texas City presented to her, that white supremacy was a lie.

His Momma told him that God would take care of them. That

whatever God had in mind for them, that would be their fate. She attended mass every Sunday. She washed and ironed the clothes of white families just as she did those of her own family and put her earnings in a quart jar in the kitchen cabinet. She would take out a few coins and buy Shana clothes from the secondhand store when needed. She scrubbed her creaky, wavy floors, and she washed and ironed her white linen dress for Sunday church. Before going to sleep, she prayed the rosary.

But Clayton lived outside his mother's God-directed world. He respected her and loved her. But behind his placid brown eyes, lived a different picture of the world. He could be patient, but his plans did not include Shana staying in Texas City.

Clayton was not always on edge. Sometimes he went to the movie house a few blocks from Texas Avenue, even though he had to enter through a ticket booth for Coloreds on the side of the theater and sit upstairs in a segregated balcony. He enjoyed Westerns and rooted for the Indians.

Alcohol never tempted him since he had seen what it had done to his father. He had no time for women in spite of a desire that would sometimes force a walk past "Lola's Place," a tavern where he hoped to get a glimpse of the women lounging inside. At times they walked outside and sat on the porch in their short shorts and halter tops. All the women at this disreputable bar were white. Clayton knew he could be arrested for looking at a white woman. He disciplined himself against all normalcy of desire. He played his saxophone, read his books, adopted a facade of indifference and feigned ignorance.

Sometimes on Sundays, Clayton awoke early to go crabbing on the jetty that stretched into Galveston Bay. He tied a chicken neck to a rock with string, sat on a granite boulder close to the water and tossed it into the channel. When the string became taut, he retrieved it slowly and scooped up a blue crab in a net.

Sometimes he would take Shana with him when he could convince his Momma that she could skip mass "jes' this once." Shana would copy Clayton in pulling the string but soon grew bored with the routine. She would play on the large granite boulders that formed a breakwater and jutted in a thin line into Galveston Bay. She enjoyed the acrobatics of the various shore birds that flew above them. At times she would sit quietly lost in thought, watching the bay water splash against the rocks.

Clayton liked to study her silhouette as it was framed by the sun behind her. He was always amazed by her radiance and the light blazing from her eyes. He would protect that light and keep it shining.

On a slack day, he watched ships pass in and out of the channel and listened to gulls squawk, their bodies suspended in the sky above him. Briny air brought him close to a feeling of peace.

On a good day, Clayton could bring home dozens of crabs. He would put them in a wash tub. He would then put the tub of live crabs in a rusty red wagon, carefully watching their menacing claws wave back and forth. Along the way home, he would share his bounty with neighbors. Shana walked beside him and held his hand in hers, content in the comfort of her big brother.

Three

In the fall of 1946, both the ending and beginning of Grace Hanson's life approached their appointed times, borne on nine silver rail cars that were pulled by two red-and-yellow engines glistening in the sun. The Santa Fe Texas Chief, with its Warbonnet nose, rolled across a span of narrow tracks over Galveston's West Bay. The two paths of Grace's being would unite when the train shut down its engines in Galveston's historic railway station and she stepped out onto the platform.

Grace sat straight up and gripped the arm rests of her chair, afraid to look down at the water roiling beneath the tracks of the bridge. The car rocked from side to side in an audacious tease. When she had boarded the train in Chicago, the plush red-and-gold upholstered seat had provided her first pleasurable experience in years. After 31 months and 14 days in the Chicago Correctional Institute, this seat had felt like afternoon tea in the Drake Hotel.

Now she could think only of the train flipping off the tracks and sending her plush seat, with her glued in it, into the water that danced beneath her.

Grace forced herself to relax her grip and look down at her hands. There had been a time when she had kept her nails clipped and well-manicured so they did not interfere with her precise contact with the keys on her piano. The sight of her once beautiful nails humiliated her now and brought more shame to her fractured anticipation of what lay ahead for her in Galveston.

Fear about the imminent meeting with her sister Greta dominated her emotions. But a cruel irony required her to bear another, momentary fear as the train crawled across this narrow bridge high above the water. Her limited emotional capacity, filled with the shame of misdeeds and subsequent incarceration, now bordered on panic. Overcome, Grace could not pray it out. She just held on to her seat and continued to breathe.

Upon release from prison, Grace Hanson had taken a taxi straight to the train station to begin her journey to Texas. Being outside the prison walls had frightened her as much as being inside them always had. Full of shame and guilt, she had forced herself to execute her plan. She had not allowed herself a glance at another person.

As the train now crossed the bridge in its slow pace, a beautiful contralto voice across the aisle began to sing. A young Black woman, with eyes closed, softly sang:

Swing low, sweet chariot,
Comin' for to carry me home.
Swing low, sweet chariot,
Comin' for to carry me home.

Confused and unable to calm her fear, Grace thought she had returned to prison and tears filled her eyes. Black inmates on her cell block had sung that song at night after lights out. The yearning for freedom that was embedded in its words, as it had been for almost a hundred years, had echoed in the hush of the concrete prison walls.

Grace knew what it was like to be imprisoned. Physically freed at last, she did not feel free. Exhausted like a small bird on a power line during a fierce storm, feathers splayed in disarray and swaying on the wire, she hung on with all her strength. She empathized with the woman whose history carried the burden of slavery, including a sense of disruption and a fear of what the future might hold. She thought this must have been what a slave felt on being set free.

Her train passed over a rusty trestle that could be raised to allow free passage for a masted boat underneath and she could see land ahead of her. A conductor walked down the aisle to inform passengers of their impending arrival. "Galveston," he bellowed. "Galveston!"

Grace worked to control her breathing until it began to slow, allowing her to pass through the panic. She reached up to the overhead rack to retrieve the paper bag that contained everything she owned, placed the bag on her lap and wrapped her arms around it. She clutched a scarred leather purse in her hands and prepared to disembark.

With her eyes closed, the woman continued her quiet singing:
I looked over Jordan and what did I see,
Comin' for to carry me home.

Grace remembered when the song had been in her repertoire. She had sung a jazzy medley of old spiritual songs as part of her performances. But it rang a different tone now. She experienced the anguish and desperation of the hopeless. Inmates had told her of the South's Jim Crow laws, and she wondered how the woman had avoided sitting in the Coloreds' rail car. They had said that normally they had their own designated car to save a white person from having to sit next to them.

That made no difference to Grace, and she loved the woman's song. When she stopped singing and opened her eyes, she saw Grace staring at her. Grace saw a flash in the singer's eyes and easily recognized her state of being - Fear.

"Excuse me for staring. I... I got lost in a memory. You have a beautiful voice. Thank you for the song," Grace said. The young woman inclined her head slightly in response.

As the train reached the end of the bridge, Grace sighed with relief and looked out into the bay at fishermen in small boats, careening in the choppy water. The train crept like a cat toward the end of its journey.

Grace knew that Greta would meet her at the station and drive her the short distance to her home in Texas City, a small industrial town 15 minutes away. The town would be her beginning of a new… what? A new everything. What would the sister who lived a normal family kind of existence, with a child and a husband who had a job, think of her – an ex-convict and drug addict?

She and her sister had never been close, having been born ten years apart. They had last seen each other at their mother's funeral, when Grace was already far along into her addiction. They had lived separate lives and seldom corresponded. Greta had moved to Texas in 1937 with her husband George, a chemist who now worked at the Standard Oil refinery. They had a nine-year-old son Michael, born in Texas City and whom Grace had never met.

Greta's generosity overwhelmed Grace. Not only had she offered her sister a place to live, she had also found a job for her as a secretary at the Catholic Church. Most amazingly, she had not hesitated to allow an ex-junkie and former prison inmate in the same home with her young son. Still, Grace anticipated that Greta's judgment would be strong and swift.

The sisters had grown up Catholic. Grace, whose life had become engulfed in the nightlife of Chicago, had not been in a church for years except for her parents' funerals. But she was ready to embrace this job at the church. It would be the equivalent of getting herself to a nunnery, an extension of her confinement, where she could continue to repent until someday – maybe – she could be forgiven. Someday she might be able to keep the gyroscope of her life upright and find a balance she knew she desperately needed. First, she had to face her older sister: the Catholic woman who still attended church. In addition, Grace knew she had been the privileged one, pretty and petite in contrast to Greta who had always struggled to keep off those few extra pounds. There was no doubt who had been the apple of their mother's eye. Yet here they would meet, with Greta in the "royal coach." And rightfully so, thought Grace.

Her cross-country journey ended with a jolt that forced Grace to tilt forward as the train came to a stop. She had traveled from Chicago, across the breadth of the Midwest, through the State of Texas, to Galveston on the Gulf of Mexico. Worn out and mentally exhausted, Grace stood up, gave a brief nod to the woman who had been singing, and walked down the aisle as her heart beat in her throat. She exited the rail car, clutched her tattered bag, misjudged the height of the last step and almost fell.

Moist air immediately clung to her face. A briny odor held within Galveston's humidity filled her nostrils. Bursts of wind blew a few strands of hair into her mouth. She pushed her hair behind her ear.

Greta was standing near the train's bright red engine. She looked older and heavier than Grace remembered, with her hair cut short. For a moment she thought the woman might not be Greta. Then she turned and their eyes met. Everything around Grace vanished in a white light as she walked toward her sister, locked onto Greta's stare. Each step forced Grace to take another deep breath as she tried to smile through her anxiety.

Greta walked also. Both moved faster until they were running over the final yards between them. They met and wrapped their arms around one another. Tears unfurled on both of their faces. Greta held Grace tightly, allowing her paper bag of possessions to fall onto the concrete.

"I'm so sorry," Grace spoke through her sobs.

"There, there. You're home now. You're home and safe."

Grace held onto Greta, overwhelmed by sadness, unable to let her sister go, afraid she would disappear into her own grief. She had lived so long in isolation and shame that her anguish rushed out in uncontrollable spasms. Steam from an idling engine on an adjacent track mingled with salty air and swirled around them as Greta kept her arms tightly wound around her. They could have been statues on the concourse as people hurried past them. Greta gently guided Grace with her arm around her shoulders as they walked out of the train station.

"This is a new journey, Grace. We'll take it together," Greta said. "No matter the past. I don't care where you have been or what you have done, I will be beside you."

Grace put her head on Greta's shoulder, trying to stifle her tears.

"Dry those tears. We have a few stops to make before we head home."

Greta took Grace shopping in Galveston before they headed back across the bay to Texas City. She bought her clothes and shoes, and all the things she would need to start work.

Grace protested. "You have already sent me money and the train ticket. I feel like a common beggar, with you taking me into your home and everything."

"Don't worry about it. You're my sister. If it makes you feel better, you can pay me back a little each payday," Greta reassured her.

Excited about trying on clothes and having a choice about how she would dress, Grace forgot for a brief moment about prison. However, once in the dressing room, her reflection in the mirror showed her pitifully thin body. Her hair, once coal black and shiny, was now dull and unkempt, hanging down to her shoulders. A pale, waxy skin covered her prominent facial bones beneath blackberry eyebrows. Sallow cheeks and a sad mouth reflected the abasement she had endured.

Quick as a bolt of lightning, the pain returned and in her mind she heard the prison doors closing. She knew those sounds too well: steel latches clicking and gears groaning like a human voice that called her name. The doors always slammed shut in a sonorous explosion. All those months she spent in a dank cell, all the losses of normal life never to be reclaimed. Suddenly shopping lost its appeal.

The road from Galveston into Texas City passed through the industrial complex between the refineries and the dock area. It pierced an eerie landscape. Huge oil storage tanks sat in fields on either side of the road. Hissing steam and the drone of generators made it difficult for Grace and Greta to hear themselves talk. Metal cylinders several stories high stood like sentries guarding the entrance into town.

It frightened Grace to feel the throbbing power of industry so close. She had lived in the inner city of Chicago and had never heard the sounds of an industrial machine as it ground its way towards money.

They stopped for a train as it crossed the road, loaded with cargo from the docks and headed for new destinations. Grace felt claustrophobic with steel girders, platforms and towers rising on both sides of the road and forming an iron canyon. They confined her and looked down on her, like the frowning knights in *Alice in Wonderland*. She wrung her hands and watched as the boxcars and tanker cars rolled past a few yards away from her. Steel wheels squealed on steel tracks under the weight of their cargo.

"Does this place make you nervous?" she asked Greta.

"No. You get used to it…. The noise, the smell. Whew, the smell. George goes to work in it every day. He is a chemist at Pan American, on the west side of this complex. He tells me they are developing an artificial rotten egg. Corny, but he thinks it's funny. Pan American is on the opposite end of a chain of refineries that are anchored by the port. He says it is safe here, so I just never worry about it. Once we get on the other side of this complex of refineries, you'll see that it is calmer."

They drove through the plant area onto South Main Street. It did get calmer as Greta predicted, but not better. Grace could hardly believe her eyes. She had traveled from the vibrant city of Chicago to this dismal, gray downtown that was lined with plain, undistinguished single-story storefronts, and the difference could not have been greater.

She told herself that it did not really matter to her. Nothing mattered now but penance. She had to pay for her sins. Gray suited her mind. Still, the starkness shocked her senses.

She tossed her hair back with a shaky hand and watched as Greta pointed out the grocery store, the drug store, a clothing store, all the places that Greta frequented. They appeared to be a wasteland to Grace. It was definitely not what she had expected.

Greta sensed her apprehension. She had felt a similar response when she had first arrived.

"It's a blue-collar town. Practical. No frills, no attention to beauty or art. No architectural marvels. Definitely not Chicago. It is like a frontier town in a way. Basic services from a box. But we are growing. Once you meet the people, this small-town atmosphere will be comfortable for you. I know you will be just fine here. I like to think of it as an opportunity to create one's own beauty. To create one's own entertainment."

Greta's house, a modest, wood-framed structure painted white with a porch, mirrored much of the town. Two large cottonwood trees fronted the house. A small flower garden bordered the porch with only bluebell vines in it at the moment as yards displayed the initial dormancy of winter.

At the end of the driveway toward the back of the house stood a garage with an apartment over it. Grace would live there, just a few steps away from the back door of the main house. A wooden stairway attached to the side of the garage led to the entrance.

"We thought it would be good for you to have your own space," Greta observed.

Grace walked through the rooms that had been painted a pale sea-water green. The apartment had a tiny kitchen at the back, a bedroom, a bathroom and a small living room.

"It's so normal."

Before she had gone to prison, she had lived on the near west side of Chicago, in tenement houses with apartments which might have ten people crammed into them. Prostitutes, drug dealers, pimps. The poor. These had been her neighbors. This apartment with its clean smell, nightstands, and comfortable sofa and chairs, defied her expectations. It had a sense of place. Unlike the jungle of criminals and social misfits mired in addiction that were her former neighbors, this place brought a sense of peace to her weariness. And yet it frightened her.

"I don't know if I can do this." Grace sat down on the couch and stared out the window. She could not look at Greta. "I don't deserve such a place. Pictures of birds. Rugs on the floor. No screaming, no shouting coming through the walls. I'm a criminal, Greta."

"Everything will be fine," Greta assured her, ignoring her pleas. "You can take a few days to relax and rest. You will love Father Joe. I'll take you to meet him once you are settled. There is no rush to begin."

"How much does he know about me?"

"I told him a little about our family. You and me, mostly. He knows you have been in prison."

"MOM!" came a shout from outside.

"That would be Michael, home from school." Greta stood in the doorway and called down the stairs. "Up here, Michael. Come meet your Aunt Grace."

The minute Michael entered, his energy filled the room. He came straight to Grace and hugged her. This was the first child she had touched since before prison and she could not stop staring at him. His small, spindly body radiated goodness as he stared at Grace in an awkward silence. What a handsome boy. Suddenly an image of her own baby as she held her just after she was born came to her. She breathed deep and tried to focus on Michael's face.

"It's good to meet you, Michael," Grace said. She could feel her heart begin to thaw a little. It had been iced over for so long.

"Mom, I'm hungry. Can I have a snack?"

"In a minute. How was school?"

"Ugh. But I made a hundred on my spelling test."

"I'm very proud of you," she responded with a big smile.

Turning to Grace, she continued, "Let's go down to the house. We'll make some coffee and I'll show you around. I made some cookies this morning. You can come back here and unpack and rest up a bit after that."

Grace watched Greta's eyes follow Michael as he hurried down the stairs. She saw the joy he brought to his mother with his vitality, innocence and purity. The angelic aura of the child.

Left alone in the apartment later, she sat on the edge of her bed. A comfortable mattress lay beneath her in contrast to the concrete cot she had slept on in prison. Living here would be a difficult adjustment at best. Impossible at worst. All those months she had just existed, isolated from a normal world and normal people, was now a time warp that would require a major rehabilitation.

"I can do this," she told herself, hitting one fist into the palm of the other hand. "I can do this."

Looking over the table and chairs, bed and mattress, frilly covers and pillows, she acknowledged all that she had missed while in prison. This place reminded her how wrong she had been to despise normalcy, to want something more glamorous, to be more important. What had that gotten her? She felt that she did not deserve even "normal" now. With slumped shoulders and deep sighs, she began to pace the floor of the apartment. Freedom was proving to be more difficult than she had imagined.

Her desire to become a professional singer in the competitive jazz craze of Chicago had required a mental toughness that she struggled to find again. Her life had started in the middle-class

Austin community, an area west of Chicago. Her father had worked as an accountant for a roller bearing company. Her mother had taught piano lessons in their home. Ten years after Greta, Grace had come into the world, conceived, her mother said, by the grace of God and thus named. Along with dolls, playing house and other normal young-girl pastimes, Grace revealed a marvelous aptitude for playing the piano. She became her mother's most gifted pupil and won every available competition as a child. Her mother had secretly longed to be a concert pianist and envisioned that she would live that dream through Grace.

But Grace turned away from classical music and broke her mother's heart. A group of musicians called the Austin Gang, the first notable white jazz ensemble in the Chicago area, had a profound effect on Grace's love of music. Classical music became too staid, too old-fashioned. She gravitated to the exciting and hip jazz style. She went to clubs on the west side, places like Hull House, and listened to piano players such as Art Hodes and Joe Sullivan. Their sound filled her with the excitement of something new. It spoke of revolution, separating her from her midwestern, middle-class existence. When she played, she copied the bluesy jazz style of Hodes.

In the process, Grace also discovered that she had a natural singing voice: husky, mellow, both sensual and sincere. She devoted more of her practice time to playing jazz and improving her singing. Her mother tried to discourage her, saying she wanted her to go to college. Her father, who worked long hours, went straight to his newspapers when he came home and showed no interest in what she did or the decisions she made.

Jazz music held Chicago in its grip at the time. Southern jazz musicians, most from New Orleans, had migrated to the city, infusing the music venues with verve and giving a new face to a lagging bar scene. Nightlife glowed hotter than the 1871 fire. This energy stole Grace away from her mother's influence. She resolved to be a part of the hip, young crowd that showed so much vitality. She wanted this to be her life.

At night, Grace worked in clubs as a hostess. Her bosses would allow her to perform when the headliners took breaks. Soon she found singing gigs in some of the myriad clubs that comprised the jazz landscape.

Grace's choice devastated her mother. She hated and feared the jazz culture and felt that nothing good would come from this decadent bunch of be-bop musicians. She badgered Grace to give up her pursuit of the depraved music, making their relationship so difficult that they both abandoned attempts at civility with each other. Greta had married and moved to Texas. Grace and her father, always distant, became even more detached. They hardly ever spoke to each other.

When Grace returned late at night, her mother would begin her crusade. "God does not want you to hang around those degenerate people," she warned. She began to call on the power of her Catholic heritage. "They are not God-fearing people. They're sinners and they will lead you into mortal sin. You will be damned to Hell."

"They are not degenerates. They are serious musicians. They are my friends," Grace screamed back at her.

After too many raucous scenes, Grace moved out of the house, her relationship with her parents toxic and broken. Lonely and at times afraid, music and hard work saved her sanity.

Grace's star began to ascend. She played larger venues and

became a popular artist whose name surfaced in various music circles about town. *Chicago Magazine* described her as "the new kid on the block, turning heads her way; an accomplished musician with a smoky voice – and wow, a real looker." Her talent brought a new world to her and she streaked to the top of the "A List." It all came so easy – and fast.

Grace did not follow the usual style of a jazz singer that depended on a lot of improvisations. Instead, she held notes in long, controlled variations that came to the listener's ear with a sweet sadness. The silky flow of her voice, accompanied by the brilliant construction of notes and chords on the piano, mesmerized listeners. She and her audience melted together like lovers. She craved the adulation that began to fill the huge hole in her heart created by her family's disdain. Grace tried at first to stay in touch with her mother, but too much had changed. She drifted away from her parents and began a solitary life of her own.

After a few years, Grace reached a plateau. The club crowd still loved her performances. She still garnered accolades and glowing reviews. But Grace stayed anchored, moving horizontally at best, and became a "fixture" on the Chicago night scene. Maybe her naive nature, or her lack of business acumen, or not having a mentor she could trust kept her from moving into the big time. She watched as other, younger performers signed contracts to sing with big bands and travel to Europe, where American jazz dominated the music scene.

Grace remained in Chicago and settled into a perfunctory routine. She fretted about the oversights and lack of attention of agents and talent scouts and denied their hurtful slights and rejections. Slowly, she came to believe that she really did not measure up to the younger singers, especially the sultry Peggy Lee. Doubt eroded her self-confidence.

Shy and reticent off stage, still separated from her family and with no close friends, Grace saw her life begin to fray around the edges, but she did not know how to stop the slide. She did not involve herself in romantic relationships because music ordered her life.

Confusion and apathy moved into her daily routines. After work she would go home alone, smoke a joint and go to bed. During the day she would not practice or learn new material. She skipped meals and lost weight. She began a downward spiral, unable to discern her own reality.

Band members and other entertainers finally coaxed her into joining them at late night bars, to relieve the pressure of performing, they said. At these times, stories were told about performances, including miscues on stage. They laughed at and with each other, smoked pot and drank.

Grace had never had alcohol before, but with the increase in her emotional discomfort, she began to rely on vodka to relieve some of her hurt feelings.

Dave, a drummer from another trio, invited her to dance at one of their late-night gatherings. "I've caught your act several times. I love your style," he said.

"Really? Be careful. You might find it lonely there."

"What are you saying? You have a ton of fans," he said, looking directly into her eyes.

He studied her longer. "You know what? I think you are afraid of success. You have everything. You only have to believe in yourself."

The words carried magic within them. The vacuum in Grace's

heart immediately took Dave into residency. Their late-night parties continued and, swept away by his attention, they became a couple. Dave moved in with her.

Ultimately, he introduced Grace to heroin. "You gotta try this," he said. Grace, vulnerable and naive, still hiding disappointments and a feeling of failure, lost all restraint. Heroin's seductive embrace spiraled her life into a freefall as she became unreliable and unable to perform.

Dave disappeared.

She was alone again.

And pregnant.

These memories now filled her with shame. I am in Texas, she thought, but Chicago has followed me across the country. I can't let it in. I must do this for Greta... and Michael.

In her mind, she saw him scrambling down the stairs like a bottle rocket. I must make this work for Greta and Michael, she repeated to herself.

ℱour

"I don't know how you ever graduated from the seminary," observed the Bishop as he stared directly at the priest in front of him. "I have warned you repeatedly, still you push my patience. What am I to do with you?"

Father Joe Irons sat up in the straight-back chair like a private under the stare of a master sergeant. He tried to remember how many times he had been called to the Bishop's Palace in Galveston for one of these "little chats" with His Reverence, sure that his number of visits led the diocese in the inglorious department of misconduct. Since he had become the pastor in Texas City, he had been here at least half a dozen times, a fact not lost on the Bishop who, according to Father Joe and other parish priests, was a bombastic, acerbic disciplinarian, who conducted the "personal review" chat with loud, profane language that could wither the strongest of men.

Father Joe loved being a priest. The ritual never felt rote or dispassionate to him. Each time he found himself on the carpet again, he braced himself for the worst, hoping for another reprieve. He tried to follow the rules. But sometimes he found that the Church's rules defied logic. Not willing to give up his own intellect and judgment, he frequently improvised. Because he worked hard, and his parishioners loved him – informally calling him Father Joe – he had escaped any real disciplinary action from the Bishop.

"You do know that a Catholic woman who has married a

divorced man cannot receive communion, don't you?" The Bishop paused, his glare enveloping Father Irons.

"With all due respect, Bishop, this woman was weeping as she told me of her love for the Eucharist, how she yearned to be closer to Jesus. She asked if there was any way she could be reinstated to be able to receive communion. I told her the rules, which she already knew. 'Father, I was almost 40 years old, still living with my aging parents,' she told me. 'This man gave me a chance to be married, to have children. Two good, Catholic children.'"

Father Joe laid on the drama a little thicker as he continued, "She told me, 'I knew he had been divorced, but I am a woman. I wanted – no, I *needed* – children. I stayed in the Church hoping that maybe something would change. My faith is not the same without communion.'"

Working up some confidence with a deep breath, he plunged ahead. "So I thought about it. I told her if she would come to mass on Monday mornings, I would give her communion in private, in the sacristy. She is a good woman. Hard working. Altar Society and all. I decided that God would want her to have a marriage and children, and that she should not be punished because she did not have many choices. She comes to mass daily. She is happy. And her husband recently quit drinking."

Father Joe knew he had pushed the limits and now bordered on insubordination. "I know that rules are important, but God gave me a mind. Not to use it would be a greater sin than bending a few rules."

"You are always bending a few rules!" the Bishop roared. "You have taken it upon yourself to challenge me and the authority of this Church!"

Father Joe waited a moment. "I love my Church, I love God and His abundant life. I mean no disrespect to you or the Church. But I must make some decisions on my own. I cannot be bothering you with every little detail."

"This is not a little detail! This is dogma, a matter decreed by the Holy Father himself. It is intended to protect the sacrament of the Eucharist."

Protect it from what, Father Joe wanted to ask. From leading a faithful servant into a closer union with the Savior? But he knew when to wave the white flag.

Instead, he said, "Yes, Your Excellency. I confess my sins to you and will accept any action you deem necessary."

He put on his most contrite face and waited for fire to erupt from the dragon's mouth again. The Bishop sat motionless, with no emotion in his face. Red blotches crept up his neck.

"Father Irons, I order you to adhere to the rules and regulations of this Church as set forth by this Diocese and our Holy Father. This is not the first time I have reprimanded you. Don't test my patience anymore. You will find yourself.... Get out of here. Let me get on with my work."

Father Joe hesitated. He had also wanted to talk about Clayton and the Black community in Texas City. Should he mention it now? He could feel the prickly atmosphere pressing on him. Another time.... Maybe next time.

"Well, go on. Get out of here."

Outside of the Bishop's office, Father Joe exhaled, a relieved grin on his face. He sat on a bench in the foyer and expressed a long sigh. He never set out to defy the Bishop, even though he knew when he broke the rules or bent them a little. Still, it dismayed him to be called in for a "chat." Each time he vowed to become more reverent, to abide by the strict laws. He had no problem with the discipline of saying daily mass or reading the breviary. No problem of never having a day off.

It was humanity, the humanness of his parishioners and their relationship with God in which he could often find a flaw in the Church's position. Too often, Church rules ignored the realities of life. Father Joe sought to secure a practical arena for sinners and saints to be able to live with the frailties of being human. In the meantime, he had to contend with the complexities of people on this earth.

He saw life as a duality of good and evil. Souls could not experience good without the knowledge of bad and the temptations inherent therein. No one could be perfect. Not even bishops.

On the way out of the Bishop's Palace, he admired the ornate hand-carved stair rails and the floor design of inlaid oak and cherry wood. Walnut bookcases lined the walls. He passed through an elaborate entrance flanked by marble columns. Once outside, he looked up at the grandness of the building and thought of a European palace.

The house had been built for Colonel Walter Grisham, an attorney from Virginia. The diocese had purchased it from his family for the Bishop's residence. It presented a perfect emblem of the power and glory of Catholicism. But to Father Joe, it represented a divide between the Catholic hierarchy and his parishioners. As he turned toward his office, he wondered if the Bishop had lost touch with his flock.

A growl in his stomach told him it must be lunch time. He had to hurry back to his office to interview a new secretary who was coming in for their first meeting. What would the Bishop think of him hiring a woman with a questionable past, particularly one just out of prison? A young woman, too. He acknowledged the unwritten rule about young women working in the rectory.

He knew little about her except that Greta, her sister and a parishioner, had said that she needed help. Greta had described her as young, talented and beautiful, and also lost, adrift in a sea of guilt and shame because of a prison sentence in Chicago.

Not exactly the *curriculum vitae* of the typical church secretary, Father Joe surmised to himself. Something else the Bishop would not need to know. He might understand that an ex-prison inmate could use a second chance. But young and beautiful? That would raise a red flag for the Bishop.

Father Joe had said that he would interview Grace and so he would follow through with his decision, but he denied to himself that he was intrigued by her story.

When she came into his office, an aura of despair entered with her. Grace kept her eyes averted from Father Joe, staring at the floor and wringing a handkerchief in her hands. She tried to force a smile but interrupted it with a deep breath.

He immediately felt her pain. He could not help himself. She appeared genuinely wounded, her spirit deflated. He did not need to go through the usual interview protocol and question her. It was simple. She needed his help; the rest would take care of itself.

"I need you here at eight o'clock in the morning. Most days our work will be over by five. I am confident you can do this work, and I will do everything I can to make it a positive experience for you. Can you start on Monday?"

$\mathcal{F}$ive

Grace had begun her residency in the "nunnery." That was how she saw her work. She had put herself next to a holy place and she vowed that its proximity would guide her on a path of reconciliation. It would keep her safe and sheltered until she healed her spirit. Although this would not stop her depression, her workday would give her a break from the afflictions of her mind, which she hoped would allow the healing to begin.

Greta's assessment of Father Joe had been correct: He was congenial, funny and easy to please. A short walk from Greta's house to the rectory put her at a desk in a pleasant anteroom that was connected to the priest's office. She had enough busy work to keep her outside of herself most of the day.

After the first week, she began a habit of arriving five minutes early each morning to inspect the floors and waste baskets, straighten the already straight chairs and pull files she would need for that day. It was important to keep herself precisely on schedule.

Grace saw herself as the novitiate, disciplining her life as contrition for her past. In the deeper recesses of her mind, she walked a tightrope, straining to maintain her stability. Her fragile peace showed in the taut way she held her mouth and the fact that she never smiled.

Father Joe was breezy, energetic and always respectful, and insisted that she call him Father Joe. She thought he was kind and he did not push her, even though she found it difficult to look at him when they spoke. She worked to keep tight control of her life and continued to resist emotional attachment to anything or anyone.

After a couple of weeks, she felt that she was able to hold it together – at least on the surface. But memories from her past and deep-seated emotions from her unconscious mind found a way to keep her on a teeter-totter at odd times. A recurrent dream had her in a museum peering out from inside a glass box and seeking to escape. People passed by and stared at her. She paced back and forth like a panther in a cage, her eyes gazing out on the freedom of those watching her, until she slowly realized that she belonged behind the glass, that she felt safe and secure there, like the other museum pieces.

As she walked to work this morning, a light rain began to fall and a car passed by a little too fast. Grace stumbled sideways off the road and suppressed a desire to cry out at the driver. As she bent to remove a rock from her shoe, her blouse pulled out of her skirt, and she quickened her pace in the rain. She arrived at the office frazzled and afraid.

Grace could not speak to Father Joe when she entered the rectory. She went to the bathroom to straighten her clothes and do something with her wet hair. She ended the effort by throwing her brush into the sink. In front of the mirror, she held her breath to fight back tears.

She had worked hard to maintain her stability by staying on task and not deviating from her daily routine. She had focused only on the next step and the step after that. She kept changes to a minimum. Father Joe's patience and kindness had made it easier to keep her secret locked inside. She had made a little progress, but sometimes it all overwhelmed her.

She recalled the dreamy ecstasy of heroin and at times still desired the freedom it brought. The drug allowed her body to drift weightlessly, her mind to fly to distant islands where she could laugh and frolic in the sea foam that swirled around her. In a haze of heroin, she believed herself to be powerful and in control.

In reality, heroin had initiated her descent into Hell and she consciously hated that life. But she still desired the drug when the memory of her baby intruded itself.

As Grace worked to put these thoughts aside and begin her day, a parishioner came into the rectory to make an appointment for the baptism of her infant daughter. Grace turned from the file cabinet to greet the woman and saw the baby, dressed in a pink dress and booties, her cherubic cheeks matching the dress. Light radiated around her, and her sparkling blue eyes regarded everything in the room. The child startled Grace and she gasped. In a cruel instant, the infant had transported Grace back to her tenement house in Chicago and the cascading images smothered her breathing.

She turned away, then looked back at the woman. She tried to speak, stammered, and finally stood mute and staring at the mother. Her body shook. Disoriented and feeling faint, Grace rushed into the hallway. She found her way to the bathroom and held onto the sides of the lavatory as the room reeled around her.

She came out of her fog as she heard Father Joe's voice. "Grace, are you alright?"

She walked into the hall and braced herself with one hand on the wall. Father Joe reached out for her arm. "You're as white as a ghost," he said. "Let me help you. You might fall."

"I can't go back in there. I can't," Grace said, turning her head away from the priest.

"It's alright. Why don't you go outside and get some fresh air? I'll take care of things here."

A while later, Father Joe joined Grace on the back steps. She kept her eyes closed and brought a shaky hand up to her forehead. She wanted to scream. All the blackness within her memory returned. She had thought the memory buried for good but found it was only hidden, not forgotten. Now it lay there, in the blue eyes of this innocent baby.

"It's okay. We can go back inside. You need to sit down." Father Joe guided her back to her chair and waited before speaking.

"I know you have struggled with something other than being in prison. Sometimes these things work themselves out if allowed time to heal. But sometimes a problem can be so big that you might need help with it. If you want to talk with me...."

"I thought I was better. I can't hold it together anymore. I can't go on hiding it," she stammered.

"Prison must have been a hellish time for you," he prodded gently. Silence again. "When you feel...."

Grace interrupted him. "I'm still in prison. I killed my baby."

Father Joe eased back in the chair, surprised to hear those words and stunned by their implication.

"The other inmates called me 'Baby Killer.' And it was true." A sigh slipped through her clenched teeth. She could no longer deny the storm that raged inside. Her story broke out between sobs.

"I worked in Chicago as a jazz singer, in nightclubs. I wanted to be a star on a grander stage, but I wasn't going anywhere. I got depressed. A drummer I met, Dave, began to pay attention to me and to flatter me. I was overwhelmed by it. He said he wanted to protect me, take care of me. And he did in a way. I had never had a serious relationship before. I was naive. He told me how great I was and boosted my confidence. He pushed me to expand my repertoire, try new songs, even try writing my own music. Together we created a songbook for me." She paused for a breath.

"We moved in together.... Dave and me." Grace inhaled and shed more tears.

After a moment, she continued. "I had been smoking marijuana for a number of years to relax after a show. Then Dave introduced me to heroin. It was stupid, I know. Heroin addiction is an epidemic in Chicago. But I was lonely. I needed Dave.... But I had no tolerance for the drug and became totally addicted. I suppose part of me knew that Dave was already a junkie, but I didn't allow any thought of it."

She stopped to cry.

Father Joe wanted to reach out to her, to comfort her in some physical way to relieve the anguish he heard in her story. But he sat still, trying to fathom how he could help her in this gut-wrenching moment. The pain in her voice and on her face disquieted him. For the first time he felt the depth of her despair.

"Then I got pregnant. Dave, unable to cope with it all, left me. Just left, without a word. I wanted to stop shooting the stuff, but I couldn't. I had little money and what money I had went to buy more drugs. I couldn't pay my rent." She looked up at Father Joe.

"Oh, Grace. I'm so sorry."

She rushed to finish the story. "The baby came. When she was about three months old, she caught a bad cold. It was winter and we had no heat. She wouldn't stop crying. She had a fever and wouldn't sleep so I didn't sleep. After a day... or two... I don't know, she finally went to sleep. I was relieved and took a big hit of heroin. I slept for a long time. When I woke, the room was freezing."

Father Joe could feel the end of this story. He now sat stunned, bereft of any words.

Grace struggled to take a deep breath and began to cry harder. "I went to her bed. She didn't move and I thought she was asleep. When I picked her up, I knew immediately that she was dead. I sat and held her for hours, wanting to die with her."

Father Joe placed his hand over hers, still unable to speak.

Composing herself, she went on. "While I was pregnant, I didn't want to have the baby. When she came, I just fell in love with her. She was so much the opposite of me. Pure and innocent. She would look at me with her blue eyes, as if I was something special. She would smile at me like I was someone really good, and her tiny fingers would touch my face. She needed me to take care of her... and I didn't."

She looked up at Father Joe. "The prosecutor wanted to charge me with negligent homicide. But because she died of pneumonia, he dropped that. I got three years for possession of an illegal drug."

Father Joe reached across the desk and took both of Grace's hands in his. They sat without speaking. Death of such innocence carried an unspeakable sorrow and it hung in the space between them.

"I have never had that kind of trauma," Father Joe struggled to find words. "It is unimaginable to me.... But I do know about despair and loss of hope.... You made a mistake, Grace. You made some bad choices, but you had no intention of harming your baby. A mistake is not a life sentence. You have had enough punishment for what happened. You have had enough."

Grace sat back in her chair, cold, numb and exhausted.

He urged her, "You have to forgive yourself for mistakes, no matter how bad they seem. You are not able to do it now. At some point you will be. God is not an avenger. He loves you as the creation that you are."

Father Joe's words had no effect.

"I can't. I keep remembering it."

"That moment will always be in you. But with forgiveness you can move on in life. Have you told Greta about this? Anyone?"

Grace shook her head no.

"Start by telling Greta. It would be a good first step. You can't keep this inside of you any longer." He paused, still watching Grace carefully. "Can you get yourself home?"

Grace nodded in response.

"Go home. Take as long as you need. I'll be here if you need me."

Mentally exhausted, Grace left and that night she told Greta about her baby. "I named her Peggy. She's buried in a pauper's cemetery on the south side of Chicago. She was a difficult baby from birth and the nurse told me that was because she suffered from addiction…. I made her addicted in my uterus, Greta."

Slowly Grace shared the entire story of her sordid descent. "I was desperate and lived in poverty. I blamed myself for Dave's leaving." Grace paused before deciding to confess to the rest of it.

"You have to know it all. I had gone on the streets and prostituted myself. I lived in the worst of the worst tenements. I lived in Hell and got stoned to withstand the pain."

Greta held Grace in her arms for a long time, rocking her and smoothing her hair.

Greta held rock solid. She showed no surprise, no clucking, no judgment. She poured out her enormous compassion for her wounded sister.

"I love you, Grace. I love you no matter what you've done or where you've been. We will get through this one step at a time. I know who you are and who you will be again."

Grace went to her bed and languished in depression for three days, seldom getting up and eating little of what Greta brought her. Greta stayed by her side, urging her to get up or at least talk to her.

"Can you talk to me, Grace? Can I do anything for you?"

She read to her: short stories, poems and the newspaper. She brought hot tea and cookies. Grace remained in bed, mute. She stared or slept.

Father Joe called daily and sent words of support through Greta. The baby in that lady's arms with her innocent face had sent Grace back to the squalor of the tenements and that cold, icy room. It was suffocating her.

On the morning of the fourth day, one that was sunny and warm, Greta walked into the apartment determined to get Grace out of bed.

"You have to get out of bed. I know you don't want to, but you must. Come on, get up. I am taking you out today."

Grace did not protest as Greta gently helped her into the shower and then dressed her. Soon they were on the road to Galveston, Greta chatting about Michael and his schoolwork.

"He is a wonderful little boy. Very sensitive and so eager to please. And growing like a weed." She talked about George's work and activities going on around Texas City.

"It's not the most exciting place, but it's a good community for us. There are many wonderful people in the town. Once you get out more, you will find activities to enjoy. It will get better… easier."

Greta drove down Galveston's Broadway Boulevard with its oleanders, palms, majestic oak trees and stately Victorian homes. The ornate Bishop's Palace passed their view. She drove to the end of Broadway, down the seawall onto the beach, and brought the car to the water's edge. Greta held Grace's arm as they strolled on the sandy shoreline. Sunlight sparkled off the breakers as they rolled onto dun-colored sand. A sea breeze freshened the air and tousled their hair. The sound of waves curling onto the shore calmed her sister's anxiety.

"I was afraid to come here. I was afraid of your judgment. And afraid of what you would think of me. I mean, whatever you think of me is justified, but…."

Greta interrupted her admission. "That's probably because I did judge you. For a while anyway. After all, I hated you most of my adolescent life," Greta chuckled. "I had been 'the princess' for a long time when you came into the world. You showed up beautiful and talented in the middle of my reign. You usurped this princess. I felt pushed aside and it hurt me. I had to hate you to hide my jealousy. But then I saw you develop, play the piano so beautifully, be so beautiful…. Well, it all became awe. You dazzled me."

She gathered her thoughts. "Then George came into my life. Then Michael, especially Michael. Kids are wonderful teachers. Michael brought a sense of worth to my life, a knowledge of the real value of things."

Greta paused and turned to Grace. "I don't judge you anymore. I stopped that a long time ago. As for where you have been... well, I just feel great empathy at how much you have suffered. I know you well enough to know that you are not that person. You made some bad choices and you did the best you could to survive."

Grace, obsessed with her memory, replied, "How do I forgive myself? I killed my baby. In prison, I compartmentalized my shame, my sorrow and fear. I put the most painful thoughts deep beneath my awareness. I thought I could do the same here."

As they stood silent, a formation of pelicans flew overhead. Grace gazed at the flock. Despite having large bowl-shaped bills, small bodies and expansive wings, they flew with great rhythm and fluid motion, a silent masterpiece of movement.

"Those birds have such freedom. What I would give to be one of them, flying on the wind in perfect control."

Greta reached out for her. "You will, Grace. You will fly again. For now, we just need to get you through today. And I say it is time to eat."

They lunched at Gaido's where the elegant dining room quieted Grace's turbulence, with its white tablecloths and polite waiters who spoke in quiet tones. Greta ordered for both of them and summoned a feast: crab claws dipped in batter then deep fried, grilled red snapper covered with lump crab meat in a butter sauce, coffee, bread pudding. Grace sat and stared at the food.

Greta continued her careful encouragement. "You have to start enjoying little things again, like food. And maybe we can find a movie to see. You must fight, Grace. You have to get angry at what happened. You have to fight your way back to being who you are at your core."

Greta touched the side of Grace's face. "I think that salt air has put a little color back in your cheeks.... I know it is difficult, coming back from what happened in Chicago. But you are in a safe place now. We love you, Grace."

Grace took Greta's hand and managed a weak smile. Then she began to eat.

When they returned to the apartment, Michael came over to visit Grace. He held a pad of drawing paper and crayons and asked her to help him with a school project. She watched him draw and color a tepee and some Indians.

"Mom says you took painting lessons in… you know... where you were."

"I don't think you need any help, Michael. You're doing very well."

Michael stopped drawing, suddenly bored with the task. "I'm going to see my friend now." He started toward the door and turned to say, "I'm glad you're here, Aunt Grace," then dashed out the door.

Grace recalled the painting lessons the prison conducted as part of their rehab program. But she believed that nothing had helped her, not that and not the therapy. She picked up Michael's pad and a crayon. Without thinking, she drew dark swirls and rolling shapes like clouds. With a few more strokes they became a large fire with billows of smoke pushing high into the sky. Beneath this emerged a tenement house where gray, ghost-like figures rose from the windows into the cloudy mass above. Dark and ominous images flowed from the crayons, like nothing Grace had ever seen before. She continued through several pages without stopping, all of the images dark and depressing. She couldn't help herself as they tumbled from her, unbidden. The number of drawings surprised her when she at last laid the crayons aside.

That evening, Greta brought her some soup for supper with another message from Father Joe. "I told him you would be back to work on Monday."

Greta skimmed through Grace's drawings. The dark images alarmed her. "Grace, you wouldn't do anything to hurt yourself, would you?" She raised her voice slightly. "You have to promise me you won't. Promise me."

Grace sat on the edge of the couch; her eyes downcast. She did not reply.

"Grace?"

"I'm just tired now. Just tired."

With Greta's help, Grace returned to work on Monday, resolved again to put her past behind her. Father Joe welcomed her back, knowing that she still struggled and remained on a tenuous path, feeling isolated and unable to overcome the shame that haunted her.

He worried that she would relapse into addiction, and he did not want to put more pressure on her. Each day he engaged her in conversation, probing gently to find common ground that would allow Grace to talk more about her past. Later in the week, his efforts seemed to begin paying off.

As he came out of his office with a coffee cup in his hand, he stopped by her desk.

"You know, I don't see you as a rebellious person," he observed. "It is like you accidentally fell into a bad situation."

Grace paused in her work, looked at the floor and calculated her response. "I was a naive person. When life gave me bad news, I didn't have any way to cope. I sought someone to make me feel better and I found Dave. That was my first bad decision. But I became very good at making more of them." She paused again and could feel her anger rising. "Listen, I did it to myself. I did those things. Nobody forced me into it."

"Sometimes circumstances that we are unaware of set us up to make bad decisions," Father Joe said. "We all have a darkness, a shadow, so to speak, that wants to take control. It has an uncanny ability to dictate behavior sometimes."

He paused and then took a chance to ask the hard question. "Prison must have been a shock to you. What was that like?"

"Just say the word 'prison' and its sound makes you feel bad. If you can imagine something a thousand times worse than the sound of the word 'prison,' then you begin to get an idea of it. Nights were the worst. I couldn't sleep. Most of the time I stared into the darkness and listened to scratching and shuffling noises, imagining the rats running across the floor." Grace paused, the image of rats roaming through her mind.

"I think time hurt the most. You know how time just flies by sometimes? You wonder what happened to the day. Before I went to prison when that happened, I would just comment about it to myself or to whoever was nearby. In prison, time became a mental agony. Time dragged like a literal ball and chain.

"Conversely, my mind dwelled on the fact that 'doing time' in prison meant losing time. I became acutely aware that I was losing time, unable to live a normal life. Even though I knew I needed to be punished, I desperately wanted that time to be mine so that I could be me. It never happened, and I lost myself completely. I never knew how precious one minute could be until then, and the agony of those minutes passing never to be reclaimed brought an excruciating longing to be free."

As if in response to her own thoughts, Grace rose from her chair and began to pace.

"Panic at the loss spiraled into hopelessness and despair. Life in the form of time keeps on moving like the sun and the moon. It pays no attention to whether I am in prison or at Coney Island. Whoever coined the euphemism "doing time" knew that pain of loss. It's doing your life locked up."

"You must have been so relieved to get out."

"Relieved? I was scared to death. Prison made me a zombie. Suddenly I didn't know if I was a human being anymore. How could I be out here?"

"You want to tell me about it?"

Grace did not want to tell Father Joe, but the words began to come out of her. In bits and pieces, the memories came back.

"I walked out of the prison gates in bright sunshine. It was cold, but not Chicago cold. My only warmth was a light sweater. A strong wind swirled so that women crossing the street had to hold their skirts down. Men in suits and ties ran up the prison steps behind me holding on to their hats. I looked over my shoulder at the prison's entrance and held my breath, expecting that I would be called back, afraid that I had been released by mistake. I felt dizzy, thinking that all these people were doing normal human things. I knew I wasn't normal. I was not even sure that I was human.

"I saw a concrete bench, went over and sat down. I was holding a paper bag filled with everything I owned. I put my hand in my purse and wrapped my fingers around the money and train ticket that Greta had sent to me, fighting back tears, lost and alone, feeling like a tree that had been ripped out of the ground, roots and all.

"I could not get up from the bench, could not move. Car horns blared, trolley wheels screeched on their tracks with their bells clanging, vendors hawked their stuff on street corners. Noises assaulted me and people hurried by me. Paralyzed with shame and sitting in front of the prison, I knew that everyone judged me as a criminal who was just put back on the streets. I had no life and I watched the whirl of people from inside a bubble.

"Several small birds pecked the grass close to where I sat. I thought of the fear that had gripped me every time I went on stage to sing. Despite that fear, I had never missed a curtain call. That thought saved me at that moment. I convinced myself to imagine that I was walking into the glare of stage lights. After that, I somehow stood up, walked to the corner and took a taxi to Dearborn Station."

"And you were on your way to Texas."

"Yes. I felt that I had no choice, that I had no place else to go. I am so thankful for Greta, but I came engulfed with fear and shame. I will admit something to you, Father Joe. I believed this job to be the equivalent of entering into a nunnery, an extension of my confinement. I didn't deserve to have a normal life anymore."

A slight smile came to Father Joe's face.

"I have never been a Mother Superior before or the head of a convent. So, don't tell the Bishop that story. He will accuse me of trying to usurp the sisters at Incarnate Word."

Father Joe became serious again. "We all live too much in the past, Grace. It pursues us and dictates how we live. But the past is over. It cannot touch you. Each day is a new creation. That's what the resurrection is all about. In time you will be able to see yourself as your own original creation. That innocent person whose life became damaged, that spirit, still resides in you. Mistakes are not counted for eternity. There will be healing.

"You are going to be alright, Grace. Your life will get better. As Churchill said, 'You must never ever, ever, ever, ever, give up.' I will help you. And Greta will be there for you."

Six

At the kitchen table, the bitter taste of defeat hovered inside Louis' chest. Surrounded by all the trappings of success, he did not feel successful. He lived as though two people occupied his body, never sure who would show up. At times, he presented a confident and competent *persona*. Suddenly the confidence would leave him and he would feel as if he was trying to push a rope uphill. He played at the charade, an actor in the burlesque of his own life.

He told himself that he understood this dichotomy, but in reality, he did not have a clue as to who really inhabited him. At times, an unconscious spirit haunted him like a ghost rattling chains and disrupting his thoughts, wanting to get his attention. At other times, he perceived only a discomfort like a minor itch or rash that had not been diagnosed.

He poured a glass of bourbon, too distracted to remove his jacket, and drummed his fingers on the ceramic top of his mother's old table. It matched the stark white of the cabinets and walls trimmed in wainscoting. White appliances adjacent to a white ceramic sink lined one side of the room. Outside, fallen leaves covered the lawn. Cool fronts came with regularity now as the year-end approached.

He turned off the kitchen light and drenched the room in darkness except for a few shadowy shapes thrown from a hallway light. In the early gloaming, he could barely see the bay through the back door window, its surface serene up to the shore.

Marsh grass, curving down on slender stalks, bunched close to the water's edge. Louis often sat here in the dark in total silence, sipping bourbon, smoking cigarettes and thinking.

He made a sandwich from leftover steak and poured another bourbon. He ate in the dark. It had been a big week, resulting in their largest net income ever.

What do you think of that, Alcid, he thought? He knew it would not have been enough for his Daddy, who never stopped pushing, pursued by a maniacal drive for more.

Louis should have been happy and puffed up by this latest success. He enjoyed what the money allowed. But money did not quiet the other voice in his mind: his Daddy still hovered there, fueling the uneasiness which required significant amounts of bourbon to relieve.

Finally falling into bed to quiet his mind, Louis slept fitfully. He awoke before daylight with perspiration soaking his pillow. He sat up feeling hot and lightheaded. His hands tingled as if a mild shock was coursing through them. He laid back down and tried to exhale the tightness in his chest.

Louis had always been healthy, too busy to be sick. But now a cryptic fear churned his body. He sat on the edge of the bed and realized that he did not feel ill. He was suffering from fear: an awful, difficult-to-breathe fear.

What the hell is this, he thought.

His mind fought the confusion. He considered calling Dr. David Morgan but decided that the hour was too early. While his symptoms faded, the experience frightened him enough that he knew he should at least talk to his doctor and made the call as soon as the office opened. They told him to come in right away.

Dr. Morgan's office was connected to the clinic hospital, a

small 20-bed facility that served Texas City. As a precaution on his arrival, the nurse made him lie down on the treatment table. Louis grumbled as he waited for Dr. Morgan to arrive.

"So, Louis, why did you get me out of bed so early?" They had been friends for a long time. "There is a surcharge for calls before nine o'clock, you know."

With a slight acknowledgement of his friend's attempt at humor, Louis described his symptoms. Dr. Morgan listened to his heart and flipped through his chart.

"Has this happened before?"

"No," Louis said, not exactly lying, but avoiding information about the symptoms of his self-diagnosed indigestion.

"Your blood pressure is a little high. But your heart sounds good and your pulse is fine. Let's get an EKG."

Louis paced back and forth across the small room as he waited for the results. He held an unlit cigarette between his fingers. Whatever he had experienced had passed and he was feeling fine. Louis never liked being around hospitals.

He checked his watch. He knew his secretary and Mack would be on board to handle the office. Still, it annoyed him to be detained.

"I have to get to the office, David,"

Dr. Morgan leafed through Louis' file.

"Just settle down a little, Louis. The good news is that your heart appears to be healthy, no major blood pressure issues. But I think we should run a few more tests. I'd like to draw some blood and get a urine sample, and I'll call you when I get the results."

The next day, Dr. Morgan's nurse called Louis and informed him that he should come by the office after work.

"What did he find?" Louis probed.

"I don't know, Mr. Broussard. He just said to tell you to drop by after work," was her only response.

Louis grumbled about David not talking to him personally, but he went to the office as directed. He wondered about his tests and thought of the worst, most exotic, diseases he could have, none of which would be good news. He did not feel that bad. But then, what if it was cancer? The Big C. Or another disease which could not be cured. Louis convinced himself that his trouble indicated heart problems and could not be cancer.

Dr. Morgan wasted no time when he entered. "Here's the deal, Louis. Your tests are normal. You have a slight elevation in your liver enzymes which can be corrected by cutting down on your drinking. Your heart is sound, your lungs clear. That's the good news."

"And the bad news?"

Dr. Morgan hesitated, struggling not to offend his friend. "We've known each other a long time and I have never seen you so withdrawn. It's like you crawled into a shell. You are depressed and your body has alerted you to the fact that you are ruining your health. Too much alcohol, too much smoking.

"In addition, I hear things from mutual friends who are worried. You have isolated yourself. You work all the time. I think you had an anxiety attack, which can be like an alarm to make some changes in your life. Stop abusing yourself, Louis. Actually, without changes, in the long run you could be killing yourself."

"Ah, hell, David. Things are not that bad with me. Maybe I just need to take a few days off."

"I could give you some medication for depression. What I

want you to see is your need for a lifestyle change. "

Louis shifted in his chair, wanting a cigarette. "So that's it?" Louis lifted his hands and waved them in the air. "No medicines? No treatments? No surgeries?"

"What I am prescribing is that you stop smoking, stop drinking so much, lose about 25 pounds. More importantly, stop working so hard. Find something that you enjoy doing. You're stuck, Louis, not sick. You have symptoms related to stress, not disease."

Louis promised David that he would try to change his ways. But by the time he opened his car door, he had thrown that advice to the wind and now wondered why he had spent so much time on a trivial matter. He lit a cigarette and forgot about it.

After work, the sky was darkening as Louis pulled into his driveway. Shadows starkly outlined the two-story brick-and-stone house. Once inside, he sat at the kitchen table with a glass of bourbon and his bluster faded out along with the light. Gloom enveloped him as darkness and silence filled the room. He heard creaks from the walls as they cooled along with the night air.

He tried to remember when he had started this habit of sitting alone, drinking and thinking. Maybe he should have paid more attention to David. Maybe he should be happy there was no disease – no Big C. Agitated and ill at ease, Louis needed to get out of the house.

His car tires crunched the gravel as he parked in front of a plain square house on the east side of Main Street, across from the Hallows, close to the entrance of Dock Road. Light from a refinery flare cast shadows on the front porch. A single red light bulb burned next to the doorway. Sounds of the nearby industry droned through the night air, a constant reminder of the relentless processing of oil and chemicals.

Lola's Place, sailors called it. Once a residence, the house had been converted into a small honky-tonk bar that provided another gathering place for crews from the port, as well as those locals who were unconcerned with their reputations and town gossip.

Lola's Place had a bar with a small dance floor off to the right, as well as a jukebox. "Vargas Girl" posters lined the walls. Besides being a gathering place to drink and dance, Lola's Place provided "hostesses" for customers. Louis occasionally went to a back room with one of the women. Most often he came to drink and visit with other patrons. He belonged to the local country club where, in the past, he had played gin rummy after a round of golf or drank in its small bar. Now he preferred the seedy atmosphere at Lola's with its subdued light and neon beer signs.

The women wore gauzy see-through tops and short shorts, and lolled around the bar, or sat on a couch and chairs by the dance floor. Louis found the conversation here more enjoyable than the country club. He might sit at the bar next to the fire chief, or even the police chief, who were there "attending to matters of town ordinances," of course. He could also listen to a French ship's captain tell stories about life on the water. Stories of stormy seas or collisions with whales on the downside of a deep swell brought a vicarious surge of excitement to Louis as he imagined himself at the helm.

Two seamen on the frayed, sagging couch talked quietly with two women. One seaman spoke French to the woman next to him. She laughed at the incomprehensible words, and her response broke the quiet in the small room. Men at the bar turned to look their way. A radiant, coquettish smile curled her lips as she shook her head in bewilderment at all the eyes trained on her.

Louis thought the other man on the couch might be Russian. The tall, buxom blonde next to him caught Louis' eye. She returned his glance with a smile as he briefly stared at her.

"Who's the new girl on the sofa? The blond one," Louis asked the barman.

"Her name is Tina. She started last week. Says she is from California, but I don't know. Said she got tired of the weather out there."

Cigarette smoke clouded the room as Louis looked around. T-Bone Walker blared out "Call it Stormy Monday" from a jukebox edged with red and blue lights. A couple danced in the small space between the jukebox and the couch.

Louis saw Steve Nader, the fire chief, further down the bar. A small man, Nader was built taut as a violin string and spoke in a hoarse voice that sounded like a growl with words. Louis knew Steve well, appreciated his blunt honesty and welcomed the chance to talk with him. Carrying his drink, he joined his friend.

They sipped bourbon and chatted with the barman, who reminded Louis to pay his liquor locker dues. Turning to Steve, Louis brought up his conversation with the Coast Guard about potential new safety issues.

"Yeah, I heard some rumors about that. They haven't talked directly with me yet."

"Do you think we need changes in our safety rules on the docks, Steve?"

"Hell, yes! First of all, we need more firemen. And equipment. But there are obstacles. We must generate money to get more men and equipment, and nobody wants to pay more taxes.

"What bothers me most is that our firemen have absolutely

no coordination with crews out on the docks. Nobody is in charge except Russo, and he's so concentrated on making money for the Terminal that he's oblivious to any real safety issues."

Louis quickly responded, "I think we have a good system, Steve. We've handled all of the accidents, all the fires," Louis offered. "I think the Coast Guard is just looking to flex a little muscle."

"I don't know," Steve drawled slowly in disagreement with Louis. "True, we haven't had any really big problems. But you're thinking in the past. My job is to anticipate the future. I have to think of what might happen. The bigger that complex grows out there, the more I have to expect the unexpected. And that gives me nightmares. Sometimes I dream about burning oil and fire rolling out of refineries in waves to engulf our entire town. In the dream, it looks like the fires of Hell, consuming every piece of ground and leaving only the smoking ashes of Texas City in its wake. It's an awful thing.

"During the war, I dreamed of airplanes bombing the complex. Explosions one after the other, as all those storage tanks disintegrated into pieces of metal and flew like V-2 rockets over the town. I used to wake up sweating. I don't worry anymore about being bombed, but who knows what could happen out there.

"Oh yes, I would like to see changes made. And we can't be dragging our feet on this forever. The busier this port gets, the more opportunities for mistakes. I know Russo wants to keep it as it is, but he has a limited view of the picture." Steve rubbed his thumb and fingers together while looking directly at Louis. "The worst part of this whole situation is that someone besides Russo will have to pay the fiddler."

Louis waited a moment to speak. "You're just a natural worrier. I say we are okay as we stand."

Steve's response was short and simple. "I get paid to worry."

Louis now realized that he had stoked the embers of a smoldering fire. Steve, normally reticent to talk, continued to lecture.

"Take that New London school explosion, or the Hindenburg. If someone had thought ahead, maybe they could have prevented – or lessened – those disasters in some way. You can't keep your head in the sand and wait for something bad to happen. This petrochemical beast resides barely 100 yards from people's homes. It belches flames and gases out of its mouth 24 hours a day. All those pipelines? They carry oil, gasoline, kerosene, toxic chemicals that can peel the skin off your bones or kill you with one deep breath. You're damn right I worry."

Louis bought another round. He thought Steve's tirade was overblown and blamed it on the bourbon. His mind wandered back to the blond on the couch. He watched as she stood up, her long, willowy legs attractive and sensual. She took the young French sailor's hand and walked him toward a back room, his face locked in a sheepish grin like it might have been his first time. Steve sat quietly in thought, smoking his cigarette.

Coming back to their conversation, Louis asked, "What do you think could happen?"

"I don't know. Any number of things. But something will happen. I just hope it is not too big for us to handle."

Louis playfully mocked Steve. "Well, I'm going out tomorrow to buy more insurance."

Steve chuckled. "Good. Maybe, if you're lucky, you'll be around to collect it."

Louis drove home thinking about what Steve had said. He knew Steve to be a worrier and so he tended not to couple much reality with Steve's words. The industry's safety record was a good one.

He did have trust in Mack though, and his cautionary words came back to Louis now. What if...? began to hang in his thoughts.

In a night of disturbed sleep, Louis wrestled with his pillow and was awakened several times by bizarre dreams before falling back into agitated sleep. He awoke before daylight with his heart racing, pounding against the inside of his chest. Fear gripped his body.

At the foot of his bed was a dragon, tall as the ceiling. Its glassy eyes glowed a menacing red, its head swayed on a serpentine body that was covered with luminescent green scales. The head moved back and forth and exposed its fangs toward Louis. He felt his body being dragged to the edge of an abyss. Louis grabbed the covers and fought to keep from plunging down a precipice.

He clutched at the bed and shut his eyes tight. When he slowly opened them, the dragon no longer towered at the foot of the bed but had been replaced by an old Chinese man who sat on a marble pedestal. Strands of his gray beard hung down to his chest and a peaceful smile creased his face.

Louis blinked and edged to the side of the bed. There was no abyss. The same frayed oval rug covered the wood floor as it had for years. The dragon and the Chinese man had both disappeared.

Louis wobbled to a chair, sat down and took in short gasps of air. He tried to recall what he had eaten or drunk the previous evening and wondered if he had been drugged. Maybe someone had slipped him a mickey. Bewildered and still scared, he dialed David's number at home, even though he knew his friend – and doctor – would still be asleep.

When they met later at the hospital, Louis immediately described his feelings.

"I'm telling you, my heart was pounding in my chest like never before. When I saw that dragon, I was awake, David, wide awake. There it was. I thought I must be losing my mind. I could feel myself going over the edge. Then the Chinese guy showed up!"

"Do you have any chest pain now? Any dizziness?"

"I was awake, David, totally awake, and trembling with this awful fear. I saw that dragon in my room at the foot of my bed. It scared the hell out of me!"

After a thorough examination, including another EKG, Dr. Morgan took Louis to his office and talked to him in a quiet voice.

"You had a hallucination, Louis. It was not real. It happened in your mind, a manifestation of what we previously talked about. I'm not a psychiatrist, but I did a turn on the psych ward when I went to med school. I know what kinds of weird things can happen in your mind.

"I know a dragon did not come into your room. Your subconscious mind created that dragon. It came out of a little black box in your mind. A dragon is an archetype. It is the archetype of mythic fear. You personified the tremendous anxiety that you have suppressed in your mind. The Chinese man, then, symbolizes wisdom or knowledge. He wants to reassure you.

"None of it really happened. It all came from your unconscious mind. It is similar to daydreaming except it is information that you know nothing about. All the tension of not being who you really want to be has been causing these symptoms. You are living the life of your father while still wanting to be Louis. Look, I know this sounds like mumbo jumbo to you. It is something that not many people ever experience. But you are not insane."

Dr. Morgan waited for Louis to respond, but he remained silent.

"Physically you checked out fine, but you had a terrible fright. Your symptoms were the same as if you had encountered a gunman intent on shooting you or if you had been chased by a bear. Except this time the culprit came from your mind. Very real to you and just as frightening. You experienced a big-time panic attack."

"It was real, David. I saw it," Louis insisted.

"Hallucination displaced your reality. You could feel its presence, but you never actually touched it. Your feet went onto the floor, not into an abyss."

Louis sat silent, working to resolve the real and unreal in his mind.

"I think you should get some counseling. See a therapist. Maybe a pastor? Someone you can talk to about what's going on inside of you. The only thing I can do is give you an antidepressant or tranquilizer. It may ease your symptoms, relieve some of the anxiety and get you over a few rough spots. But it's not a complete solution."

Louis' response was soft and searching. "It was so real, David. That feeling of going over the edge. Are you sure I'm not going crazy? I have been working hard. I got pretty angry with the Coast Guard recently and Steve Nader is telling me we need more safety regulations. I guess I am a little uptight. But this was really scary."

"You are not crazy, Louis, but your concept of reality has been challenged. The unconscious is a powerful force that we don't give much attention to. It exerts itself when our lives get too far out of balance. Something inside of you is calling for a change. But your ego, also very powerful, doesn't want it to happen."

Louis stared at the floor as he felt the size of the room get smaller. He became dizzy again and could hear David's voice echo off the walls.

"Look at me, Louis! Listen to my voice. You are here with me. You are alright. You have had a terrible fright. It will pass."

The fear did pass. But the memory of the dragon convinced Louis to follow David's advice. He knew nothing about dragons or Chinese men. He did not understand how his "awake nightmare" happened, nor what it meant. But the next morning he sought a counselor. He found that he would need to go to Galveston for a certified professional. He quickly decided that would take too much time away from work and therefore put the suggestion aside. He didn't like the idea of seeing a shrink, anyway.

At dinner he talked with Demetrios about what David had advised.

"Louis, you don't need to go anywhere. You come here. We have a few drinks. You tell me your troubles and I listen. After a few more drinks, we dance the *Hasapiko*. Dancing takes away all troubles in the mind. It frees your spirit and lets it laugh." He threw his head back in a hearty chuckle.

"Not for me, Demetrios. I don't dance. I'll leave that to you Greeks."

"Ah.... But Louis, we are all Greeks at heart." Demetrios laughed again.

Louis did not laugh.

Demetrios had another idea. "Why don't you see the priest then? Father Joe. He'd be a good man to talk to. He counsels lots of people. Maybe you just need a good confession." Demetrios tilted his head, looking at Louis with his eyebrows raised. "You been a bad boy, Louis?"

Louis drove home along the bay after dinner. He stopped beside the seawall and got out of his car. Mosquitoes buzzed and lightning bugs blinked in the air around him. The Milky Way, a luminous river of distant stars, dominated the southern sky.

Louis stared into the depth of night, wishing a message could be sent through its vast space telling him what to do. A message from whom? He scoffed at the idea. But he had never before doubted his own sanity, his ability to function rationally. He knew how the world worked and it did not include things unseen. Life worked like a mechanical device, an engine. Time moved through a logical structure of cause and effect.

His world now rocked with something unseen yet real. A force capable of influencing his mind and body existed without his knowledge or consent. It forged new doubt and anxiety. The dragon experience had allowed a glimpse into another world, like dreaming but not dreaming. It introduced him to another Louis, a lost twin, someone he had not known existed.

Later, Louis sat in his kitchen and tried to sort through his thoughts. With his inability to explain this mystical phenomenon, nothing made any sense. Was it like magic, but in a real way?

He took a deep breath and worked to focus on his choices. He considered taking pills a sign of weakness and he hated weakness. He also did not think it smart to go back to the church that he had brushed aside so long ago to seek the aid of a priest. Go to the dancing priest? The thought made him chuckle. What could a priest, allegedly celibate, know about real life? What could he know about dragons?

But to see a psychiatrist? That would be total abdication. Not a good choice for a man in control of his own destiny. What would people think? Louis knew that he must do something.

Just make a choice.

Louis pulled a coin out of his pocket. "Priest or pills. Priest or pills.... Heads it's priest, tails it's pills."

He flipped the coin into the air and watched it spin, its silver sides flashing in the dim kitchen light. The nickel bounced and clinked on the table then lay with the Indian head gazing up from the face of the coin, holding Louis' fate in its mesmerizing stare. In the dim light, the Indian's eye peered back at him.

"Oh, God! Priest!" He looked again, shaking his head and confirming the results. "Priest."

Memories of his boyhood years in church flooded in. Serving mass as an altar boy; the anxiety that overcame him when he waited in line to make his confession; being scolded for his sins as he knelt in the dark box; confessing his ever-present thoughts about sex; and the priest telling him that those thoughts could send him to Hell.

He had believed it all back then but had abandoned the Church when he went off to college. He had never told his mother that he no longer believed and never again worried about going to Hell.

Despite Louis' doubts, the priest presented the most convenient approach. And because he had experience talking to priests in confession, he reconciled his choice with that thought: It is just another confession. No big deal.

After arriving at his office the next morning, he called to make an appointment with Father Joseph Irons at St. Mary's Church. Lingering hesitation and fear resulted in his stammering through the explanation of why he needed to come. "Counseling. My doctor said I should be counseled," he whispered to the lady on the other end of the phone.

"Father Joe can see you in two weeks, on the nineteenth."

After he hung up, something about the lady's voice lodged in a corner of his mind. It sounded clear and kind. The voice did not fit with his image of a church lady. The women he remembered from his altar-boy days appeared elderly, somewhat frumpy. She sounded efficient and young. And something else. As she talked, she sounded like she cared, like it was important for him to have an appointment. Either way, he liked the sound of her voice.

At the appointed time, Louis walked into the anteroom to the rectory office wearing a freshly starched white shirt and a gold-and-blue tie with diagonal stripes. He removed his hat. He felt perspiration under his arms and on his forehead and took out a handkerchief to blot his face.

Feeling the urge to light a cigarette, he looked around the room. His gaze stopped on a painting that hung on a side wall. The 13th hole at the Master's Golf Course in Augusta, brilliant flowers of azalea bushes growing in profusion behind white sand traps which bordered three sides of a lush green. He had seen the image before and thought it an odd picture for a church office.

Grace sat at her desk. Louis thought her pretty, but sad. He wondered if he was in the right place.

"I'm Grace." She greeted him, asked him to have a seat and

offered coffee, which he refused.

"I'm Louis Broussard. This feels kind of like going to the dentist," Louis offered, trying to ease his tension.

"Father Joe is expecting you. He will be with you in a few minutes, Mr. Broussard."

In the last few weeks, Grace had gained some needed weight and her skin had regained some of its healthy softness. Her hair had recovered its luster. Louis studied Grace as she shuffled papers on her desk, went to the file cabinet and moved back around behind her desk. She stood about five-feet-six. Thin. Shoulder-length, shiny black hair framed her face. He thought her pale face needed some sunshine. Louis judged her to be in her thirties.

"Are you the lady I spoke to yesterday?"

"Yes."

"You have a nice phone voice."

"Thank you."

He had expected an older woman, someone more... "churchy." She seemed out of place in a church office, more appropriate to be working for an insurance company.

He watched her hands as she handed him papers to fill out. She had long graceful fingers. Her hands reminded him of his mother who had loved to play the piano.

"Do you play the piano?" he asked.

Surprised, Grace did not look up as she responded, "I did. For a while."

"I asked because you have long fingers. My mother did too, and she played the piano."

After a few minutes of uncomfortable silence, Louis tried to fill the void. "Did you play professionally?"

Grace quickly looked up. Louis saw her lips narrow in a taut line. Her eyes focused on his face as if trying to decide if he somehow knew her.

"No," Grace replied, and turned her chair toward the file cabinet.

Louis waited for her to go on talking, but she returned to her work without further comment. Father Joe appeared in the doorway to his office, a broad smile on his face. He stood taller than Louis, but his rounded shoulders made him appear smaller. A middle-aged man with graying hair beginning to show on the sides of his head, Louis immediately recognized him as the dancing priest at Demetrios'. He again noted the depression on his jawline and felt awkward when Father Joe caught him staring.

"Mr. Broussard, please come in. I had a lymphoma," he said with a smile to ease Louis' curious stare. "A smart young dentist caught it early, but they had to take part of my jaw. To the dismay of my parishioners, it didn't shorten my sermons."

The priest sat down behind a beautiful ornate desk topped with inlaid leather in small squares. Front panels on the desk prominently displayed carved Japanese pagodas and flowers. Louis noticed the neat, cleared desk and mentally contrasted that to the mounds of papers that covered his own at work. A crucifix hung on the wall behind the priest and a bronze Buddha in the Lotus position sat on a bookshelf. Books lined both sides of the room in cases up to the ceiling.

"Well, beginnings are the hardest. You can call me Father Joe. Having been a priest for so long, Joe seems a little abrupt. But if it makes you more comfortable, I don't stand on ceremony. I'll call you Louis if you don't mind."

Louis cleared his throat and began to tell Father Joe about the dragon incident and Dr. Morgan's thoughts that his physical symptoms were the result of anxiety. He said that Dr. Morgan had advised him to see a counselor to help him sort that out.

"I'm telling you right now that I don't believe in a devil, or anything like that. I'm not crazy, I'm not possessed and I don't need an exorcism. I'm here because you won the coin toss."

Father Joe smiled. "Well, I promise you, no exorcisms. That stuff scares me." He smiled again. "I know a little about you from talk around Demetrios' Cafe and people who work around the docks. I frequently visit the Seamen's Mission out there. Your name comes up among my parish members occasionally. Were you born in Texas City?"

"Born and raised in Texas City. My Daddy came to Galveston to work on the wharves. He worked for a ship's chandler until he saved enough money to start his own ship supply company. He married soon after that. My mother had several miscarriages, so I am an only child. I went off to college, then came back home."

"You came back to work in your father's business?"

"On the day I graduated from the university, my Daddy had a heart attack. Three weeks later he had another one and died. I had no choice but to take over the business. I had just passed my 21st birthday.

"I had always wanted to go to sea and be a ship's captain. I grew up around ships on the docks. My Daddy let me hang around down there. I had books about life in the merchant marine, so the thought of adventure on the seas excited me.

"He was a devout pragmatist and worked all the time. He bought land because he knew the port here would grow and become an important part of the shipping industry. And it did. He built a successful business and I studied business to please him. But I still dreamed of going to sea."

"And your mother?"

"After my Daddy died, she lost interest in everything and started drinking heavily. One night she overdosed on her sleeping pills. I don't know if she did it on purpose or if the alcohol…."

They talked for almost an hour when Father Joe recommended that they meet again the following week.

"I don't want to keep coming here for a long time. How many times will this take?"

"We'll see. It depends on how much you want to tell me. For now, let's take it one week at a time."

In the outer office again, Louis stopped by Grace's desk to set up another appointment. He bent over the desk next to Grace to look at the appointment book and caught the aroma of her perfume. Trying not to be too obvious about his interest in her, he couldn't keep from lingering a little.

On his way back to work, Louis thought about how easy it had been to talk to the priest. His thoughts also returned to Grace and the excitement he had felt when standing close to her. The attraction left Louis bewildered. He was used to having women be attracted to him, and that always made him feel in control. But Grace was different. The thought of her was more intense and more persistent than he had expected. Louis began to feel the tension of an emotional revolution stirring in his mind.

Seven

Father Joe stood in the doorway of his office, coffee cup in hand, and lingered longer than usual. In the two months that they had been working together, he and Grace had arrived at a place of mutual respect. He wanted to help her but knew it would take patience. He saw so much potential in her that he could not hold back easily. Having her confidence and a vision for her future drained away in prison had seriously affected her well-being. Father Joe knew that her spiritual recovery would come with an improvement in her mental health. So he walked a tightrope between patience and gentle nudging.

Grace, being naturally shy, kept their relationship on a strictly professional plane. But, more importantly, her sense of shame instilled in her the belief that she did not deserve anything more.

"I played the piano a little, too," Father Joe recalled as he sipped his coffee. "Not professionally, of course. I took lessons until I discovered golf."

Grace squirmed in her chair. She looked directly at his face and knew he wanted to help her. Slowly she began to talk.

"The memory of that time is too painful for me. I don't play anymore. Not playing the piano has been part of my resolve, part of my penance. I'm afraid playing the piano again would tempt me back to that old life."

"You must have enjoyed some of that time."

"Actually, I did. Early on, I lived a wonderful kind of naive existence. When I got started, I was a young girl living a dream.

I knew nothing about life.... I mean, real life. I got caught up in a pretend life, in adulation, and I thought I knew everything.

"I suppose it was all too much too fast. I set no boundaries: I couldn't see anything wrong. I thought I was happy, but there was an underbelly to all of my hubris that the need for recognition blinded me to. I thought I was hot stuff, you know? What's that old saying, 'The higher you go, the harder you fall'?"

Father Joe waited for her to say more but Grace remained silent. He started back into his office, paused and turned, and came back to the doorway.

"But you remember the scales, don't you? You must be good at notes." He did not wait for her to answer.

"I just had an idea and I need to ask a big favor from you. You know Clayton, the young man who keeps the grounds here? On Saturdays I meet with him in the choir room. I'm trying to help him learn to play the saxophone. He is a fine young man, very eager to be a musician. Unfortunately, I have a meeting tomorrow morning. Do you think you could substitute for me? You would be perfect for Clayton. I know he would appreciate your help."

Grace had not touched a piano since before prison. To even think about breaking her imposed exile from anything resembling music left her speechless.

Father Joe moved closer to her, speaking softly and gently. "You have to start somewhere, Grace. You must go back to music because it was such a huge part of your life. You must come to peace with that. And helping someone else would be a way to ease back in." He paused briefly.

"It could be a gift to Clayton and to yourself. You are doing so well. It's time for you to take a chance. I think he has a talent for the saxophone, but he needs a real musician to help him. What do you say, Grace? I know you would be good for him. Please?"

"I don't know, Father Joe. That makes me very nervous.... But you have been so good to me. Do you really think I could help him?"

"Yes. I think it will help you as well."

"Okay. I'll give it a try. Just this once."

The following morning, Grace entered the church. Despite her respect for Father Joe, she sensed some collusion put her there. Greta most likely. The more she thought about it, the more irritated she became.

She hesitated before the choir room door. She could see the piano through the window. Grace felt panic leap into her chest. She stopped suddenly, too afraid to risk going through with her promise to Father Joe, and she turned around to leave. Then she heard the soft notes from a tenor sax coming from the room. The honeyed strains of "Body and Soul," a song she had once loved to sing. She stood entranced as the notes melted her discomfort. The melody awakened the thrill of music's magic that had been hibernating in her. She turned around and put her hand on the doorknob. With a deep breath, Grace pushed through the music room door.

Clayton stood at attention when he saw her, apprehension flowing through his taut body. They both froze for a moment, uneasy at their sudden meeting.

"I'm Grace."

"Yes, ma'am. Father Joe told me you would be here." Clayton spoke slowly, choosing his words carefully, working to avoid the casual, slangy speech he spoke at the docks.

Clayton's muscular body dwarfed Grace. His big hands

curled around the sax. She looked at his handsome face, his deep-set eyes that betrayed the fear beneath his efforts to be cool. He waited for Grace to speak again.

"So, you want to be a sax player?"

"Yes, ma'am."

"Do you read music?"

"No, ma'am."

When Grace moved toward the piano, Clayton took an awkward step back.

Grace paused and looked in his eyes. "If it helps Clayton, I'm nervous, too. But I don't bite."

"I've never been around a white woman much. Never alone."

"Well, no one needs to know. You'll be just fine here. The important thing is your music. Would you play something for me?"

After a few false starts, Clayton settled into a smooth, short riff. Grace listened as he played, impressed by the quality of his sound. It was uneven at times, but she immediately recognized his natural talent and believed that he would be able to learn a more focused tone with practice.

She could see the struggle in his face, and it reminded her of her own efforts when learning to play piano. Each new level required an increased effort, and that effort would create a new history to draw from and become a step to the next level. An odd feeling came over Grace. She realized that as she focused attention on Clayton, she was becoming less nervous and that she could actually feel tension leave her body. While she could not have described it, a small sliver of light emanated through a crack in her broken heart.

Grace sat down and touched the keyboard's cold ivory and

quickly put her hands in her lap. She approached the keys again but abandoned her effort once more. Slowly she brought her right hand up to the keys and played a few chords. Then added her left hand. Each note softened her touch, her fingers finally moving smoothly over the keyboard.

She stopped as quickly as she had begun.

"That's a nice horn," she observed, turning to face Clayton.

"My father won it in a dice game in an alley in New Orleans. He said he was gonna pawn it. But one day he left and never came back. I started playing around with it while listening to the radio."

"What do you listen to on the radio?"

"I like the blues. The jump blues. T-Bone Walker. Dinah Washington. I like some of the pop singers. Ella."

Names of musicians and singers from her past rolled across Grace's mind, as she recalled her own beginnings. The rush of being on stage, the mesmerized audiences that melted into the music. These images loosened the grip of fear. Little by little, Grace felt her body's rigidity morph into a downy softness. She positioned her body in a comfortable posture on the bench and placed both her hands over the keys.

The piano cast its spell as magic from the inert keys silently slipped into her fingertips and spread throughout her hands. She began to play a short melody. She closed her eyes and gently swayed, lost in a moment of reverie. The room appeared to brighten. Her eyes opened and she abruptly stopped playing again.

She turned her attention to Clayton. "I can teach you to read music," she said. "I can give you some exercises to improve your note recognition, to tune your ear. It will take a lot of practice, but you have a real natural talent. Do you have a mirror at home, one you can stand in front of and play? You should practice the notes and focus on their sound while you watch your fingers. Thirty minutes. Every day. An hour would be even better."

"Yes ma'am, thank you. I can do that. Thank you, ma'am,"

"Father Joe had a meeting today. But I think I may have inherited you, Clayton. Will that be okay with you?"

Clayton measured his response thoughtfully. His eyes rested on her, but thoughts in his mind flew to the Jim Crow laws he lived with every day. How would he negotiate the invisible boundaries around his blackness and her whiteness? What were the dangers? Was he being too bold? He knew she could help him with his dream.... He had no choice except to show up. Ultimately, he decided that he would take any chance to pursue his dream.

"You tell me when to be here. I will be here."

Eight

"We have a fire on the dock!" Mack yelled as he burst into Louis' office. "Down at Slip A!"

Louis and Mack sprinted to the docks. Gasoline spewed from a hose writhing and dancing wildly on the dock. It flooded the platform and the road next to the slip. Flames ate at the front of the dock house.

Mack grabbed a dock worker. "What happened? Where are the fire crews?"

The man pointed to a ship moving down the channel almost out of the turning basin. "That ship left the dock before our loading hose got disconnected and it ripped loose. Gasoline flowed into the dock house and something in there ignited it."

Mack's eyes followed the fire's path. Beyond a shallow ditch next to the road stood a dozen storage tanks filled with oil and gasoline.

"Get that value shut off. Now!" Mack yelled.

"We're working on it!"

A fire crew from the Terminal arrived and frantically fastened their hoses to a fire hydrant. Mack rushed to help unravel hoses and get water started on the blaze. By now, gasoline had flowed across the road and into the ditch, just yards from the storage tanks. The fire crew aimed a plume of water at the dock house, but it lacked enough pressure to get much water on the flames.

"We need a pumper! Get another hose going up there by the road," Mack screamed.

The torn loading hose continued to flail, turning its spewing head toward the burning dock house. The stream of gasoline ignited and burned its way back to the hose connection, causing a small explosion. Fuel on the dock burst into flames and fire raced toward the ditch, now filled with gasoline.

Mack pulled on Louis' shoulder. "If that fire gets to those oil tanks it will burn all the way to our warehouse and destroy the whole place! We have to get to that valve."

A siren's wail interrupted Mack as the town's fire engines came roaring up behind them. Steve Nader jumped from the lead engine, yelling orders to his men.

"Where the hell have you been?" Louis shouted at him.

"Picking my nose. Shut up and get the hell out of my way!"

He directed his men to hook hoses to the engine's pumper. They flooded the flames with a powerful surge of water. Fire erupted in the ditch. Louis backed away but Mack stood his ground. A workman hollered that he had secured the valve. Fire in the ditch raged on.

Heat from the burning ditch increased as flames danced high into the air. Steve Nader ignored the flames and heat. He took a wire cutter and whittled a hole through fencing behind the ditch, led his men through the hole and positioned them with their backs to the storage tanks. They directed their hoses into the burning ditch to block fire from getting to the tank farm.

Flames ignored the torrents of water. Suddenly Steve Nader yelled at a gathering crowd of workers to get away from the dock. "Louis, get those goddamn gawkers away from here!"

Louis and Mack led the crowd up the gravel road to a safe distance. More firefighters arrived and fought the inferno in the ditch. They funneled a chemical foam on the raging fires and were finally able to smother them out.

Louis angrily accosted Steve. "What took you so long to get here?"

Steve pushed his blue fireman's cap to the back of his head. "I don't know a fire's burning unless someone tells me about it."

"What do you mean?"

Steve shouted, "I came as soon as I got the goddamn call."

"We almost had a disaster here. This whole tank farm could have gone off like a string of dynamite."

Steve turned his back on Louis and walked away. "I don't make the rules out here."

Louis, shaken and alarmed, walked back to the office with Mack. He went directly to the cabinet and pulled out a bottle of bourbon. He tilted it at Mack.

"I believe I will," Mack responded.

Louis mulled over the fire in his mind. He remembered his smug exchange with the Coast Guard Captain about safety regulations. Louis had thought the young Captain wrong and misinformed, and he had treated him rudely. Now his hubris stung, knowing how easily that fire could have erupted into a much bigger problem. Flames had grown so quickly, and they had died just a few yards away from a major disaster.

Another thought erupted into his mind. It could have been much worse: The fire could have destroyed his business. Maybe the entire waterfront.

"Dammit, Mack, that was too close to getting away from us. We could have had a serious situation there. It happened so fast." He paused while a new thought took shape in his mind.

"To hell with Vincent Russo. He may be president of the Terminal, but something must change out here. We could have lost our warehouse, and no telling what else. We need a faster response. We need Steve out here instead of in town. Maybe I acted too hastily to dismiss that Coast Guard fellow. I'm going to have another talk with him. Let's see what ideas he has for us."

Later, as he sat in his darkened kitchen in the evening, the day's events played over and over in Louis' mind. The fire carried a rude awakening. In the quiet and safety of his home, he cursed his own stupidity and questioned his own decision making. Why did I think I should be the one to arbitrate safety procedures? Who am I to say when we have enough safety?

The turmoil brought his Daddy to mind. What would Alcid have said if Louis had lost his warehouse?

Exhaustion followed, coupled with a sense of relief, allowing his memories to return to the beginning of it all. Many years ago, Alcid had stood very near where the fire had burned, trying to imagine his dream into reality. He had followed on the coattails of Captain Augustus Wolfe and the Manon brothers, adventurers who had crossed the country from Minnesota to the open spaces of the Gulf Coast. They envisioned a port rising out of marshes on the mainland north of Galveston. With the advantage of railways connecting their port to the interior of the country, and acres of land to develop ancillary industries, they saw opportunities for great wealth.

Alcid, with the need for adventure in his blood, had followed on their heels and dreamed his own future. He had never understood why Louis did not march to the same drummer.

Louis had heard these stories often, stories about hard work and sacrifice, grit and determination. But he had never seemed to live up to his Daddy's vision and drive. Alcid thought his son soft and spoiled. Louis acknowledged that he had become complacent, one of those men his Daddy called "fat cats," someone who sat back and watched the money roll in. He worked hard, but his heart had never been encased in work as was his Daddy's.

Alcid had dreamed of an empire. He had bought land in the town and on the prairie with profits from his business. He had built a Victorian mansion for Cecile. It rose three stories, with a turret on top to watch for ships in the bay. A wide porch wound around the front and sides. It stood haughty and alone, an exquisite example of the style of the times, built with cypress boards cut and milled in Louisiana and brought by ship to the port. The interior walls and stairway were fitted by gifted craftsmen with fine woodwork. A spacious entry hall waited to meet the many visitors who were entertained in their home.

Alcid and Cecile had expected to have many children, but Louis had been the only child. A large family was the only missing piece in Alcid's dream.

The bustling port had increased in size rapidly since Louis had taken over the business. Growth of the adjacent industrial complex originated with the oil boom in Texas in the 1920s and 1930s and continued to grow, creating an expansion for refining and storage of the hugely profitable resource. Oil from the bounteous fields discovered all over Texas became "king."

Louis had heard the mythic stories of men digging in their fields and oil wells spouting forth. The abundance of oil brought with it not only riches, but a way of doing business in which money became the barometer of success. It brought with it a rush to get to the next boom of oil gushers. "Work fast" became a common mantra and everyone worked as fast as possible to get ahead or to just keep up. As a result, if success required a lie or a little rule bending, so be it.

Money stoked a lack of conscience and ethics in many cases. "Whatever it takes" described a new morality. Wildcat fever mirrored the 49ers' gold rush mania and oil became known as "black gold." Millions of barrels of oil came out of the ground as fast as drill bits could reach the vast underground reservoirs.

That kind of pace did not appeal to Louis. The sea had always called him. Ships rather than oil were his passion. But Alcid would not let that dream come true, and Louis watched as refineries replaced marshes and prairies surrounding Texas City in order to process the many barrels of oil coming out of the ground. Refineries, petrochemical plants, even a tin smelter, rose from the land on Texas City's prairies – land that Alcid and his partners had acquired years before the boom. He ultimately sold the land to other developers who were driving growth within the industrial complex.

Soon, oil brought more jobs. Thousands of workers constructed a maze of pipelines and processing vessels. Refineries piped the black gold through columnar furnaces and distilling towers and separated it into valuable components. Chemical plants manufactured plastics, detergents and fibers such as nylon and polyesters from abundant oil.

All of this activity resulted in products that needed ships to move them – ships that needed Tiger Ship Chandlers to supply them.

The start of World War II had increased pressure on the entire complex to produce more and faster. New workers arrived daily and the town grew rapidly because of the oil industry. But Texas City itself had not shared in the wealth produced by the oil. The gargantuan industrial complex south of town, online 24 hours a day and seven days a week, existed outside of the town limits, so it paid no taxes to Texas City. Louis had heard rumors that the town leaders wanted to incorporate the docks and refinery areas, but it was a move that had been fought hard by the Terminal Railway Company and the other corporations.

Louis, barely turned 21 years old and a reluctant recruit, had had little time to formulate his own course of action and had continued to follow the powerful bosses who set the climate of business, as well as his Daddy's work ethic.

Louis ran his fingers across his singed eyebrows. The explosion and subsequent fire troubled his mind. While it was a small fire and explosion that had physically shaken his body, it threatened more than he had at first admitted. He imagined what a huge disaster it could have been. And he realized that annexation by the city would be the only way Steve Nader and his firemen would get what they needed to protect the massive complex.

With a huge sigh, Louis began to take stock of his own feelings as a result of the fire and its dangers. What if he had died? Who would have cared? He had become so reclusive. The thought surprised him and made him uneasy. He believed himself to be a man of independence, with no serious ties other than his business.

Now his life suddenly seemed shallow and unimportant. What had he ever done for anyone besides himself? Grace's face appeared in his mind. He had never heard her laugh, never touched her, did not even know her last name. But he had seen her each time he met with Father Joe, and he could no longer deny that what Grace thought of him did matter.

A wry smile creased the dimples in his cheeks as he began to connect the dots. Grace *did matter.* She was not just another woman to pursue. He had to admit his interest in *her,* his concern for *her,* to recognize that he *cared* for *her.* Caring had not been a long suit in his relationships. Grace had unwittingly become a new experience for Louis. She raised his awareness to another level and his armor-clad heart began to soften.

Nine

The fire at Slip A shut down all loading at the docks, giving Clayton the afternoon off. He walked through Monsanto's parking lot to the seawall where he sat and stared at the bay. Fire unnerved Clayton. It vividly brought to memory the accident that had changed the direction of his life ten years before. Any unintended fire fueled a nauseating fear that momentarily paralyzed him. The fear brought with it confusion and an inability to think clearly. It did not linger, but always left him with a replay of his calamitous meeting with fire and its accompanying images.

Clayton had excelled at football in high school, and he had been offered a scholarship to Southern University in Baton Rouge, which he had gratefully accepted. On a midsummer day after graduation, he had just finished a workout to keep himself in shape for Southern's upcoming fall football practices. He had been walking home on the side of Texas Avenue when a drunk driver plowed into the rear of another car, catapulting it into a telephone pole with a terrific force.

Clayton had rushed to the damaged car to help. The woman driver lay slumped over the steering wheel, unconscious from the impact. Her body had set off the raucous horn. In the backseat lay a child who had been thrown onto the floorboard.

Gasoline from a ruptured fuel tank quickly ignited and Clayton frantically pounded on the window glass and tried to open the door, unaware of the fire burning his shoe and pant leg.

The child saw the flames and started screaming, "Mommy! Mommy!"

He turned his back to the car and kicked in the window like a mule. Ignoring the flames that now engulfed his lower leg, he lifted the crying little girl from the car. Other people arrived and quickly removed the mother from the front seat. They all scrambled away just before the car became filled with fire.

Clayton's burns required him to stay at John Sealy Hospital in Galveston for two months as the healing and recovery required multiple skin grafts and related surgeries. He would walk again, but injury to the tendons in his ankle would never allow him to run again. He would not go to Southern University to play football. And, without a scholarship, there would be no college.

He reconciled himself to that because he had saved the little girl. It was when his father returned home shortly after for one of his infrequent visits to try to coax money from Ella Mae that the bitterness was ignited in him. His father had been at the house only two days when he came home in the afternoon drunk on cheap whiskey. Clayton, still on crutches and rehabilitating his healing leg, became the target of his father's rage.

"You a dumb ass. You know that, boy? You think some white man would save you from a wreck? Shiiit. He woulda let you burn. Look at you. You ain't never gonna work. How you gonna take care of me? I'm stuck with a cripple. Ain't nobody gonna give you a job. You can't work on a garbage truck or dig ditches. Now I gotta take care of you!"

"When did you ever take care of anybody?"

"Don't you sass me, boy. I'll kick your ass even if you are on those crutches."

His father lit a cigarette and wobbled unsteadily on his feet. "You ain't never gonna work."

"I CAN work! I WILL work!" Clayton screamed at his father.

His father raised a clenched fist.

"STOP IT, EARL," Ella Mae rushed to Clayton's side.

"I CAN WORK," Clayton screamed at his father.

Earl walked toward the door. "I'm leaving. I can't stand looking at you!"

Clayton followed him outside, screaming. "I CAN WORK. BUT I AIN'T NEVER TAKIN' CARE OF YOU!" Tears rolled down his cheeks as he watched his father drive off.

Memory of that scene brought the bitterness back into his throat. Reliving that demeaning conversation threatened to drag him down again. But now, as he mused in the breeze coming off the bay, he realized again how Shana had saved him. Earl had left that night and had never come back. But he had left his seed in Ella Mae that would grow to be the gift of Shana. The image of her big brown eyes and innocent radiance allowed the bitterness to drain out of Clayton. She needed him.

Clayton's physical prowess had long been his main focus, but he was also smart. He had found joy in learning and become a voracious reader. He had begun to live mostly in his own head. Eventually, he was able to get the job as a longshoreman, tolerating difficult physical labor because of its pay, even though it was grueling and sometimes dangerous. He told himself maybe after a year or two he would try to get into college. Eventually, a "year or two" rolled into ten.

"This was just a small dock fire, never any danger to me," he told himself, as he tried to gain control of his emotions. He knew he would go back to work there. He had no choice. He had always known in the back of his mind that something could go wrong at the docks. He lived in the midst of dangerous stuff. Fortunately, most of his work was concerned with dry materials like cotton sisal or, lately, bags of fertilizer. He had learned to ignore his fear through discipline and need.

Ten

Saturday, February 8, 1947

The dock fire continued to occupy Mack Hale's mind. He began a process of enumerating questions, more or less curiosities, about the cargoes passing through the port, current working conditions and safety precautions around the docks. He allowed his mind to wander freely, bringing him images and ideas randomly about Tiger Ship Chandlers' warehouse and its surroundings. He tried to imagine the implications of each idea both to Tiger Ship Chandlers and the surrounding communities.

One thought kept returning like an ignored person tugging on his sleeve. Fertilizer. Ammonium nitrate. He knew little about it, except that the port had been shipping tons of the stuff to Europe to replenish their agricultural lands. He also remembered something about its use in explosives. Those two facts kept nagging at Mack. He decided to get more information.

On Saturday morning, Mack put his full weight on the cranking pedal of his prized white-on-silver Harley Davidson flathead motorcycle. The engine roared its guttural pulsation. He sat for a moment to let the engine warm. On most weekends, Mack rode to feel the wind in his face and to experience freedom that only a two-wheeler gave a rider.

This morning he headed up to Kemah to visit Zach Foley, an old Navy buddy who owned a waterfront bar and curio shop on the cut between Galveston Bay and Clear Lake. The conference with the Coast Guard Captain, and then the recent fire, had left him with an itch, an uneasy feeling that he couldn't resolve.

Mack had enlisted in the Navy at age 19 in 1941 and served with the 1st Marine Division as a medic for four years in the Pacific Theater. He had survived amphibious landings and fierce fighting on the island of Tulagi, and later at Guadalcanal. The war experience had brought him wisdom beyond his age. It had forged mental and physical discipline, so he always paid attention when his mind set him astir.

He knew his current job and he did it well. He looked at the warehouse as his "ship" and kept it uncluttered, with nothing in the "gangways." He took great pride in its organization and cleanliness, prioritizing every detail, each important in itself.

Mack organized his life in the same way. He lived alone in one unit of a small duplex on 2nd Avenue, just off Main Street. This old, white clapboard structure reflected its low-rent status. He kept a set of barbells and a weight bench in the small bedroom and worked out daily to keep his trim body at 175 pounds.

This morning, he raced past egrets that exploded out of the marsh grass as he incised the wind along the two-lane highway. He knew he drove too fast, but that was part of the joy of a motorcycle. No traffic impeded his ride and he turned up the accelerator to full throttle.

He soon arrived at Foley's Bar. Ceiling beams and wooden walls covered with photographs created a warm welcome to its visitors. Mack had not visited Foley's in a while. After a vigorous back-slapping greeting, he and Zach reminisced about their wartime memories, shore leaves and drinking exploits. It was a bit early, but Zach popped open two beers.

"It's almost lunchtime somewhere," Zach remarked. "Besides, we haven't had a beer together since that time in Galveston when the bartender started that insane 'Mack and

Zach' routine. I didn't know whether to laugh or deck him. Luckily you stayed calm and steered us clear of another brawl. You always had a cool head. I think too many Howitzers have rattled my brain."

Their stories echoed with camaraderie and humorous anecdotes.

"We had this certifiably crazy commander on board," and "Remember when we went into this bar in…." Or "This rookie ate the banana…." Only the long pauses between memories referenced the things that the trauma of war would not allow them to mention. They laughed and then turned quiet, as images of dying comrades flashed up from the corners of their minds.

Mack sipped on his beer and arrived at the question he had come to discuss.

"Zach, you were involved with munitions, all those shells your ship poured onto the landing sites. You had to have handled them many times. What do you know about ammonium nitrate?"

"Are you planning on building a bomb?" Zach laughed. When Mack didn't reply, he continued. "Oh, come on now. No job can be that bad."

Mack finally laughed. "I'm not building a bomb. Our port has been handling huge amounts of this stuff as fertilizer. I remember something about ammonium nitrate being a component of explosives. But we don't handle it with any particular precautions. We had a meeting with the Coast Guard recently about reviewing our preparedness for accidents, which started me thinking about some of this stuff. Mr. Broussard kind of flipped the Coast Guard guy off. But I just have a feeling… something…. I can't really say what."

"Well, nitrates are used in explosives. Most of our ordnance used potassium nitrate. Both potassium and ammonium nitrate are oxidizers," Zach said. "They have a couple of things about them that are good for use in explosives. One thing is that they release oxygen when they burn. What does a fire need to keep burning? Oxygen. So, this shit is hard to snuff out. And second, when nitrates burn, no ash is produced. Nitrates turn into a gas and the gas then vaporizes. There is a lot of energy released when that happens. When they get hot enough, nitrates detonate – in other words, explode – with a force faster than the speed of sound. Supersonic, amigo. Very powerful."

He thought a bit more. "One other thing. Nitrates require other things to go from simple burning to detonation."

"What kinds of other things?"

Zach tilted his head left and right. "Sensitizers. Like maybe another explosive or a fuel that burns and raises the heat. And they need containment. You know, like when you put gunpowder in a shell casing. Containment creates pressure, which raises heat. When the fire – deflagration – gets hot enough to increase the speed of a fire's burn, detonation can occur.

"Let me summarize it this way. Deflagration is a sudden and violent fire that produces large amounts of heat. An explosive force occurs when solid nitrates decompose very rapidly into nitrous oxide and water vapor. Detonation – the explosion that comes from the deflagration – although difficult to attain, produces supersonic shock waves because of the high energy produced in the transference into a gas."

"Deflagration to detonation is not entirely understood. But at some point, that energy has to go somewhere. And if you have a large enough supply, it creates a tremendous force.

Zach continued with a new, serious look on his face. "This is powerful stuff. It will knock your dick off. But it has to be made into the right package to do that. How is the fertilizer shipped?"

"It's packaged in heavy-duty paper bags," Mack said. "One-hundred-pound bags."

Zach shrugged. "I think it should be okay. Pure ammonium nitrate is actually difficult to irritate. You almost have to ask it to burn. Like I said, it takes a lot of steps to make it into an explosive. It has to be contained or compressed in some manner like in a shell casing."

He thought a minute before asking a question. "This stuff you're talking about, it is used as a fertilizer, right? If so, that should be pretty stable. Sounds like your stuff is lying around in paper bags. It should be okay. Of course it can burn, but...." He left the thought with a vague shrug.

They shared a few more stories and some laughs. However, Mack left his meeting with Zach asking himself the same questions he had asked before he came. Was it a hazardous material or not? The answer seemed to be "maybe it is, and maybe it isn't." There were no directives from the Coast Guard or the Fire Department that said it could be. Apparently, no one at the Terminal considered it dangerous.

Mack did not feel entirely satisfied. But, with no place to turn, he let it slide out of his mind and turned to consider how his Saturday would unfold from here. In his spare time, when not cleaning and polishing his Harley, Mack fished on the jetties or read Jack London and other adventure stories. Solitary life suited him just fine. He had been orphaned at a young age and had grown up in foster homes. After high school, he had applied for a job at Tiger Ship Chandlers. He had impressed Louis by looking directly at him when they talked. In less than a year, Louis had made him foreman of the warehouse.

But the call of patriotism had captured Mack soon after that and he had enlisted in the Navy. Louis had promised him a job when he returned from the war, to which he had quickly agreed. The war had not hardened him. Rather, it had made him more appreciative of life. He felt fortunate to have survived and returned to Texas City with his body intact. War had taught him not to sweat the small stuff and to address the difficult first.

Mack had exchanged letters with Louis during the war and appreciated that Louis had saved his old job for him. Now Louis kidded him that he felt like a surrogate father, happy to help Mack follow his dream.

In some ways, Mack also became Louis' mentor, filling a few of the gaps in Louis' character. They made a good team.

Beneath his placid appearance, Mack carried a fierce courage. Nothing could shake him. Fundamentally, he believed that if he could survive the war in the Pacific, he could survive anything.

Eleven

Thursday, February 13, 1947

A bouquet of fresh cut flowers came with Louis for every counseling session he attended with Father Joe after that first visit.

"For the office," he said, as he handed them to Grace.

She accepted the flowers with a breath of surprise and a hint of a smile on her face every time. Flowers brightened the room and brought a new energy to her surroundings. Louis noticed a slight change in her attitude in the last three months. She seemed less distant, a little more genial, more responsive to his presence. Her original reticence had made it difficult for Louis to read her and he had not felt completely at ease in her company. The fact that he now wanted her to show an interest in him kept him a little off balance, unsure how he should respond. The awkward moments created an uncharacteristic shyness, another new experience for the bold and often aggressive bachelor.

Lately, Grace's softened approach allowed Louis to drop some of his defensiveness. He enjoyed the feeling of not needing to impress or intimidate her. It became obvious that she, too, was enjoying the bouquets.

Talking to Father Joe had become easier for Louis, also. In their latest talk, he was able to share his childhood, his mother's rages and his father's absenteeism.

"I think my mother loved me. But she cared little for being a parent. She loved the Catholic Church and never missed Sunday mass. She wanted me to be a good boy but basically abdicated my moral training to the church. She insisted I become an altar boy, but I rebelled against all of that Hellfire stuff."

Louis talked about his love for ships, how he had hoped to become a master mariner so he could captain ships worldwide, and how his parents conspired to discourage him.

"I spend much of my downtime now sitting in the dark of my kitchen, thinking and talking out loud to myself," he said in response to Father Joe's probing.

Louis stared out of the window behind Father Joe's desk where he could see the back door of the church. The door had wooden steps leading up to it, steps he had taken many times as an altar boy on his way to serve at morning mass.

"I used to go through that door, sometimes every day for weeks, to serve mass. Six-thirty a.m. on weekdays and Saturdays. I rode my bike. On cold winter mornings, my mother had to practically push me out the door."

He talked about his gradual disillusionment and then his separation from all religious ideas, and how he had turned to hedonism for a time in college.

"I'm just an ordinary sinner now, Father Joe, no more wild parties. I am not a religious person. I find it impossible to take it all literally."

He took a deep breath and opened up about the visit from the dragon and the Chinese man, and how much fear they had engendered in him.

"I really thought I was losing my mind. For a moment the concept of a devil loomed very real."

Father Joe thought for a moment, then responded respectfully. "The dragon experience frightened you, but historically having visions is not uncommon. The Bible is full of apparitions and visions. It was not rare, just uncommon. Today, stories of apparitions or voices are more likely to be associated with schizophrenia. But after the fear you felt abated, you returned to normal behavior. And it occurred just once to you. So, please don't worry. You are not psychotic, Louis.

"I see the dragon as a gift to you, like an angel's whisper. There is much about the mind, as well as the ways of God, that we do not understand. There are mysteries in life that are inexplicable. Can you accept that? I think that is an important step. Jesus said the Kingdom of God is within you. That implies there is something in each of us that is sacred, something core to our being human. From all the things you have told me, your life has been, can I say, a bit unruly, with lots of anxiety and maybe longing for something different? In fact, you haven't talked about any joy in your life.

"So, I call the dragon a gift, let's just call it an energy. Because of the dragon, you are here with me exploring who you really are meant to be. Without this acceptance, you would deny what you experienced and not gain any knowledge from it. So, can we say that it was real in an unreal way, a way that is not understood at this time?"

Father Joe hesitated for a moment before continuing with a stark question. "I also wonder what you are hiding from in that dark kitchen?"

Louis looked up in surprise. "I'm not hiding. I just like to think. There's nothing to hide from."

After a moment's pause, Father Joe observed, "Let me share a few more thoughts with you. Your mother's possible suicide is a big part of your current experience. Suicide can bring intense shame and guilt to those left behind. We can talk some more about that later. But you must know that if she took her life, it was not in any way an indictment of you."

He paused to let Louis absorb this perspective before continuing. "Another source of intense guilt to be dealt with is that you were raised in a strict Catholic theology. Due to subsequent events in your life, religion no longer fits you. You have not been able to make it work. You, no pun intended, went overboard to the other side, away from the church.

"Parallel to that, you have been suppressed in the expression of your deepest wishes. You have never been allowed to act on your dream and find your sense of place. You feel like you have been paddling upstream your whole life. Suppression hangs around below the surface of the mind and a part of your mind works hard to keep that suppressed stuff down."

A queasy sensation rose into Louis' throat and the color drained from his face. He wanted Father Joe to stop and for the session to end. He wanted to stand up and leave. He was having trouble breathing.

"I can see this makes you uncomfortable, Louis. Take a few deep breaths. Breathe…. Is there something you want to say?"

Louis demurred with the shake of his head. Father Joe could see Louis begin to relax, and he waited a few moments more.

"A wise part of you wants to reconcile your life with what you hold as truth. That truth, call it intuition or internal wisdom if you wish, does not coincide with what you were taught. In its desire to protect us, our Church has covered us up with so much theology and so many rules that it can be difficult to be self-reliant. Your desire to find your own way in life clashed with the fear of disobeying your mother's strong beliefs.

"Your father did not have the power of the Church behind

him, but he created his own share of guilt for you through his patriarchy. Your mother, the Mother Church, and your father all created strict boundaries around you and left no room for your own human experience or your point of view. You were never given a choice. Hell is the great ogre created to keep us from examining the validity of our own experience. Hell became bigger than Heaven in your mind. To handle this burden, you felt that you had to deny, suppress or project it away. And those memories are persistent. They hang around.

"You don't have to understand all of this right now, Louis. But if Dr. Morgan can find no physical reason for your symptoms, you must admit that there is a power within you that can create havoc with your health. 'Confused' is a good place to be at times. Confusion helps loosen your grip on what you think might be real. Trusting your own experience gives you the opportunity to make a choice of what to believe in.

"This is a process that not everyone has the courage to consider. That is why I say the dragon is a gift to you. It is a friendly dragon wanting to help you make your own choices, to get your attention on the possibility of change in yourself."

After a moment of silence, Father Joe spoke again in a less serious tone. "What do you do for fun?"

Louis shook his head, "I haven't been having much fun lately.... I used to play golf for fun."

"Good! I also play golf. Why don't you set up a game for us?"

On his way out, as Grace made him another appointment, Louis studied her face. God, she is beautiful, he thought. He felt a sudden urge to touch her but hesitated. Instead, he pushed past his hesitancy and spoke to her.

"I want to take you out to dinner. I would like you to go out with me. How about it?" Tiny beads of sweat formed on his brow as he waited for her response. He swallowed, thinking she would never reply. He paused longer but received only silence. He rushed through a response to fill the void. "Just think about it.... You can tell me next week. No hurry."

Grace kept her eyes on the desk. Part of her wanted to say yes. She could not stand up to the force of shame that still gripped her when her routine was threatened with any disruption.... Just having Louis stand beside the desk filled her with anxiety.

"I'm not... I'm not doing that sort of thing right now. I've...." She stopped, lifted her head to look at him. "Maybe another time... maybe... some other time."

Louis stammered over his words and rushed to reply. "I am a little rusty at this, too, asking for a date. I hope you are not offended. Maybe you have a boyfriend?"

"No. I don't," Grace replied.

As he left the office, Louis felt relieved and happy that he had asked her but bewildered at his awkward behavior. He never had trouble talking to women. And Louis considered her choice of words encouraging.

After Louis left the office, Father Joe saw the flowers on Grace's desk. "Hmm, looks like someone around here has an admirer."

"What?" Grace tried to look surprised. "Oh, Mr. Broussard brings those for the office."

Father Joe tilted his head. "I know. I have seen them before. Grace, you are a vibrant young lady. It is not surprising that Louis finds you attractive. You should go out, have some fun. What do you think of him?"

"He is a handsome man." A rosy blush invaded her cheeks.

"He does seem like a nice man. I don't know." Grace paused and her lower lip quivered as she struggled to put words to her feelings.

"The truth is…." Tears came into her eyes. "The truth is, I'm afraid. I am afraid of anyone – of everyone – especially a man – knowing the truth about me. Some days I think I am getting better. But then the shame devastates me and I can't shake it."

"Grace, you don't realize how far you have come. I am impressed with your progress. You are doing great. The fear will not go away in one great release. It wants to remain like a bad habit. Yes, it can still frighten you, but you are stronger now. You have the resolve to face it and not turn away from the responsibility of what happened. Maybe accepting flowers from Louis is a good start. Try it on for a while," he finished with a smile.

Twelve

L ouis met Father Joe at the golf course on an unusually gorgeous winter's day, a warm sun smiling on the morning, making it a perfect day for golf. He welcomed this casual time together with his new-found friend. His game would not be sharp because of the long absence from playing, but he assumed that Father Joe was a pure hacker anyway. To protect Father Joe from an assumed sense of embarrassment, he secured an early tee time, thinking fewer witnesses would mean less pressure.

Louis began to get an inkling that something was afoot when he greeted Father Joe and noticed his smart Ben Hogan lightweight windbreaker.

"After you," Louis said on the first tee. He glanced at Father Joe's clubs, an old set of Ben Hogan irons and woods. A full set, but they showed their age. Father Joe said little at first and Louis thought he might be nervous about playing. He took a few slow and deliberate practice swings that showed stiffness in his movements.

Louis heard the thwack of the driver and watched Father Joe's ball arc high, long and straight down the middle of the fairway. It rolled along the fairway to a stop more than 200 yards away from the tee box in perfect position. Louis looked at Father Joe, then back at the ball, his face contorted somewhere between disbelief, confusion and amazement.

"My dad was a golfer," Father Joe explained with a huge grin. "I started playing at five. It has always come easy to me."

Louis shook his head. "I never thought I would be playing with a sandbagger priest. Does the Bishop know you play golf?"

"He doesn't know I'm playing today. He hates golf. I told him that God loves golf, that He invented it. The Bishop didn't buy it. And by the way, just to clear the air, I had a girlfriend in high school, too."

An embarrassed grin formed on Louis' face. "It doesn't surprise me, although I never thought about it."

Louis hit a good drive, though not as far. They walked down the fairway, pulling their handcarts, and laughed away the nervousness of first-tee shots. In the bright sunshine, a light wind drifted across them and ruffled the flags on the greens. Louis admired Father Joe's skill at the game. He attacked the golf course with natural athleticism and the same gusto and joy as the dance at Demetrios'. Louis delighted in the magical energy that emanated from him, similar to a child's exuberance. Just being alive brought this priest so much joy.

In the counseling sessions, Louis had witnessed both Father Joe's depth of thought and a stability that balanced his response to the world with his religious beliefs. To see this playful spirit at work in him had brought Louis to a greater admiration.

On the sixth hole, Louis stepped up to the tee box and hit his drive. "Oh man," he cried out. The ball flew with a slight hook, traveling high and long before its graceful descent to the fairway, like a duck landing on the surface of a pond.

"Great shot," Father Joe said.

"That's the best contact I've made all day. Vibrated out of the top of my head and through my toenails."

"It's a real joy to find that sweet spot," Father Joe added.

Both men hit short pitch shots to the green. Louis' ball stopped four feet away from the hole. Father Joe then pitched his shot inside of it and finished with a short putt for a birdie. Louis missed his putt.

"Divine intervention," observed Father Joe

Louis groused again, "I'm reporting you to the Bishop."

"Sometimes life is just not a fair... way, Louis," he returned with a grin. Louis responded to the bad pun with a smile and a groan.

After nine holes, they entered the clubhouse for coffee.

They sat at a small table with a view of the 18th green, away from the counter, the only guests in the room. Father Joe silently stirred cream and sugar into his coffee while Louis studied him.

"I have been bothered by what you said about finding my own truth," Louis spoke. "You remember that?"

Father Joe nodded.

"What keeps me from making up stuff and saying it's true?"

"Because if you did that, you would be a politician," said Father Joe, that impish smile anchored by a nod of the head. "But seriously.... When I say 'truth,' I'm talking about primary things, like gravity or oxygen.

"Here's an example from today. That drive you hit on the sixth hole, that feeling of perfect connection between golf ball and club face? You knew what that feeling was before you ever hit a golf ball. No one had to teach you that. No one could teach you what it feels like. They might try to tell you what it feels like, try to explain how it happens, write some formulas to show the physics. But no one can make you feel it. You just have to hit enough golf balls to make that perfect connection and experience it. When you do experience it, you know that club face and ball met in exactly the right spot to create a perfect vibration.

Harmony in your body is what signaled to you that it happened.

"I know this is complex. But that feeling of striking a golf ball in the sweet spot resides in you. It comes with the knowledge that it feels good; it is good. It provides a remarkable moment. You then want every shot to feel like that.

"Truth is like that. It is harmonious. You feel the truth throughout your body and you just know. Truth is more than answers in the Baltimore Catechism. It is existential. To put it simply, you know when you know. Like that golf shot."

Louis sipped his coffee. "For the moment I will take your word for it."

"It is a paradox. So just stay open to new ideas."

"Let me get you out of the pulpit for a minute. I also want to ask you about Grace."

Father Joe smiled. "Ah, let's get back to earthier conversations. You mean Grace, my secretary? Not Divine Grace?... Well, the 'mortal' Grace came from Chicago to live with her sister. She is intelligent, efficient and organized – a great help running the office. You're not wanting to hire her away from me, are you?"

"No, no." Louis waved his dissent. "I was just curious since I see her every week. She is nice to look at."

"She's finding her way around in new surroundings. I think you should ask her out. She could use some company."

"I tried that. No luck. I'm a little intimidated by her. I can't tell if she doesn't like me or is being professional."

"Give it another try. You might be surprised."

As Louis drove away from the golf club, he knew he was more than just curious about Grace. He acknowledged to himself that he was thinking about her every day and wanted to spend time with her and get to know more about her. Like a schoolboy crush, she commanded much of his attention. Her diffidence was something new to him. He had seldom been denied. Maybe he enjoyed the mystery of her. Whatever the reason, he found himself in new territory.

Louis' counseling sessions continued. He became more and more comfortable, and the appointments seemed like the continuation of a conversation. In a subtle way, his meetings with Father Joe created and nourished a friendship between them. They both led lives that dictated singularity. Louis, even as a child, had never had a close, best friend with whom he could share everything. Deep down, Father Joe had become a real father figure for Louis. For his part, Father Joe, surrounded by his congregation and positioned as leader of the flock, felt that he needed this personal interaction, too. They both found comfort in the company of each other.

Louis had learned much about himself and admitted that he had begun to look forward to each new visit. He cherished the new friendship with Father Joe. Trust in the priest began to build self-reliance and a new confidence in himself, opening avenues that had been closed off by his solitary existence. He grew more aware of weighing his decisions and acting out of a new internal resource. Grace, however, for the moment remained unfathomable to him.

Thirteen

Saturday, February 22, 1947

Grace continued to work with Clayton and admitted to herself that she enjoyed the sessions. Now sure that she had been slyly manipulated, she laughed to herself at the thought. She found the darkness lifting from her spirit in small increments. On her better days, she joked with Father Joe, and accused him of purposefully sleeping in on Saturdays when she met with Clayton, knowing of course that he arose before dawn every day to read his breviary. But her personal demons had not abandoned her. She still had dark days of doubt when she could not shake her shame. The frequent ups and downs, more than she wanted to admit, kept her wary of ever declaring herself free.

As she got ready to meet Clayton for their weekly lesson, Grace found herself evaluating the impact he was having on her. Teaching Clayton and watching him progress provided relief from dragging her own past around. The irony of her teaching music like her mother shuffled her emotions like playing cards: appreciation, guilt, confusion, sadness. Although she recognized jazz as her place, she now regretted not being more appreciative of her mother's efforts to make her a concert pianist. She was beginning to understand now that her path would have been very different and a lot more suitable to a stable and harmonious life. Over time, Grace had begun talking more openly with Greta, now able to share her doubts and fears. They even talked about Louis.

"He must have problems of his own because he has been

getting counseling from Father Joe. He seems nice, though. Older than me," she shared with a slight smile.

"It might be nice to have an older man to talk to."

"He's only a little older, and he's definitely not the confessor type."

"It wouldn't hurt to have him over for a visit. You could invite him to Sunday dinner," Greta gently offered.

This idea both intrigued and frightened Grace. Her early determination to become an ascetic and hide herself in the "nunnery" had become less rigid. She had begun to notice the world around her, like the sky when it was covered in silver gray clouds or polished clear by the sun's rays. On her walks to work, she heard birds singing. But she still felt unworthy of a normal life.

The flowers from Louis discomfited her and weakened her resolve to… to what? The question hung in her mind. Punish herself? A new energy buffered her thoughts. Her determination to live in isolation had developed small hesitations. At times, she could feel a glimmer of normalcy squeezing itself into her mind.

She walked briskly to the church, stretching her arms above her head and enjoying the warm sunshine on her face. Instructing Clayton relieved some of her introversion. She now played the piano whenever they met for his session. The feel of the ivory keys beneath her fingertips brought a fleeting release from tension in her body. Thoughts of playing and singing again also found their way through her defenses for brief moments. But, for now, she contented herself by concentrating on Clayton's progress.

Clayton was working hard and developing rapidly with her assistance. He showed a natural proclivity to technique and quickly improved his tonal quality. Grace thought he might have perfect pitch, but to gain further mastery he would need to learn vibrato.

"Vibrato," she told Clayton, "is a variation in the pitch of a musical note. It is subtle and creates a deeper sound. You hear a sweet, warm tone as opposed to a less rounded note. It can be created by an up-down movement of the diaphragm, by modulation in the throat or by movement of the lower jaw and lip.

"I don't quite know how to teach this to you. It is like an athletic skill. Sometimes you need to be intense, sometimes you need to mellow down. At one time I could sing it…. So, that's the next level for you. Just keep practicing and we'll muddle through it."

As Grace sat at the piano, he leaned over her shoulder to see notes on the sheet of music and, without thinking, put his hand on her shoulder. It would have been innocent ordinarily, but both of them felt a shock from their contact.

Clayton's heart raced. He lingered over her and breathed in her freshness. He wanted to pull away, but he also wanted to lay both of his hands on her shoulders, to be able to be a normal man expressing his gratitude for Grace, even if only out of appreciation for her kindness.

Their work together over the past Saturdays had created a closeness that neither had thought much about. But the touch brought a physical presence into the room that could not be ignored, and it charged their relationship with an unsuspected energy.

Grace stopped playing and held her hands over the keys.

"Ahem. Well…." Her face flushed.

Clayton knew he had made a mistake. He quickly pulled his hand back. He spun around, threw his head back and walked away.

"Grace, I apologize. I'm sorry. It's jes'.... I just want to say thank you."

"It's okay, Clayton. We've been working so intently these past few weeks that things can get misinterpreted."

"Nobody ever helped me so much. Nobody ever cared about what I could do. I have been invisible all my life and now you see me. You see me as a real person. It's just that I am so grateful. Not only for the music lessons, but for the confidence you give me. For the first time, I can see myself as a real person being treated like a real person. That's all it is, really. Gratitude. I owe you too much. Thank you, Grace. Thank you."

Grace did not turn around. Sadness overwhelmed her. She kept her gaze on the piano keys, unable to deny the wave of emotion that followed his touch, forced to acknowledge feelings that she had worked hard to suppress and that she had hoped no longer existed. She had denied her loneliness for so long. Surprised and afraid of her emotion, she felt the sadness of her imposed isolation, and the fear that commingled with so much of her life. Even the touch of a grateful admirer froze her for the moment. Grace struggled to compose herself.

"You're welcome, Clayton. You have been good for me, also." She paused to catch her breath. "You're the best pupil I've ever had. Of course, you're the *only* pupil I've ever had," she said with a smile.

They both laughed, ill at ease with the tension in the room. Grace stood up, straightened the sheet music and eased herself toward the door.

"Clayton, you are a beautiful man, inside and out. In another place, another time – no, probably another universe – maybe things could have been different. But for now, there is only music. I know how important it is to you because I have been to that place. Nothing comes before the music. Nothing interferes with that, no matter what other feelings show up." She paused and looked up at him.

"That's enough for today. See you next week?" she asked gently. He nodded silently in response.

On the way home, Grace chewed on the raw emotions that were churning in her. The renewal of her spirit that had begun to surface carried companions of sensuality that she was not ready to admit.

Fourteen

Tuesday, February 25, 1947

Vincent Russo, president of the Terminal Railway Company, phoned Louis and immediately came to the point.

"I hear that you are taking some new proposals to the Safety Board. That is a foolish idea, Louis. You know how those things go."

After the fire and some serious introspection, Louis now agreed with Mack on the need for a coordinated safety plan that would include the different emergency crews on the docks as well as Steve Nader's Fire Department. The decision now energized Louis to fight for better safety on the docks and he began to badger other board members about these ideas. Louis discussed greater enforcement of the existing rules and went so far as to mention annexation of the port and refinery properties by Texas City.

No surprise: word had gotten back to Russo. And Louis was ready for his call.

"Oh, really? Why do you say that is foolish? We came close to a major fire that could have destroyed all of the warehouses along Dock Road. I think we have room for an assessment of our procedures."

Russo's response was immediate.

"Let me be perfectly clear. You start talking about changes, you have to include the Coast Guard and other federal regulators. More rules mean more interference with our business. More importantly, you draw attention to the port. You are aware,

I am sure, that Texas City is already talking about annexing the whole complex. Taxes! That's what that means. More money to feed the insatiable appetite of the government."

Louis' dislike for the port boss leaked out and he found himself baiting him. "It seems inevitable to me. Besides, we owe something to our community, don't you think?"

"We don't owe the government a damn thing! We built this industry and we can sustain it without outside help. We can grow it bigger and better. It is safe enough here. The Terminal does not need more rules. Neither does Monsanto, Standard Oil or any of the other corporations out here. We have good safety standards now and we can handle our problems on our own."

"I don't agree," was Louis' retort. "I think we got lucky this time. We need better emergency response time, a central port authority, and better communication with Steve and his men in Texas City. What we currently have has been adequate so far – maybe – but it would not be enough in a major catastrophe."

Vincent Russo's voice turned cold. "You know, Louis, arrangements could be made to bring supplies in from Galveston chandlers with just a phone call."

"Is that a threat?" Louis stood up at his desk and knocked over his chair. His anger spilled out. "Are you threatening me?"

"I'm just saying you also have a business to protect. I am just trying to help you keep the enterprise your father built, to keep it growing like the other hard workers out here. We have a good climate for business and it runs smoothly. The fire was just a little hiccup. It got handled. Those things happen in industrial complexes." Russo's gelid voice purred over the phone. "I'm saying you need to think carefully about what you are doing."

Louis slammed the phone down. A sinister smile took form

on his face. It felt good to be angry. He had forgotten how anger prickled his skin, how it brought new energy, an aliveness, to his body.

"You're right!" Louis said out loud to the office walls. "I will certainly think more carefully about what I am doing! You can't threaten me, you little son of a bitch! Truth is truth and right is right!"

Louis picked up the phone and called the church office. "Grace, this is Louis Broussard. I need to talk to Father Joe. Can I come in this afternoon?"

"He just stepped out of the office. Are you alright, Mr. Broussard?"

"No! I'm not alright. I'm angry."

"I think he has an opening later this afternoon. Hang on," Grace said.

Louis picked up a pencil and tapped it on the desktop while he held the phone. Mounds of paper sat on his desk that he could not attend to in his agitation. He needed to work, but a new sense of urgency kept him waiting on the phone. He had awakened to a cognizance of his own feelings. A few weeks ago, he would have poured himself a drink, muttered to himself and let this skirmish with Vincent Russo slide. Not anymore.

"Mr. Broussard, can you come in at four this afternoon?" Grace said.

"I'll be there. Thanks, Grace."

Later that day, Father Joe stood in the doorway to his office as he and Grace waited for Louis to arrive. He took the opportunity to talk quietly with her.

"Grace, you've been here a few months now. Do you have any thoughts about the future? About what's next for you?"

Grace seldom thought about the future. She had wanted nothing more than to work here, live with Greta and keep herself invisible to the world. Still feeling brittle and breakable, and on some days just hanging on by a thread, she thought it best not to think of the future. While living one day at a time came more easily to her with each passing day, in her mind, she had no future. Her heart, through sheer will, had been hardened against that possibility.

By now she had learned to recognize Father Joe's efforts to steer the conversation where he wished it to go, and she waited for his next comment.

"Do you think about going back to Chicago? Singing again?"

Grace had thought briefly about going back to Chicago. But the sting of shame put a stop to that. She feared that she would not be strong enough to take care of herself and that path would direct her into a black pit again. She was not sure of what that meant, but for now she needed Greta, her job and Father Joe to give her the support her fragile life needed. Helping Clayton had added one more purpose to follow.

She recognized that fear still ruled her decisions and she did not think it a good way to live. But in spite of that awareness, shame retained its grip on her behavior. She did not have the resolve to fight that battle yet.

Her response was slow and quiet.

"No. I don't think about it. I mean I have briefly thought about it. But no, singing again is out of the question."

"Have you thought about making some new friends here? I've told you all the jokes I know. You must be getting tired of hearing them." Father Joe dropped his wily tone. "I think it is about time you inserted yourself back into society. There is a big world out there that you are shutting out. You would be a great addition to it."

Before responding, Grace's eyes moved without conscious thought to the vase of yellow roses that Louis had brought earlier in the week and that now colorfully decorated her desk. The thought of him was her first response to what Father Joe had said. She moved to the file cabinet to put away papers.

"You are probably right. It's just that...."

Louis came through the office door in such a rush that he startled her. In her surprise, she knocked over the vase. "Oh, look what I've done," Grace said as she ran to the restroom for paper towels. Louis grabbed the stacked In and Out boxes and held them until she returned.

"I surprised you. I'm sorry, Grace."

"What a mess I've made," she said.

"No. It's my fault. Let me do that." He touched her hand as he took the paper towels from her. He kept his eyes on her face as he blotted the desk. Father Joe watched them from his doorway.

As he finished wiping the desk, Louis looked up and saw in Grace's eyes the desperation and pain she was feeling because of a simple mistake. He saw how shallow her confidence lay, just above a feeling of panic.

He forgot about Russo. He knew what she was feeling. He removed his hat and stood in front of her, rocking back and forth and distraught at causing her distress. He nodded at Father Joe mutely as the priest observed the interaction between the two of them.

Grace saw that the flowers were now splayed out in a puddle on the floor. She remembered how she had felt the first time Louis brought flowers. Each week they became easier to accept.

They no longer presented a threat to her. But his personal attention to her was another matter.

Louis stood before her, all of his attention on her, longing to help. She saw compassion in his face that she had not seen before.

"It's alright," she said softly as she bent to pick up the flowers. "The papers will dry. The flowers will live."

Father Joe smiled. "Ah, catastrophe averted. Thank you, Grace. Come in, Louis."

Once in his office, Father Joe steered Louis to understand the source of his anger with Russo.

"It is okay to get angry. It is the dimension of the response that can get you into trouble. For instance, if it passes into rage, it can become violent and uncontrollable. Rage usually comes from anger at yourself for your own misdeeds or your own frustrations. Then you project it onto someone else in an attempt to make that person guilty. You may see that you had cause here because Russo threatened you. Your response seems okay to me, normal, not out of control. It is another part of this process of understanding your emotions and recognizing that it is a process. Recognition is an important part of healing. The good news is that you have given yourself permission to be in that process."

"How long will this last?" Louis asked, feeling his frustration still swirling.

"I don't know. You are doing fine, Louis. Don't be too concerned with how long."

After the meeting, Louis stood at the desk and waited for Grace to make another appointment for him.

"Maybe I could come by your house. We could talk or take a walk. Maybe you could just call me Louis?"

Louis assumed Grace's silence was a rejection and awkwardly

tried to back out of his request.

"I just thought I would ask again. No harm in asking, okay?"

"No. It's alright," Grace said. "I mean, I appreciate your asking. Greta... my sister... said you should come for dinner... Sunday."

They looked at each other, both astonished at her invitation. Louis broke into a big grin. "I'll be there. What time?"

"Two o'clock. Greta likes to eat at two o'clock on Sundays."

On the following Sunday, Louis dined with Grace, Greta, her husband George and their son Michael. Greta had prepared a fine meal of fried chicken, mashed potatoes, green beans and hot rolls. But time moved glacially through the natural awkwardness of first encounters. Louis and Grace fidgeted with their forks, endured embarrassing starts and stops of conversation, and seldom made eye contact.

They each probed to find a topic of conversation. Louis talked about his ship supply business. George told about his work as a chemist at the refinery. Greta played the gracious hostess, passing the rolls and fried chicken mounded on a platter.

"Do you like to fish?" George asked Louis.

"No. My Daddy never fished so I never developed an interest in it. Do you go fishing?"

"Yes. I'm pretty regular at it. Michael goes with me some. Greta did once but can't find the time anymore."

"I like fishing," Michael said. "I caught a big redfish. Real big."

"I remember that redfish, Michael. He fought you very hard, but you reeled him in like a professional. I tried to get Grace interested. No luck in that department," George said, smiling in her direction.

"He's right," she replied. "I can't stand to see that poor fish dangle with that hook in its mouth. I'm too much of a city girl for that foolishness." Grace cast her eyes down. "At least I was once."

She looked up and smiled. "Maybe I will become a fisherman – a fisherwoman – at some point, though."

"I guess I was too bookish," Louis said. "I read a lot and I collected arrowheads. But most of the time I worked. My Daddy could always find a job for me."

"Real arrowheads, from real Indians?" Michael sat up in his chair with interest.

"Yes. Tribes of Karankawa Indians roamed this area and lived around the bay. You might have fun digging for arrowheads up by Moses Lake. It's a small bay really, but it's called a lake. I have collections of arrowheads mounted in frames. I'll bring some over to show you," Louis said as he shifted his eyes to Grace. "That is if I get invited back."

Grace blushed and turned toward Greta. "That would be up to Greta. You have to pass muster with the cook."

"Of course, you are welcome. I love to watch people eat my cooking. And you are good at it, Louis." Greta smiled with her genuine invitation, and laughter eased the moment.

Louis asked Michael if he liked pirates. Michael, his fork twirling in mashed potatoes, sat up tall again and focused on Louis.

"We had a very famous pirate that lived right across the bay, named Jean Lafitte. He used Galveston as a base while he raided ships in the Gulf of Mexico. He built a house on Galveston Island and started a small community of people who were part of his gang of pirates."

"Really?" Michael asked, wary that he might be getting

tricked. "Did he have a patch over his eye and a big sword?"

"For sure he had a sword. I don't know about the patch. There is an interesting story that he was actually a spy and that the government let him roam free to track Spanish ships."

Louis had Michael's curiosity aroused now and entered into a comfortable conversation with the young boy while the others talked about dessert. Grace could see that Louis enjoyed talking with Michael and it made her wonder if he had ever had any children of his own.

"Do you have any family here?" George asked. "Have you ever been married?"

"George! That's none of your business," Greta scolded him.

"It's okay," Louis replied. "I have never been married, and my parents are both dead. I don't have any family." The question didn't bother Louis, who knew that unmarried men of his age raised questions, including questions about their intentions, premature as they may be. "I guess I never found the right woman, like your Greta."

Greta deflected the compliment, sensing Grace's embarrassment. Rising from the table she said, "Let's have dessert."

They completed their meal with coffee and bread pudding. The pudding along with the lace tablecloth reminded Louis of his mother. She had loved to set a fancy table with lots of plates and her fine silverware. She had considered bread pudding one of her specialties and always served it with a splash of sherry on the top – a generous splash for herself. She and Alcid had entertained frequently. Their dinners were more somber and formal than Greta's family. And his Daddy always did the lion's share of the talking.

"We do this every Sunday. You're welcome to come back, Louis, if you don't mind fried chicken every time," Greta said.

Grace stood at the door as Louis walked to his car and Greta joined her. "He seems like a good man. Although I think Michael made more points with him than you did."

Grace gave Greta a wan look. But Louis had impressed her with the way he engaged Michael. He had made a stalwart effort to be accepted. Grace had grown very fond and protective of Michael. Louis' kind regard of him revealed another surprise to her.

"What do you think?" Greta was eager to see some enthusiasm from Grace.

"I don't know if he is a 'good man' or a 'clever man,' but he is a good-looking man. Someone who might be able to curl your toes."

Greta gasped. "Why, Grace! I never heard you talk like that." They both began to giggle as Grace covered her face with both hands to hide her blush.

Greta stopped laughing and stared at Grace. "Honey, I believe that is the first time I have heard you laugh since you got here." They laughed again. It warmed Greta's heart to see Grace show some glimmer of a return to normal.

"My, my. Curl your toes. That's a new one for me.... Maybe he's just shy. Talking to Michael might be easier for him."

"Don't get your hopes up, sister," Grace replied. "I'm not looking for a man. I'm okay the way I am." Grace knew as soon as she said the words that it was not true, however. She did get lonely and still fought periods of depression.

"Oh Grace, I don't mean to imply that you need a serious relationship with Louis. I'm not a matchmaker. I love having you here. It's just that me, Michael, George and Father Joe are about the only people you see. I think you would enjoy having someone else to talk to you." Greta put her arms around Grace. "I know you have to go at your own pace. I don't ever want you to leave here."

Fifteen

Louis' feud with the Terminal Railroad had cooled with his mind on Grace and his meetings with Father Joe. But his attention returned when reports began to circulate of covert maneuvers initiated by Russo. He had coerced other members of the Safety Board to vote "no" on Louis' proposals for a central port authority. He had rejected other suggestions such as expanding some rules, including a heavy fine for employers of workers who smoked on the docks. When the news reached Louis, he met with Mack to discuss these new developments.

"He is circling the wagons, Mack. Russo won't let go of that power." Louis walked behind his desk as he talked. "It is interesting that this fight over regulations is coming up now. I think I have had my head in the sand. As you know, we have shipped ammonium nitrate through the port for several years, but I notice that larger amounts have been arriving lately. Tons more are being shipped to Europe."

"I agree," Mack spoke up. "We have been thinking so much about the gasoline fire that I wonder if we have not overlooked a much larger problem."

"I'm thinking the same thing. What are your thoughts?"

"During the war, the Army regulated shipment of ammonium nitrate. But they no longer consider it their responsibility, even though it is still used in explosives. Regulations and safety directives over its shipment now belong to the Coast Guard, and they haven't said anything to us. I talked to several foremen, but I couldn't find anyone responsible for regulating its movement. Despite its history in explosives, ammonium nitrate is not treated as a hazardous material. It is simply fertilizer and tons of it are loaded onto ships here every week. After I talked with Zach, I just kind of put it out of my mind."

Louis knew Mack to be meticulous. Normally Louis paid little attention to what went into the ships that Tiger Chandlers served, being mostly concerned with his own bottom line. But Mack now had Louis' full attention.

"What are your concerns about all of this? Why haven't you said more about this to me? Is it unsafe to ship? We've never had a problem before."

"I guess I just dropped the ball. The foreman told me it had been declared safe, even though he had little information about it. So, I called Russo's office and, apparently, they are aware of its previous history. His secretary told me that Mr. Russo had consulted with a representative from the manufacturer who emphatically asserted the safety of ammonium nitrate. But I don't know. I have an uneasy feeling about it now."

"Maybe we all have fumbled this one, Mack. I'm not blaming you. This whole business has made me irritated. Why can't we get a simple answer? Do you think it has explosive capabilities?"

"Well, yes and no. My buddy Zach served as a gunnery mate on a battleship during his tour in the Navy. He explained explosive reactions to me. Certain events have to occur to create an explosion with this stuff. Deflagration-to-detonation transition, he called it. It is all very technical. Maybe I should have said more about it to you sooner.

"He said that nitrates need sensitizers and some kind of

confinement to achieve that transition to detonation, and to be effective as explosives. He talked about shock waves and zones, subsonic and supersonic waves, pretty much over my head. Basically, his view is that ammonium nitrate as a fertilizer is stable and should not be treated as a hazardous material. Maybe he's right. But I can't shake the idea that there is information about ammonium nitrate that we don't have. In the overall picture, we have plenty of other volatile substances out here to worry about, so we still need changes in our safety procedures."

Louis leaned over his desk, propping his chin in his hands. "We need an independent third party, a proper port authority that is separated from the people making the money out here. I admit that I, too, have been caught up in this web of profits with all this booming business. Russo's right about one thing: I have a big stake in this.

"However, one of the board members asked me who had made me the watchdog at the last meeting. Do you think I'm pushing too hard, Mack? No one else seems to care. Just us and Steve Nader." Louis paused for Mack's response.

"Oh, I think there are lots of others who are concerned. It's just that the port lacks any leadership other than Russo. I have become complacent, too. It's like cancer: The thing grows silently until it hits something major. Are you pushing too hard? I don't think so. Me, I've always enjoyed a good fight. Maybe we're moving too slow."

Louis abruptly stood. "God damn it!" He picked up a metal paperweight and threw it against the opposite wall, denting the wood paneling. Mack had never heard him raise his voice.

"I've been a fool hanging onto my Daddy's coattails and

playing Russo's game." Louis picked up the phone and called Steve Nader. Steve answered in his gruff voice.

"Steve, I've had it with Russo. He's blocked everything I've tried to do out here. The son of a bitch is getting under my skin!"

"Good," Steve responded. "It's about time somebody besides me got angry."

"Do you have any ideas where we should go from here? Russo is not going to cooperate with any changes."

"I don't think you have many options. It's damn hard to get around Vincent Russo. About the only avenue I see is to get that whole area annexed by Texas City. Then we could have some input into regulating it. We could sure use some of that money in the community. You need to talk to the mayor about that. I've been worried about the docks ever since you brought it up at Lola's Place."

Steve paused before changing the subject. "Where the hell you been, Louis? Haven't seen you around much."

"I've been busy, Steve. But I'll buy you a drink soon, I promise. I miss talking with you."

Louis realized that he had been living in a cocoon too long. This snubbing from Russo raised a red flag about his own indifference. A voice had awakened inside of him. Now he knew both the question and the answer. What have I been doing all these years? I have been running with the pack, blaming everyone but myself, he concluded.

He turned around to face Mack. "I think it is time for me to stand up to Russo. He doesn't want change. I blame him, but I have not done anything to help the situation, either. I'm going back to the board. We are going to keep this conversation alive. Steve is right about needing an independent overseer. We can't keep the status quo. The port is getting too busy."

His resolution calmed Louis' anger and Grace suddenly came into his mind. It happened frequently now – her face appearing to him at odd moments. He did not understand it all, but he knew Grace catalyzed many changes in his life. She was becoming a more important part of his landscape every day, which brought unheard-of ideas to Louis' mind.

"Have you ever been married, Mack?"

"No, sir."

"Me neither."

In the evening, Louis sat at his kitchen table analyzing the situation further. Father Joe, who had admonished him for hiding here in the dark, had pointed out that he had not gotten what he had really wanted out of life, that the dragon had come searching for the real Louis Broussard and scared the hell out of him. For Louis to be his own man meant rejection of the big boss: his Daddy.

All the questions pursued in his sessions with Father Joe now gave Louis the confidence to make an uncomfortable examination of himself. He knew the counseling had helped him and the future had become important to him once more. That included simple things like listening to the radio again, which he had stopped doing long ago. He learned that a Black man was signed to play baseball in the major leagues for the first time. True to his habit, he talked out loud to the kitchen walls.

"What do you think of that baseball player, Jackie... Jackie something, up there in Brooklyn? *He* broke out. *He* won't let people tell him how to live. He is showing that he is free. I wonder how they feel about that in the Hallows. Do they even know about this player?"

Louis spoke as though Jackie Robinson stood before him. "What's it like to be the only Black man in an all-white league? You could be bringing a ton of trouble on yourself. How did you make that choice? You must be a courageous man…. And tough. You would have to be tough. You could have just stayed in the Negro leagues. You have more courage than I have.

"But on the other hand, I think it is more than that. I think it's bigger than you. You knew that it was bigger than you and you chose to take it on. For the others…. You did it for all those others stuck in places just like the Hallows, didn't you? My hat's off to you, Jackie. You have the right stuff. I need some of that courage myself." An image of his Daddy hovered over his internal dialogue.

His thoughts moved on to Grace and he saw her as dreamy and elusive, in and out of focus. At times he saw her as a fragile child. Other times he recalled the scent of her perfume and saw the woman in her. Grace awakened him to the silence of his existence, to the fact that he did not have joy in his life. Maybe he had never really known what joy looked like. Maybe he never had the courage to look for it. In this darkened kitchen, he had separated himself from everybody and everything, He had avoided anyone who had any real feeling of lasting importance. During all those years of closed-minded arrogance, he had never thought that his way could be the wrong way. What did it get him? What price had he paid to be right? Grace made him want to change all of that. In spite of whatever troubles she had experienced, her presence flooded him with confidence and a desire to do better.

"I have been like a slave," he said to the darkened kitchen. "I have been shackled by my history. I have not been a free man!

But I do not want to live like that any longer. By God, I am the captain of this ship! I will be a bondsman to no one. Vincent Russo cannot dictate my ideas or my actions. I stand with Steve Nader."

Sixteen

Sunday, March 9, 1947

Greta's invitations to Sunday dinner continued and Louis took advantage of them, both to enjoy her cooking and to see Grace. Afterwards, he sometimes chauffeured her around town in the big Chrysler or they enjoyed walks around the neighborhood. They often sat on the seawall and watched birds flying over the bay.

Grace, always cordial, remained distant, however, while Louis did most of the talking. He tried to find things to do to entertain Grace and gave her plenty of latitude. His level of patience surprised him.

During one Sunday drive, on a whim, Louis turned down an abandoned blacktop road on the north side of town by the lake. The road went straight to nowhere for about a half mile. Tall marsh grass grew on either side. No other cars, no people, no movement except the sway of the tall grass in the wind. The isolation brought an uneasy feeling to Grace.

Louis spoke first. "This road led to a proposed development that never made it off the drawing board. Too far from town, people said, so it has remained unused."

Louis shut off the engine and they sat in the quiet for a while.

"It's sort of eerie out here, it's so silent." Grace looked around and could see nothing but grass and old barbed wire fences.

Louis got out of the car. He opened the door for Grace. "Come on."

"Where are we going?"

"Come on. It's alright."

Louis guided her behind the car to the driver's side. "Get in. I'm going to teach you how to drive. You can't live in Texas and not know how to drive."

Grace, surprised by the novel idea, went along with Louis' plan. He showed her how to start the car, how to use the gas pedal and the clutch.

"Give it some gas and then slowly... slowly let out the clutch."

She pushed hard on the gas and revved the engine too high. She stopped and looked at Louis.

"Try it again. Just push lightly on the gas pedal."

She again pushed too hard. In her confusion, she pumped the clutch and the gas at the same time. The car leaped forward, slowed, leaped again and bucked like a wild mustang. Louis' head banged into the windshield repeatedly when the car roared forward, until mercifully the engine died and the car rolled to a stop.

Grace threw her hands over her face. Louis thought that he had made a mistake and brought her to tears. But she was laughing.

"I am so sorry. Are you hurt?"

"You're laughing. I have a concussion and you are laughing," Louis feigned indignation. Then he could not hide his laughter and his joy at seeing Grace laugh.

"I'm okay. It's worth a few knots to hear you laugh."

Grace tried a few more times and was finally able to steer the car in a zigzag path down the road, avoiding the shallow ditches on either side. She quickly decided she had had enough. Louis then made the short drive to the low seawall that separated Texas

City from Galveston Bay, where they sat and talked, looking at the water.

"I was driving a car when I was 12 years old," he commented with a final chuckle, then turned serious.

"I don't really know anything about you," Louis said. "I know you came from Chicago. You must find life here very dull, coming from such a big city." He paused, hoping she would begin to talk about herself a little more openly.

"A little quiet can be a good thing," Grace said. "Chicago had too much excitement for me. I needed something different. Do you find Texas City dull?"

"I thought it was very boring… that is, until I met you. I never really questioned it, I just accepted it."

Louis paused, then asked, "What did you do in Chicago?"

Grace continued to stare at the water. "I worked. I…," she stumbled over the words for a moment. "Some things, Louis, a woman wants to keep secret. That part of my life? It's not anything I want to talk about now."

Questions hung in his mind. But he appreciated her honesty and let the questions lie quietly. He was so attracted to her that nothing could have deterred him. Her past did not matter.

A few Sundays later, they lounged on Greta's front porch after dinner. Louis leaned over and kissed her. It surprised Grace, but she did not resist.

"You know I am crazy about you, Grace."

An awkward silence followed. "I enjoy your company, too." She rose and walked to the edge of the porch, keeping her back to Louis. "It's just that… it's complicated, Louis. I can't explain it to you. I had not planned on this sort of thing."

Grace shrugged, wanting to say more, but her confused

emotions kept her stuck in indecision, and the strain rattled her.

"Complicated? What's complicated? It's a 'boy meets girl' kind of thing. Simple to me."

"You said yourself that you don't know anything about me."

"It doesn't matter."

"It matters to me."

Louis heard anger in her voice, as Grace receded into herself again.

"You could tell me about it," Louis said. He leaned toward her and continued. "Listen! I have a past, too. But this is different. I've never felt this way before. It scares me, too. But I can't ignore what's happened to me."

"I'm sorry, Louis. I can't do this right now. Please, can we drop it?"

"Okay. Okay. But I'm not giving up. I can wait. I know there is something you are working through. You didn't come here from Chicago just to be with Greta. I'm telling you that it does not matter to me. I'll let you think about it. But I am coming back."

After Louis departed, Grace sat in her apartment and sorted the day out in her mind. I enjoy his company, she thought. And he is attractive. It is natural for him to want more, and I can see the relationship moving to a place I had hoped to avoid. Sometimes I want him to touch me. But I am too afraid.

Her eyes swept around her small apartment. These pale green walls, with their gaily painted flowers, had provided shelter from the world. But her determination to remain an ascetic now wobbled in the light of Louis' attention.

Grace undressed and stood naked in front of the mirror. She had regained some of her prior normal weight. Her small waist still curved into her hips. She ran her hands over her breasts, lightly touching them.

With her desire came shame, which quickly spiraled downward into depression. Oh, I can't do this, she thought, watching in the mirror as tears began to fall down her cheeks. She grabbed her robe and tied it tightly around herself, her thoughts whirling.

I can't see him anymore. He should not expect to see me anymore. She pulled the lapels of the robe tighter against her throat. I will end this flirtation before it becomes another episode that I regret.

She lay in bed and depression drew her body into a tight curl. Her hands pulled repeatedly on the ends of the robe's belt to tighten it. She saw herself, on the inside of her closed eyelids, looking down from the ceiling as if she had left her body behind. Grace no longer belonged to the figure on the bed. Confused, frightened and lonely, she cried herself to sleep.

Grace fought through a difficult week, each day slipping into a deeper depression despite her efforts to stay on an even keel. Frightful dreams began to interrupt her sleep. By Saturday morning, she had devolved into a fragile mess trying to hold onto her sanity; she awoke nervous and unsettled. She had progressed so much in turning her attitude positive these past few months that she had believed herself to be over days like this. But she could not control her internal dialogue. In no way could she meet with Clayton for his lesson. She would just have to stand him up today.

Memories of her addiction surfaced. She cursed her dependency and remembered how she had become an unprincipled, shameless person who lied, stole or begged while under the influence. Memories of heroin oozed out from her brain. Smiling demons beckoned her to join them in the ecstasy of pleasurable obliteration. Her own grinning image summoned her.

Will I never get away from that accursed person? Grace fought to remain objective, acknowledging that Louis' advances ignited this turmoil. He had been kind and generous. No one, outside of her immediate family and Father Joe, treated her with such dignity and respect. But she could never reveal her past to him. Her fear escalated as she paced across her tiny living room. She became more removed from reality with each step.

She heard a car door slam and the real world muscled its way back into her consciousness. As she ran to the window to see who was there, Louis stood outside with his foot on the first step looking up, searching for Grace at the door or the window.

"Grace," he called for her.

"Louis, what are you doing here?" She spoke, looking down at him through the open window.

"Good morning," Louis replied. "I thought we could go on a picnic. It is a nice day and I have a basket full of food."

"I'm not even dressed yet." She shielded her eyes from the morning sun.

"You've been working too hard. You deserve to have some fun."

"You don't know anything about what I deserve." Grace tightened her robe and walked out her door onto the landing. She could feel anger growing inside her as she folded her arms across her stomach.

Louis took one step up. Grace turned and went inside, slamming the screen door.

"Wait a minute, Grace."

"No, you wait a minute." She cried as she spoke through the screen door. "I want you to leave me alone."

"I don't believe you. I think you enjoy being with me. Tell me what you are afraid of, Grace."

"I want you to leave me alone!" she screamed. "Go away! And don't come back, Louis."

Louis spoke toward the window. "Grace, this is unreasonable. Grace, talk to me."

"Go away, Louis." She slammed the window shut. Moments later the car backed out of the driveway and she heard tires squeal on the asphalt road.

Grace sat on the edge of her bed. She never should have come to Texas City. She should go back to Chicago to be with her kind of people. She could get on a bus to Galveston and be on a train heading north today. She could start to sing again.

Grace blamed Louis. He had awakened that person she was desperately trying to avoid. It would be impossible to see him again.

She began to pace the room and her resolve to be an ascetic dissolved. The fight to remain rational exhausted her and she coursed into deeper depression. As she paced, her mind kept repeating, I can't do this anymore. I can't. I can't. Returning to Chicago offered no hope. Sing again? What a joke! Me, a normal person? Impossible!

Grace walked into the bathroom, her body torpid, her mind exhausted. She stood before the mirror, her face twisted in a cruel mask. She took the old bottle of sleeping pills from the cabinet, removed the cap and poured out a handful. I must stop the voices in my head.

A knock startled her. She turned to see Michael standing

outside her door.

"Aunt Grace, can I come in?"

She stared at the pills in her hand. Michael rapped at the door again. "Aunt Grace?"

She stared at the door, then back at the pills. The pure innocence of his voice softened the turmoil that churned inside of her. She put the pills back in the bottle, held it tightly in her hand and went to the screen door. Michael stood before her with his pad of paper under his arm, a box of crayons in his hand.

"Not right now, Michael. I can't right now."

"Aw.... Mommy is busy, too."

He stared at her as tears rolled down her cheeks.

"Uh oh. I'll go get Mommy." He dropped his pad and crayons, scampered down the stairs and yelled for his Mom.

Greta found Grace sitting on the edge of her bed. She put her arm around her. "Michael is so fond of you that it scared him when he saw you crying. He doesn't know how we women can be sometimes, with our hormones and all. He thinks tears really mean something." Greta looked at the pill bottle still in Grace's hand and a sliver of dread pierced her heart.

"I was just going to take a couple to get some sleep," Grace said.

"That's fine. You have not been sleeping well all week. I can see those bags under your eyes. You wouldn't mind if I kept the rest of them with me for a few days?"

"That would be good. Do that. Oh Greta, I am so tired of failing." She laid her head on Greta's shoulder and sobbed.

Greta held her tight. "You have been in some terribly dark and difficult places. It takes time. One day at a time.... One day at a time, sweetheart. I believe in you, Grace. I'm in this fight right here with you. We're going to get you back, Grace... the real Grace."

Greta held Grace tightly, fearful that she would disappear into her past. Greta did not know how much more either of them could take of this tightrope walk between the highs and lows of unmanageable emotions, but she would not relent.

"Maybe you should go back to counseling."

Grace breathed in and then released a mournful sigh. "Maybe. The past just slips up on me so fast. I'm okay for a while, then everything fractures into little pieces. I can feel something melting inside of me. I feel life draining out of me.... And I can't stop it."

Greta tightened her hold on Grace. "You and I are all that is left of our family. I will not let you drain away. I will not. You will get better. This is just a bump in the road. Together we can get past this. You have to hang on, Grace. I will be here. I will stand by you. You can hold onto me."

Seventeen

Friday, March 21, 1947

Good days and then bad days again had kept Grace on a roller coaster. Dark moods continued to overtake her, but she was able to avoid total despair. Greta kept close to her. Father Joe continued to nurture her with gentle reminders of her many talents. He taught her how to meditate, how to pivot her thoughts when she started downhill.

She forced herself to start going out more often in the warming spring weather and agreed to Greta's invitation to drive to Galveston and shop for bright dresses in floral prints and spring colors.

She began making progress again and felt better on most days partly by determining that she would not give up tutoring Clayton. The weekly task became her lifeline. His rapid progress boosted her confidence in the approach they were using. His success provided a bright spot in her life, and it infused her with much-needed energy.

They never mentioned the touch, nor the feelings that it had evoked in each of them. Excitement for the music channeled into gratitude and trust between them. Grace believed it would be possible for Clayton to play professionally.

This morning, Grace walked into the office with a question for Father Joe. "Have you ever heard of Arnett Cobb?"

He pursed his lips and asked, "Did he play outfield for the Chicago Cubs?"

"Nooo. That was Ty Cobb and he played for Detroit. I went

to a few White Sox games…. Comiskey Park, you know? I know baseball," she concluded with a smile.

"Oh, I knew that. Great second baseman," he responded with a grin. "But a rough player. Is Arnett a brother?"

Grace laughed. "Well, in a way, yes. As in all Black men call each other 'brother.' But he is not Ty Cobb's brother. I can see you don't know anything about Arnett Cobb. He is a well-known Black musician I met in Chicago. Actually, he was born in Houston. In the music world, he is known as one of the best tenor sax players, and a good technician. I met Arnett when he played at a club where I worked and we crossed paths many times over the years. We're friends. I believe he can help Clayton. He told me about a place in Houston called the El Dorado Ballroom, where he directed a house band occasionally. I heard on the radio that Arnett is coming to Houston and I want to take Clayton to meet him."

Father Joe stood quietly and then frowned. "I don't think his mother would want Clayton in a dance hall in Houston."

His answer surprised Grace. She started to speak when Father Joe interrupted, a smile on his lips. "…Unless he went with a priest. So…, I'll just have to take you. But we can't let the Bishop know." A wry smile curled his lips.

"Thank you, Father Joe. Thank you so much. I had not thought of how we would get there."

"I think it will do you good to hear a live band. It might get you back into music. Did you ever think about joining the church choir?"

Grace turned the question over in her mind. "Not now. Maybe… someday."

They talked about arrangements for the journey to Houston.

"This is great, Father Joe. I know it will be important for Clayton. I'm excited to see Arnett again but a little nervous, too. I wonder if he knows I have been in prison?"

"What was it like, being a 'star'?" Father Joe asked.

"You know, Father Joe, I have not allowed myself to think about that in a long time. I'm still frightened by the memory. First of all, I was never a star. Peggy Lee is a star. Stars sing with Benny Goodman, go on tour to Europe with the big bands. But I loved singing. Connecting with an audience captivated me. I loved playing the piano, too. My mother did me a big favor by pushing me the way she did."

Sadness stole her enthusiasm. "But I screwed it up because I wanted more. My ego played me by whispering in my ear. 'You are a star,' it said. I bought the lie and my life faded to black. It turned into a bad movie with no way to change the ending. Drugs and… well, you know the rest.

"I miss the music at times, but my memories always end up in an icy apartment. It's too painful. I can't go back there. I recognize that it shuts down the rest of my life, but that's the way it is."

"Like a relationship with Louis," Father Joe observed.

"Yes. That's part of it. Outside of high school crushes, Dave was the only serious relationship I ever had and that didn't turn out so well. Why would I want to do that to myself again?"

"Grace, you have to go back to the beginning," Father Joe urged. "You have to go back to the music, to that place where your soul began to soar. Renew that person and you will gain the strength to take on your fears. You are not a failure, Grace. Believe me. I have heard many confessions and I know a lot about the human condition. I know that the dark night of your soul can drag you to an abyss that appears inevitable to avoid.

"But you can back away from the edge. Greta is here. I'm here. Lean on us. We need you. The world needs you. Get back to the music and you will find yourself again. Stop depriving yourself of what you love. It no longer makes any sense."

On the night of the concert, Father Joe drove them to Houston. He had been an assistant at St. Teresa's Church, so he knew his way around downtown.

"Dowling Street," he explained to Grace and Clayton. "That's the heart of the Black community. All these businesses you see here are owned by Black businessmen. On both sides of the street." He waved his hand to emphasize the broad swath.

Clayton sat in the middle of the back seat and turned his head from side to side, amazed at what he saw. Modest wood-frame houses, neat and well tended, fronted by trees, shrubs and even flowers. In the evening twilight, he saw mowed lawns and weeded flower beds. He did not see a single house with peeling paint. The houses gleaming white in the green yards reminded him of pictures from a garden magazine he had once rescued from a waste basket.

He beat the flat of his hand on the back seat and jutted out his jaw. Grace turned to him. She knew what he wanted to say but he kept it in. He breathed deeply and shook his head.

He chafed at his impotence to choose his fate - stuck in the Hallows, unable to live elsewhere in Texas City, by the simple fact of the color of his skin. He wished Shana could be with him to see the difference between this neighborhood and theirs. He did not know how he would get her out, but he would do it. He would not allow the Hallows to define her sense of place. Interfacing with a different world convinced him. He, Shana, his

Momma, they could all live like this if they could rise up with great courage.

They arrived at the corner of Dowling and Elgin. Father Joe drove into a parking lot adjacent to a white two-story, art-deco building. A gentle breeze greeted them as they walked toward a single doorway at one end of the oblong structure. Air heavy with the aroma of spring growth filled their nostrils. Honeysuckle blossoms dominated the myriad fragrances. A crowd of young Black men and women waited in line to pay and pass through the entrance.

Clayton stared at the beautiful women in captivating dresses and high heels. Some stood aloof, indifferent; others laughed, jostled each other, or pranced on the sidewalk. The men walked beside them, wearing cool machismo as well as suits or sports coats. Most wore ties. Clayton, who had never owned a coat and tie, glanced down at his scuffed shoes and wanted to hide them in some manner.

Under a canopy imprinted with the words El Dorado, the line found its way through a small foyer to stairs that led to a second-floor ballroom. The trio led by Father Joe followed a waitress to a small, round table. Their presence created an instant stir of inspection and whispers from the guests at tables near them. A middle-aged white man in gray slacks with a light blue shirt, a muscular and handsome Black man with a strong, square jaw who was dressed all in black, and a young white woman with pale skin and black hair – reminiscent of a movie 'femme fatale' – did not fit in with the normal party goers at the El Dorado. Surprised and suspicious looks followed the procession as they took their seats.

They sat near the dance floor, with its smooth and shiny oak planks that were permeated with the spirits of dancers from bygone years. A multi-tiered bandstand occupied space at the far end of the room. The musicians began to gather, tune their instruments and organize their sheet music.

In a few minutes, the lights dimmed and a mirrored ball in the middle of the ceiling began to turn. Dancing dots of light cascaded as if the moon had fractured into tiny pieces and fallen to the hardwood. Couples rushed onto the floor to dance, giddy with expectation.

Arnett Cobb stood at the front of the bandstand with his saxophone tethered to a cord around his neck. The crowd applauded and held its accumulated breath. He tapped his foot, snapped his fingers, counted down: three… two… one. The band jumped into a vigorous "It Don't Mean a Thing" and dancers filled the floor. Some laughed and some whooped with excitement. Arnett began to play a solo riff and his saxophone roared to life.

The music washed over Clayton like a genie emancipated from Arnett's horn. In that instant, he saw Arnett Cobb as the ultimate pinnacle. The gloom and anger that occupied his life lifted. A broad smile creased his face. He lost himself in the notes as waves of sound carried him right up to Arnett Cobb. He hadn't known that such a place existed, a place that felt like a magic carpet ride, a place that thrilled him beyond his wildest dreams.

Clayton rejoined Father Joe and Grace with a huge grin on his face. All three of them shifted in their chairs to watch the dancers, spellbound by the joy and freedom expressed in their movements. Jim Crow laws and the heavy hand of segregation in Texas City denied access to anything like this fantasy island. Grace had never seen such freedom of expression, even in

Chicago. Nothing she had experienced generated the energy that was being unleashed in this ballroom. People were set free here. Surrounded by the walls of the El Dorado Ballroom, they were sequestered from the chains of a white man's society. In this freedom of dance, they touched the joy of authenticity.

As Grace watched Arnett play, a tendril of fear crept into her mind. *What if he does not remember me? It has been so long. I look different.* Without hesitating or second guessing herself, she took a pen and paper from her purse, wrote a short note and asked a waitress to deliver it to the leader of the band.

Minutes into the first break, Arnett Cobb came toward their table. Grace stood to greet him and he embraced her. They talked privately for a few minutes as Grace wiped tears from her cheeks. She introduced Father Joe and Clayton.

Clayton unwound his large frame and stood over Arnett Cobb. He took Cobb's extended hand, pumped it several times and nodded his head up and down with excitement.

"I work for Father Joe in Texas City," Grace told Arnett. "He graciously volunteered to bring us here tonight. I wanted Clayton to meet you because you have been a great friend and teacher to so many young musicians. He has a talent for the saxophone. I hoped you might be able to encourage him to keep working on his music."

Arnett smiled, his arm around Grace. "Anything for you, little lady. I am so happy to see you again.… And looking so beautiful. We miss you in Chicago. When are you coming back to us? You know I could get you some gigs right now. In fact, you could sing for me…. No. You have too much talent for that. There are plenty of places that would be happy to headline you."

Grace lowered her eyes as her cheeks reddened. "I don't have any plans to return to Chicago. I've learned to be a Texas gal."

"Lookie here. I heard you had some troubles. I just wanted you to know we all love you. Be happy to see you back on a stage in Chicago."

Arnett glanced around the room and patted the sides of his shiny black vest with his thumbs inserted into the pockets, deep in thought. "I tell you what. Clayton, come on up to the stage with me. We have some time between sets here. Let's go up there so we can talk."

Clayton, filled to the top of his head with excitement, beamed his agreement.

"I have my sax in the car, sir."

"That's okay. I have plenty up there you can work with."

Arnett said a few words to Father Joe, then guided Clayton to the back of the bandstand. He handed him one of his saxes and listened to him play.

Grace could see Arnett talking and gesturing to Clayton with both hands. He made motions around his chest and his throat, tapping lightly on the bottom of his chin as Clayton played. Clayton nodded eagerly. Arnett played a short piece, then listened to Clayton play. This exchange went on until the band returned.

Clayton smiled at Arnett, nodded again and smartly shook his hand. He returned to the table with a big, satisfied grin stamped across his face, like it could stay there forever. Grace looked at Father Joe. It was the happiest either of them had ever seen Clayton.

"Mr. Cobb said I showed a lot of promise. He said they have a talent contest here every month. He wants me to enter the contest... said I could win it."

The band started again with the mellow tune "Mood Indigo." Clayton put his hands in his pockets and let his body slide down in the chair. He swayed in time with the music, never taking his eyes from Arnett's fingers as they caressed the sax.

Grace nodded her head up and down, drenched in the euphoria that radiated from Clayton. She knew the joy of having someone validate the hope sheltered in one's heart. She understood the glow on Clayton's face, knew that Arnett Cobb had verified his dream and promised that tomorrow would be a new day, that he could pursue his dream with renewed vigor.

Arnett gave Clayton a real father figure for the first time. Someone who praised him, made him feel worthy and gave him a reason to be proud of himself. Grace stood as the song ended and blew a kiss to Arnett, applauding both his music and his kindness.

Grace recalled what Father Joe had said about her getting back to music. In this moment shared with Clayton, she could feel the freedom he wanted for her. The pleasure of performing filtered through her. She felt the tug of Chicago on her heartstrings for the first time since her train had rolled out of the station to begin her journey to Texas. Grace did not fight the notion. The music of the night carried her on wings of rhythmic harmony to a place where, for the moment, anything could be possible.

The exhilaration of the music in the El Dorado began to soften as they neared Texas City on their return home. As he drove, Father Joe's thoughts turned to his sermon for the next day. He knew this event to be more than just an evening on the town, and he wondered how he could use the experience and reflect its real importance to his parishioners. Social justice remained a shadowy presence around the pulpit. The joy that lit up Clayton's face at the club brought conviction to Father Joe of the Church's need for greater awareness.

Grace nodded in intermittent sleep and Clayton slept soundly in the back seat. At the midnight hour, Father Joe steered his aging Ford into the outskirts of Texas City, with its empty streets and paltry lighting hanging from poles near the corners. To the south, flares burned as always, reminders that the refineries never slept.

Revolving red lights in his rear-view mirror jolted Father Joe out of his reverie. He eased the car to the edge of the road and stopped. The rear-view mirror framed a policeman getting out of a patrol car. Tired and eager to get home, the stop nettled him. He knew he had not been speeding.

The officer, a big, barrel-chested man, spoke with an ill-humored voice. "Sir, did you know that you have a defective taillight on the driver's side of this car?"

"No, I didn't. It must have just happened."

The officer shined his flashlight into the face of each passenger as he talked. He held the light on Clayton longer than the others. His light illuminated the saxophone case.

"You a musician?" he said to Clayton, now awake in the back seat.

"No, sir. I mean, I'm learning." Clayton shaded his eyes from the bright light as sweat moistened his palms. That tone of voice meant trouble. He had never been in trouble with the law, but he had heard stories: Don't argue. Keep your hands in view. Make no sudden moves.

"You wouldn't be carrying any of that marijuana now, would you? I hear musicians do that sometimes. "

"Officer, we're just trying to…." Father Joe tried to intervene.

"I'm talking to this boy here. You just stay quiet." He kept his light trained on Clayton as he spoke. "Get out of the car, boy."

"Officer, we haven't done anything wrong. You have no right to do this." Father Joe spoke as he rushed out of the car.

Once Clayton exited the car, the officer twisted his arm behind his back and forced him against the trunk of the car.

"Put your hands behind you," he demanded as he manacled him. Clayton did not resist even as the officer roughly pulled his hands to be sure the cuffs were secure. Clayton lay bent over with his chest on the trunk. Sweat came off his head now and his heart beat rapidly. His fear kept him still, waiting for the next word from the policeman.

Grace scooted out of the car and moved toward the policeman.

"He has done nothing wrong. What are you doing to him?" She tried to place herself between Clayton and the officer, who raised his arm to block her and inadvertently shoved her.

Grace fell backwards into a shallow ditch. Clayton was looking right into Grace's eyes as she fell. He spun around, rushed the officer and headbutted him in the chest. Air rushed out of the policeman's mouth. He staggered and almost fell, but recovered, grabbed his nightstick and bludgeoned Clayton several times on top of the head. Clayton fell face-down on the ground.

Father Joe ran to the back of the car as the officer attacked Clayton. The officer pulled his revolver and held it against Clayton's cheek.

Father Joe yelled, "No!"

"You come at me again, I will shoot you dead! You hear me, boy?"

"Officer! Stop it! Stop it!" Father Joe shouted. "I'm Father Irons, the pastor at St. Mary's."

"Yeah, and I'm the Pope," came the caustic response. He forced Clayton to stand and led him to the police car. "I'm taking this boy in. You two get back in your car, go on home. Maybe I'll forget that I saw the 'pastor' with a young woman half his age and a nigger boy in the back seat."

Father Joe hesitated. He glanced at Grace who had gotten to her feet and appeared to be unharmed. He knew it would do no good to appeal to the officer.

With barely contained fury, Father Joe warned, "You had better take him straight to the jail because I'm following you. If you don't, I will go directly to the mayor's house and have you charged with police brutality. I will have your badge. I can and will do that! I will have you fired!"

Father Joe and Grace followed the squad car to the station and watched the policeman take Clayton inside. Father Joe then took Grace home. Her body was visibly shaking. "What's going to happen to him? We have to get him out of there!"

"I'm going back to the police station now. I'll see that he is okay. You go on inside. We'll talk tomorrow."

Father Joe returned to the station. By a stroke of good fortune, the night supervisor, Sergeant Pete Maxwell, happened to be a parishioner. He told him the story and asked the sergeant to immediately release Clayton.

Sgt. Maxwell read through the papers in front of him. "Father Joe, the arresting officer charged him with disorderly conduct, resisting arrest, suspicion of possession of an illegal substance, and assaulting a police officer. That's pretty heavy stuff."

"Oh, come on, Pete. You have a rogue cop there. I'm telling

you the real story. Clayton did nothing to merit the officer's behavior."

"Did he assault the officer?'

"He was provoked. He tried to protect an innocent lady who this officer had pushed into a ditch! He was handcuffed and afraid for his life. Pete…. Look, Pete. Give me a break here. It was all a misunderstanding. You've seen Clayton around church. He works hard to support his mom and his sister. I can verify he did not have or use any drugs. You give a little and I won't file charges against the officer. You know what it will mean if I take this to the mayor's office."

It took more talking and cajoling, but Father Joe persuaded Pete to release Clayton to his custody, with a promise to come back and pay a fine for disorderly conduct.

Clayton sat silent on the way to his house. Father Joe knew rage was seething beneath his sullen face.

"Life is not fair, Clayton. I know you have heard that far too often. I know you are angry. Furious and hurt. You want a way to get even. Sadly, you have no way to do that. No way, except to rise above this. You must be the man here. You are better than him. You must find some way to hold onto that. Don't compound this travesty by thinking you have to get even. You cannot get even. You can only hurt yourself. Your mom and Shana need you. Think of them. I'm angry, too. I don't understand God's plan in all of this. But it must be for some reason. You have to let it go."

"God got nothin' to do with this. You think this is the first time a Black man been assaulted by a white policeman? What you know about it? Nothin'. You don't know nothin'!" In his anger, Clayton slipped into the English patois that he tried hard to avoid with white people.

Father Joe stopped in front of Clayton's tiny, unpainted shack. Devastated, feeling helpless and hardly able to control his own rage, the priest felt the disparity of their lives like a giant stone around his priestly neck.

Clayton remained angry but grew thoughtful as he grabbed the door handle. "For a while, in that club, I felt free, like I deserved to be there. I deserved to be there! Like a magic wand had passed over me, changed the world. People could see me. I was not invisible.

"But this is my real world." He waved his hand toward the houses outside of the car window, his anger returning. "This stinkin' Hallows. I'm condemned by this Black skin. Your God is white. Your God don't care nothin' about no Black man. He don't care about us folks here in the Hallows." Clayton dropped all pretense of politeness and threw away his careful turn of words. "Where's the justice in that? God ain't interested in justice. We still jes' invisible." Clayton pushed his way out of the car and slammed the door.

"Clayton, wait a minute!"

"You wait a minute. You don't know nothin' about being Black. You got no message for me. Can you make me white like your Jesus? No? Then you can take your white God and shove it. I ain't havin' none of it!"

Clayton grabbed his horn from the back seat and disappeared through the torn screen door of his house.

Light danced from torches over the hissing refineries, a ballet of flaming demons mocking Father Joe's world. He thought about his elegant rectory, his prepared meals and his housekeeper. It tolled a dirge to his vow of poverty: he lived as the best kept man in town. He would never be able to reach Clayton now.

"Where is my God?" he asked the night sky, helpless to answer the question himself.

Eighteen

The port and the supervising Terminal Railway Company continued their kinetic activity. The area hummed with the efforts to both import and export the products that defined the growth of a modern post-war economy. Minds freed from the toils of warfare pivoted to the creation of developments to enrich lives and bring more comforts to the human experience. From the outside, the future of Texas City beamed brightly.

On the inside, at every level of work, bottom lines were the guiding force. More products, more shipments. More loading and unloading. More overtime. Haste continued to apply more pressure to the system and brought less attention to detail.

Louis had little success in confronting Russo and nothing had changed in regard to safety policies. Louis remained committed and often reflected on what it would take to make progress. But he found few avenues to tread upon.

He buried himself and his mind in work. Louis had not seen Father Joe in several weeks. He had stayed away by design because seeing Grace would have been too awkward. He told himself that, if she did not want to see him, it was fine. But underneath his bluster he missed her and wanted to be with her. He had never really been in love, had never endured the rawness of being so easily dismissed. He tried to make it not matter. But it hurt, and his only defense lay in working harder.

On this placid Wednesday morning, Louis fumbled with his

tie and wished the weekend were already here. Impatient and irritable, he drove along Bay Street to his office. A surprising image splashed onto a clear blue sky in front of him. A brilliant orange smoke coiled over the area above the docks.

That's odd, he thought. Oil fires produced thick black smoke that set off alarms immediately, quickening anxiety with their appearance. This orange smoke generated curiosity more than anxiety. He had never seen such a sight. Bright orange clouds of smoke billowed against the bluest sky he could ever remember.

"What's going on here?" he said out loud. The beauty of it fascinated him, much like a Monet painting might. A free-form orange and blue picture floated in a swirl onto the canvas of sky. The fire could not have been burning long because Louis had not seen it when he brought in the milk at 7:00 am from his front porch.

By the time he reached Dock Road around 8:10 am, he could see that smoke was rising from a ship in Slip O adjacent to the loading crane. No flames showed above the ship's deck, but huge volumes of orange smoke rose up from inside the hold into the sky. When Louis arrived, Mack was standing beside the warehouse and watching the fire. A new fire engine belonging to the Texas City Volunteer Fire Department was parked nearby.

"There's a fire in a hold in the *Grandcamp*, " he said to Louis. "I don't know what's burning, but they loaded ammonium nitrate yesterday and today. Steve is here with two trucks and most of his men."

"Let's go take a look." They hurried up Dock Road, almost breaking into a run.

Steve Nader and the captain of the ship stood on deck near the prow. Steve was shouting to be heard above the noise and clamor of activity.

Louis perked an ear, listening hard to hear their conversation above the din of pumps and shouted orders. The captain spoke in French with a smattering of broken English. He clearly said, "Non, non, non!" Both men waved their arms and hands during what became a heated argument. Steve threw his hands up in surrender and hurried down the gangway, angrily talking to the captain over his shoulder.

Louis intercepted him near the bow of the ship. "What's going on, Steve?"

"That Frog son-of-a-bitch refused to let me put water on the fire. He has a large fire going on in Hold #4 but doesn't want water down there because it might ruin his cargo."

"What's down there?"

"Fertilizer, mostly. Twenty-three-hundred tons of it loaded yesterday, plus whatever went in so far this morning. Some of the bags caught fire. There is other cargo of cotton, sisal and a small amount of ammunition. I don't know what kind. Hold #5 has fuel oil."

"How did it start?" Mack asked.

"I don't know yet, but I would bet somebody was smoking in that hold," Steve responded through gritted teeth.

Louis knew that the captain, God on a ship, held total authority for decisions concerning his vessel. "Did you suggest that he pull his ship into the turning basin?"

"They had removed the turbine casing for inspection. That leaves the propeller inoperable so he can't move the goddamn ship. He ordered the hatches battened and turned on an internal steam system to smother the fire. All we can do is put water on her and try to keep the hull cool. But that's a bad idea to me." Steve stormed off, shouting more commands to his men.

Louis watched as the ship's crew closed and locked down the hatches. Firemen streamed water on the hull. The captain moved from hatch to hatch, bending close and pulling on each lid to check that it had been locked securely.

Louis and Mack walked back to the office. Mack fumed at the captain's decision. "This is not good. I ain't likin' this at all!"

"Nothing we can do about it. The captain is in control on his ship. Maybe what they are doing will snuff it out."

Louis' words did not quiet Mack's anxiety. He tried to recall what Zach had told him about nitrates. In spite of efforts to stay calm, a growing unease replaced his usual stoic demeanor.

Louis knew that Mack was a difficult man to rattle. He noticed the furrowed brow and distraction in Mack's face. Fear now funneled its way into Louis.

At the same time, away from the docks, Clayton awoke in the Hallows. When he heard his Momma talking to Shana in the kitchen, he knew he was late. They were talking about a strange orange smoke in the sky over toward the docks. He was never late for work as a rule but accepted that he would not get to the docks on time this morning. He did not want to work, anyway. In addition to fighting his usual back pain, the police incident continued to consume him and the lumps on his head still ached. Father Joe had paid the fine, but the lawman continued to be on patrol. Nothing had changed. No one took on the concern.

In the end, Clayton absorbed all of that nightmare police encounter alone. He acknowledged that Father Joe had rescued him, and some credit was due for that. But the realization that he had no ability to protect himself, no way to voice his version of the story, left him depressed. A sudden awareness flooded his mind; the white community had their collective knee on his chest and, until and unless that changed, he would never be able to leave the Hallows. He knew this morning that they needed him to be Black. They needed a dog to kick, and being Black left him no bargaining chip. It left him powerless. He glanced at the clock on his dresser. It ticked to eight o'clock.

Clayton dragged himself out of bed. He picked up the saxophone and played softly, pretending to be Arnett Cobb. He was standing in front of an orchestra. Athletic couples on the dance floor twirled their bodies and strutted their fancy footwork. His music set them free. Whether he played smooth and mellow or jumpy and fast, he controlled their world. He dictated the mood, carrying all those happy dancers in the palm of his hand. From the bandstand, visible to all those happy feet, he set them free.

He put down his horn, thinking he never should have picked it up all those years ago. Never dreamed. Never hoped for liberation. Nothing hurts like the pain of shattered hope. He put away the sax and dressed for work.

Clayton heard his Momma in the kitchen and, when he walked in, Shana was sitting at the table eating her breakfast, her hair already braided in pigtails.

"It's after eight oclock. You goin' to be late for work this mornin," Shana chided her big brother.

Clayton ignored her taunt.

"Looks like we got a fire this mornin' out on the docks. Come see this orange smoke," his Momma said. They could now hear sirens screaming through the window. "Never seen nuthin' like that before."

Clayton didn't stop to respond to his Momma. On his way through the kitchen, he picked up the lunch bag waiting on the table and walked briskly out the door. "I'm gone."

When he saw the orange smoke, Clayton fought the agitation in his body. Another fire. Good God, what's going on in this place, he thought. Fear churned in him. He kept moving, but he did not like it. A fire engine roared past as he walked toward the docks and the mesmerizing smoke that was cavorting above the *Grandcamp*. He had seen fires before around the docks but never from a ship. Never anything like this dancing genie that hovered over the waterfront.

He forgot about his aching back and lighter thoughts came to him. The fire might disrupt all activity today. At least it would stop work on the docks until the fire came under control. Maybe he could skate through the day without any heavy labor.

He joined his crew. They stood around and watched fire fighters hustle hoses and connect their bright new pumper to pour more water on the *Grandcamp*. Clayton's crew talked, laughed and played grab-ass on unsuspecting friends, as they awaited word from the foreman.

"Hey T-Bone, 'bout time you showed up," one of the co-workers shouted as Clayton ambled up to the group.

Clayton growled, "It's barely 8:30. Ain't no business of yours, anyway."

The crazy fire danced out of a storage hold on the *Grandcamp*. Clayton scanned the docks. The *Wilson B. Keene* sat serene in the adjacent slip, high in the water. Clayton thought he would be working two slips over on the *High Flyer* this morning. But he doubted the fire would be out soon enough for the crews to load today. He walked a short distance away and turned his back to the ship. Memories of the car fire crowded into his head. The noisy chaos rattled him and he moved even farther away, turning behind a dockside warehouse. Clayton resisted the urge to leave. He, too, came under the spell of the menacing orange smoke.

As the amount of smoke increased, the nerves of the fire fighters tightened like bow strings. They sensed the fire growing and stepped up their pace. Steve Nader ran up the gangway of the *Grandcamp* to talk with the French captain again. A new strategy was needed as tongues of flame slipped through closed hatches and the heat became more intense.

Nineteen

Wednesday, April 16, 1947
8: 20am

Fire engine sirens wailed as troubling smoke increased over the docks. The number of sirens and the strange orange color of the smoke quickly alerted the town to an unusual event.

Grace observed the smoke as she walked to work. Michael ambled alongside her, as usual, talking about whatever came into his happy, young mind. About halfway to the school, he realized he had forgotten his science project, so they had turned around and hurried home to pick it up. Grace would be late for work, and Michael would miss his kickball game in the schoolyard, but the first school bell did not ring until 8:30 am, so he would make roll call just in time. Grace knew Father Joe would not be upset if she was a few minutes late.

"What's on fire?" Michael asked when he noticed the orange smoke.

"I don't know what's burning, honey. I'm sure it's nothing for you to worry about."

"I think it's cool. It looks like orange Kool-Aid." Michael skipped ahead and paid no more attention to the glowing spectacle.

By the time they reached the church, they heard more sirens and watched as two more fire engines sped down Main Street toward the docks. Grace grew nervous and she considered walking with Michael all the way to his school. She decided against it even though the pace of cars and trucks going toward the docks was increasing.

"Look both ways crossing Sixth Street," she advised him. "There's more traffic this morning and there may be other fire engines."

Grace hugged Michael and watched as he skipped away. Michael moved down the block and kicked at stones, adrift in his own world. Grace followed him with her eyes until he was out of sight.

Being with Michael often made her think of her baby. Sometimes when she awoke early, still drowsy with sleep, she thought she heard her cry. She envied Greta having Michael. He was such a joy. They had the perfect home for him. She wondered what her baby would have become at this age, what life would have been like for her without a father.

In her office, Grace found a note from Father Joe saying that he had gone to the docks. He would be at the Seamen's Mission in case someone needed him. Grace glanced out the window at the orange ball of smoke. Louis would be at work. That he might be in danger because of the fire worried her. Grace remained confused by how she felt about him. Now past her crisis of suicidal thoughts, she hated the fact that she had returned his kindness with anger. She wanted to apologize for her behavior. She missed his attention even though desire still frightened her. Maybe he will come in next week, she thought. She would apologize the next time she saw him. She could not deny missing Louis' attention.

She hoped Clayton would come in this week for his Saturday lesson, too. He had not come since the police incident. She enjoyed those moments of teaching so much and hoped he had recovered fully from the horrible beating he had experienced.

She tried to focus on work but the fire burned in the back of her mind. She pictured Louis in his office so close to the docks. Could he be in any real danger? In the small frame of reference provided by the window, the morning appeared to be normal. She sat at her desk. Sharpened pencils. Stood up. Sat down. Tried to focus.

Outside, she heard more sirens. The urgency of their sound stirred a panic in her. She thought of Michael at school.

Michael entered his fourth-grade classroom on the second floor of Danforth Elementary School as the first bell rang. Students were standing in front of the windows that lined the east wall and watching the blaze that was clearly visible through the glass. They tittered, then gasped at the beautiful orange smoke, asking each other what was burning. It created an unusual buzz in the room.

The second bell rang. They glanced back at the spectacle and went to their seats. Miss Jones had difficulty getting them settled. It was close to 9:00 am by the time she organized health class and started down the aisle to check hands and nails for cleanliness.

Michael loved Miss Jones and waited patiently for her to walk down his row of chairs in the middle of the room. He had meticulously cleaned his hands and nails and combed his hair to impress his teacher. Miss Jones smiled, approached his desk and bent over to get a closer look. Michael raised his hands above his desk. She had on a light brown sweater and pretty red lipstick. Michael thought she smelled of baby powder. He smiled back at her, eager to please.

Twenty

F iremen furiously pumped water onto the *Grandcamp*. Engines whined as trucks moved rapidly up Dock Road. Sirens and a chorus of voices reverberated through Louis' office wall, a discordant symphony of sound.

Two more fire engines sped toward the docks. Louis could not concentrate and gave up trying to work. Mack's worry about the ship's cargo agitated him. Although he acknowledged that it was not an ordinary fire, he did not know what made it feel so ominous. He had confidence in Steve Nader and his men. The fire would be put out. It would be only a matter of inconvenience for his business. Other ships would come and go.

But his anxiety continued to rise. No matter what he told himself, he could not rid himself of Mack's concerns, nor Steve's worried comments from a few months back.

Louis heard the piercing shriek of three short and one long blasts from the *Grandcamp's* horn. It was the warning signal to abandon ship. He bolted outside and up Dock Road toward the fire.

Cliques of workers watched as more people and more vehicles crowded into the dock area. The ball of orange emerging from the *Grandcamp's* inefficient hatches had increased in size enormously, now reaching hundreds of feet in the air. It began to resemble a shroud over the entire dock area.

To the left of Dock Road, the sight of hundreds of people

stunned Louis. The last time he had looked at the site around 8:30 am, there were a few people starting to gather. Now, shortly before 9:00 am, the spectacular display of orange fire had captured townspeople like a pied piper, luring them to gather closer and closer to the ship. Some had parked their cars along drainage ditches just north of the slips. Others were walking onto the parking lot of the chemical plant.

Many young people had gathered in the assemblage of entranced sightseers. Rapid growth in the community had created overcrowding in the schools, resulting in split morning and afternoon schedules. This freed many afternoon students to join the crowds. They ran or rode bicycles onto open spaces surrounding the burgeoning fire. They watched the beautiful art moving in the sky.

The parking lot resembled an outdoor movie venue. Many of the watchers snapped photographs with box cameras. Some ate sandwiches from picnic baskets intended for later outings on this idyllic spring morning. Two young boys tossed a baseball back and forth, stopping after each throw to glance at the fire. As the crowd grew, the distance between them and the raging blaze narrowed. People, most fascinated, many festive, never considered the danger hidden in the cavorting flames.

Steam engulfed Louis when he reached the ship's side. The hull had become so hot that water from the fire hoses vaporized when it hit the steel. Swirls of dense steam entangled with acrid smoke in a macabre tango that spun up into the blue sky.

Louis saw Steve back on the deck with the ship's captain. A clamor of sounds muted their voices so that only animated movements conveyed their dread. Other voices from within the smoke and steam shouted orders, squealing in ever higher pitch as tensions increased. Fire engines wailed discordant notes and Louis felt the communal concern advance to the edge of panic.

Stevedores and the ship's crew came down the gangway in bunches as they abandoned ship. Suddenly one of the hatches that had been sealed shut blew open. Blades of fire rushed out. Flames coiled together. In the core of the ship, they multiplied then blended into larger walls of fire which rushed out of the hold into a spectacular display above the deck.

Other hatches rattled like pressure cooker valves, with tops banging against the lockdown.

Louis had trouble breathing and his eyes stung as he watched frantic firemen run back and forth to change the positions of their hoses. Steve shouted at the ship's captain, jabbing his chest with a finger. The fire chief knew that he no longer controlled the fire. He knew that fires burned with a will of their own, becoming belligerent like wounded tigers. Fear ran in step with his anger. His sense of danger increased.

Mack joined Louis on the dock, stunned to see the size of the fire.

"Look at the sides of the ship!" Mack shouted over the din. The hull glowed as red as a branding iron. Mack's eyes darted from the ship's hull to the rattling hatches and over to the crowds of onlookers. His mind raced as he tried to remember what Zach had said to him about ammonium nitrate. His eyes fixed on the hull. Its cherry-red sides now bulged as if giant bellows had inflated the steel plates.

"That's it!" He screamed at Louis. "Pressure! Sensitizers!"

"What the hell are you talking about?"

"Deflagration to detonation. That's what Zach told me about nitrates. The crew closed all the hatches! They've pressurized it.

And there's fuel oil and ammunition in an adjacent hold. Sensitizers! This is not just a fire, Louis, it's a time bomb. This ship is going to explode.

"I'm going back to the warehouse. Opening all the bay doors might prevent collapse of the roof. Get Steve off that deck, and you get away from here!"

Mack ran toward the warehouse, waving his hands and shouting to the crowds. "Get away from here. Get away!"

Louis' heart rate soared. Panic closed around him and those closest to the inferno. Their movements became jerky, less calculated and more chaotic. Terror ripped away all confident, rehearsed procedures. Unsure which way to turn, they started and stopped, faces filled with confusion. Hundreds of people who had gathered around to watch – sailors, stevedores, office personnel – moved away from the heat. They passed firemen who were fighting the voracious fire and resisting the urge to turn and run themselves.

At the same time, more townspeople swarmed into the parking lots and adjacent streets. Some sat on the hoods of cars that were parked on the sides of the road. Louis eyed a young girl on the handlebars of a bicycle, a boy sitting behind her on the seat and balancing the bike with his feet on the ground. They pushed their way onto the parking lot, inching closer. Two small airplanes circled overhead.

Chemical plant employees stood behind windows on the upper floors of their building facing the burning ship. They appeared calm, more fascinated than alarmed, as they crowded in closer to the glass. Observers edged closer to rows of windows on all five floors of the plant as the battle raged less than 50 yards away.

The abandon-ship horn sounded from the *Keene* in the

adjoining slip as fire began to threaten its position. Crewmen rushed down its gangway. Louis noted two tugboats plowing full speed up the ship channel from Galveston. They churned water behind them into foamy, white waves as they came to assist in quelling the raging fire.

Louis began to grasp the enormity of the danger that was growing by the second. In minutes, this different and intriguing fire had transformed itself into a grotesque menace that threatened to ravage the entire waterfront. A circus frivolity had captured the crowd as it swelled and continued to move closer, oblivious to the possible consequences that Mack had screamed at Louis.

Louis could see that nothing the men battling the fire could do made any difference. The hull continued to swell. A fierce heat radiated over the entire dock. The fire raged voraciously out of control.

Louis yelled at Steve on the deck, "STEVE! STEVE!" But the fire captain couldn't hear him. He waved his hands to get his attention, but Steve continued shouting back and forth with the ship's captain. Louis gave up, unsure of what he should do. Surely, Mack must be wrong. Steve knew what this kind of situation required, and there were Terminal officials on the scene also. No one touted evacuation of the area.

Louis tried to convince himself that Mack had made a mistake. This *was* just a fire, albeit a big one. It could be controlled until it burned itself out. But a terrible instinct in his gut told him he was wrong.

9:12 am

Heat from the bloated hull forced Louis away from the dock. In the midst of the shouting and chaos, Louis, now terrified, ran toward his office. Halfway there, he turned to look once more at the ship. As he shifted to turn back, the earth quaked and rippled beneath his feet. The quivering crust announced an unspeakable evil. A nauseating fear traveled up to his throat.

The *Grandcamp* detonated! A supersonic wave of energy ripped people and property to shreds. Flesh and bones, wood, glass and steel vanished into motes. The wave of destruction charged in every direction, rampaging through men, women and children. Ship hulls, concrete buildings, fire engines and human bodies claimed no resistance to the power of annihilation at Ground Zero. Indiscriminate destruction rolled across a defenseless industrial complex and through the town, continuing its travels across the Gulf, flattening coastal prairies and rattling windows up to 100 miles away. In a bizarre twist, it also darted upward to destroy two airplanes flying overhead.

Its power lifted Louis off the quaking ground and threw his body backward until it slammed into the side of a car in the parking lot. He fell to his knees. An immediate second blast forced him face down into the gravel and left him unconscious.

He came awake quickly and stood up, but weaving side to side in a daze as he tried to walk. A swell of water from the turning basin rushed toward him with a huge barge riding on its crest. Oil and water curled around his body up to his head. He frantically moved his arms to stay afloat. The tidal surge, with its energy quickly sapped, rushed back to the turning basin as quickly as it had washed ashore. It dropped the barge onto the parking lot before it could get to Louis. The helpless barge came to rest askew and on top of a mass of steel and wood debris. Louis, helpless now as well, lay on the ground, too exhausted to try to rise again.

The explosion had deafened him and he shook his head to clear his brain. He saw balls of fire, pieces of wood, sheets of steel – some as large as a car, some small as rivets – falling in a hailstorm of debris as silent as a snowfall. Bodies began to fall, some without heads, some without arms or legs, creating a surreal dreamscape that fell in slow motion, lasting a few moments that seemed like an eternity.

Smashed cars with tires blown off piled on top of each other, creating a battleground of rubble and carnage surrounding him. Oil blackened all within his view, including his body and torn clothes. Seven thousand tons of ship had blasted into millions of pieces that now rained from a smoke-gorged, black sky.

Louis struggled to remain conscious as intermittent swoons overcame him. The wind now wafted and waned. With each surge it cleared openings in the thick smoke. Louis could see the slip where the burning ship had been moored. The *Grandcamp* had vanished. Nothing of it remained as if it had been a mirage, never existing in a solid form. Bay water filled the empty slip, boiling from the heat of the blast.

The hellish landscape of bodies, destroyed buildings and fires now spread out to the southern horizon. Smaller explosions continued as burning metal was propelled into adjacent oil storage tanks, igniting them into paroxysms of their own destruction.

Louis pulled himself up and held onto a crumpled car behind him. He watched the wall of black smoke swell for miles across the refineries and hundreds of feet into the sky in a berserk rush to escape its own flames. Afraid he would burn to death, Louis tried to walk, lost all sense of direction and fell to the ground, unconscious again.

9:12 am

Grace tapped a pencil on her desk as she gave thought to the peculiar fire on the dock. Her mind moved from Michael to Father Joe and to Louis, fearful of the growing maelstrom in the air. Michael would be in health class, which came shortly after nine. At the moment, he might be holding his hands out for the teacher to inspect them for clean fingernails. Father Joe would be at the Seaman's Mission chatting with men from the ships. Louis would be working at his desk.

The force of the exploding ship roared through the church office. Grace turned toward the windows when she heard the blast and the concussive force threw her back against the wall. She bounced off the wall and crumpled into the well of her desk. Crawling across the floor to the door, she stood up and went outside. Tongues of fire darted through hideous black smoke as it boiled upward. She recoiled as serial detonations of oil storage tanks convulsed her body. She stumbled forward, groggy and in a fog of confusion. What the hell just happened?

"Michael," Grace screamed into the air. Her senses returned and she dashed toward the school. As her mind cleared, she ran as hard as she could. She gasped for breath and prayed as she went.

"Oh God, not Michael. Not Michael! She struggled to keep going. She took off her shoes and carried them as she ran, ignoring the stones and rough concrete beneath her bare feet.

"Michael, Michael!" she called out loud as more exploding oil storage tanks rocked her body.

9:12am

As Miss Jones reached Michael's desk for his health check, something made him turn his head toward the windows. He saw a curious white wave coming toward him in slow motion. It appeared to be water thrown from a bucket, separating into long droplets and flying horizontally just above the desktops. The whiteness cruelly morphed into thousands of shards of glass. The students around him sat at their desks frozen, like stone sculptures. He turned away from the bright light. The ship's explosion shattered the school's windows into tiny pieces and hurled them into the room like rain propelled on a hurricane's forceful winds. Glass cut into the back of Michael's head.

Dazed and crumpled on the floor under his desk, he heard the cries and screams of his classmates as they filled the room. The air smelled of dirt, and dust swirled in floating eddies. At the front of the room, Miss Jones frantically pulled on the door, but the force of the explosion had sealed it shut. The entire class funneled toward the door, pushing against her and each other. Terrified and panicked, some bloodied, they shrieked for their mothers.

Miss Jones could not free the door. A huge scrum of children blindly continued to push forward. Michael stood at the back of the mass of children and realized that the door could not be opened. On the west wall facing the hallway, transom windows opened just below the ceiling. Michael pushed a desk against the wall and stacked another on top of that. He climbed the desks, stood on the top and steadied himself against the wall. He reached up and pulled himself into the transom, squeezed through it, then crouched on top of the hall lockers. He had freed himself from the classroom, only to see the panic that was growing in the school's hallways.

More screams and cries for help assaulted his ears. Crumbled walls blocked half of the stairway. A teacher at the top of the stairs directed students to the other end of the building. Michael looked down the long hallway where children shoved and fought to get out, mired in confusion and fear. He dropped from the top of the lockers, tumbled, jumped up and raced past the teacher. He jumped onto the flat stairway banister and slid to mid-level. From there he was able to run down the remaining stairs and out through the destroyed school doors.

Once in the schoolyard, he moved in slow motion, struggling to make sense of what he was seeing. Students, parents and teachers ran in every direction. He had no thought about what he should do. He put his hand on the back of his neck and when he pulled it back, blood covered his fingers. He studied the blood, wondering where it came from. Bedlam surrounded him in a swirling mass of terrified children and adults frantic to find each other.

He continued to stare at his fingers. The sound of someone screaming his name brought him back to the schoolyard. Searching through the crowd, he tried to put a face to the voice that called him. Glare from the sun blurred his vision. It sounded like his Mom, her voice high pitched and urgent, but from a distant place. What was happening? he wondered. Why was she screaming?

Grace neared collapse as she entered a nightmare of desperate parents jumping out of their cars, leaving doors open and engines running. They ran onto the playground and gasped at the battered building. The shattered windows and crumbled walls brought more fear to their feverish search.

Terrified, hysterical children stumbled through the school's mangled doors. Sirens screamed in the air as more oil storage tanks detonated and sent waves of heat and concussive energy rolling across the schoolyard.

"Oh, God. Oh, God. Let him be okay," Grace prayed. Men and women yelled their children's names, some screaming hysterically. When they found their children, they grabbed them, held them tightly, then quickly retreated to their cars, speeding away wildly through the throng of vehicles and distraught searchers.

Grace saw that many of the children on the schoolyard were weeping and wandering in circles. Blood streamed down their faces onto their clothes. Some limped or held their arms in pain.

Grace searched each face. She touched some of the children and asked if she could help them. A girl asked Grace if her face was bloody, her features completely masked with it. Grace hugged her, walked her toward the school building and continued to look for Michael. The girl pulled free. "I wanna go home," she said and staggered toward the gate.

Grace moved toward the main entrance of the school. Broken glass littered every inch of ground around her. A wave of children continued to stream out. They came through frames where doors had been ripped away and she could see collapsed walls through the frames.

Boys and girls ran, some screaming, some crying uncontrollably. A boy rushed out and fell at Grace's feet, blood streaming from a gash on his arm. She knelt to help him. He looked at her and she saw terror in his eyes. She felt faint, but managed to blurt out to him, "Stay still." She wanted to tie a piece of clothing to stop his bleeding, but he scrambled up, panicked by the chaos, and ran toward the street.

She turned back toward the school. As she moved toward the building, Greta came up behind her screaming Michael's name. They both zeroed in on him at the same time, ran to him together and threw their arms around him.

"Are you okay?" they asked. They felt his shoulders, arms and legs, and inspected him for wounds.

"What happened?" Michael asked, fighting back tears.

"We don't know, sweetheart. Something terrible. An explosion of some kind." They ran toward the idling car, holding Michael's hands.

"Where's Daddy?"

"We'll go home and wait for him. Everybody get in the car."

With Michael safe, Grace began to think of the docks and she looked toward the south where fires rolled into the air.

"No," Grace insisted. "I have to find Father Joe. And Louis. You take Michael home."

"No, Aunt Grace. You come with us," Michael pleaded with Grace. "Don't stay here. Come with us."

"Grace, there could be more explosions. The whole town could burn," Greta pleaded with her.

As if in response to her fear, more explosions shook them, and waves of heat passed over their bodies as missiles of burning steel ignited some of the more than 400 oil-filled storage facilities.

"Let's go!" Greta yelled.

"Take Michael home. There is no smoke coming from the west side, so we should assume that George is okay. When he gets home, go to Houston, or anywhere up the road. I have to stay. Please, Greta. Go. Traffic will only get worse." She put Michael in the car, kissed him and slammed the door. Greta drove away, weaving her way toward home.

Grace struggled to reach Main Street. Explosions from the oil storage tanks continued. New fires roared to life. Cars and trucks, with drivers leaning on their horns, rushed by her. Traffic lurched up and down side streets, dodging huge chunks of steel and splintered wood, as people searched for the quickest route out of town.

Grace made her way through crowds of people fleeing the fires behind them. Young people ran, older people walked as fast as they could. Some carried paper bags stuffed with clothes, others carried pets in their arms.

Grace turned toward the docks and raging fires without a thought as to what she would do. She walked quickly now, focused on getting to Louis' office, carried forward in the fear of Death's near hand.

She crossed Texas Avenue and passed injured survivors who ran, limped, or stumbled and fell. Some did not get up. Men with missing arms and terrified stares struggled to keep walking. She saw others holding arms with protruding bones and a young boy with an eye hanging beside his nose.

All of those coming from the docks were covered in a sludge of oil, mud and blood. Their faces frozen by demented fear, their only thought was to escape the fire and incessant explosions. People jumped on the backs of pick-up trucks or the hoods of passing cars to get away. Explosions erupted with waves of heat that intensified the urgency to escape.

Grace searched faces, trying to identify Father Joe or Louis. She fought against the stampede and thought only of the two men. She pleaded with God that they still be alive. A motorcycle policeman at a roadblock grabbed Grace.

"Hold on, lady! You can't go that way!"

"I have to find them. Louis, Father Joe," Grace screamed above the noise that surrounded her. "They came here this morning. I must find them. Please let me through."

"Everything is either destroyed or on fire. Nothing is left in there. There is nothing you can do!" The policeman turned Grace around, held her and forced her back up the street. "Go home! Go home!"

Grace reluctantly and slowly turned and left the horror behind her. She started toward home on Main Street. Visions of Father Joe and Louis lying injured or maybe dead would not leave her.

Trucks passed, carrying injured people toward the hospital. She decided to follow them. She breathed heavily as she walked, the acrid air tasting bitter in her mouth. Sidewalks and streets were littered with glass that had been sucked out of storefronts. Collapsed store roofs and walls lay in heaps. Shop owners, most in shock, gathered in small groups and asked each other what had happened.

At the hospital, cars, school buses, delivery trucks and pickups – every available conveyance – sped up to the curb to unload the wounded and dying. Families ran to the entrance hoping to find husbands, wives and children. The uninjured moved from person to person, looking, weeping and praying.

Grace searched bodies that were lying in the backs of trucks, their blood spilling over open tailgates. Those who were conscious groaned or screamed for help.

Not finding Louis or Father Joe among the bloodied and oil-masked faces, Grace, now fighting nausea, walked through the hospital's clinic doors and into a shocking panorama. Here she confronted even greater misery, with scores of mangled bodies, and the sounds of pain and fear filling the hallways. She moved in a disorienting fog, averting her eyes and trying not to see the gore, but unable to not see it as she stepped over people on the floor.

Twenty-One

Chaos and continuous detonations roared through the smoke and fire. Louis regained consciousness with a heavy wooden beam lying across his left leg. As his eyes began to focus, he saw steel beams twisted into spires and splintered wood where warehouses once stood. The entire waterfront, now peeled and transformed into scrap, gave fuel to fires that raged across its breadth. No structure had withstood the force of the exploding ship. Everything lay in a jumble of debris.

Louis tried to get up, but the beam held him clamped to the ground. He shouted for help.

Clayton had been walking toward the main gate when the explosive force hit him from behind, knocking him to the ground and ripping off his shirt. He sat up, dazed, and tasted blood running from his forehead into his mouth. He watched the pandemonium around him like a pummeled boxer knocked on his butt, legs splayed out in front of him. He touched the cut on his forehead.

Confused and stunned, Clayton had no idea what had happened or where he was. Voices around him cried for help. He lifted himself and wobbled through the smoke, unsure of his direction. He began to sense his bearings, and concern for his Momma and Shana took hold. Whatever happened had hit them, too. Fear engulfed him as he headed for home, not knowing if he could escape the fires.

He tentatively wound his way through the thick black smoke, not sure of his direction. Suddenly he saw a man lying on the ground who was trapped by a large beam across his leg. Louis, his face twisted in fear, pleaded for help. Clayton, thinking solely about Shana and his Momma, pushed past him.

"Please. Please, help me."

Fires raged around them. Louis struggled to free himself but could not extract his leg from under the beam. Clayton paused, then turned away to move on. For a moment he hesitated, then turned around toward Louis. He did not recognize the man whose face was covered in oil and looked as black as his own. Their eyes met.

Clayton grappled with both his own fear of the fires and his worries about Shana and their Momma. He wanted to get home. But something about this pitiable, black-faced man would not let him pass by. He returned to Louis and grabbed the end of the huge beam, the effort rippling the muscles of his back and shoulders. Veins bulged in his neck and a cry came from his throat as he moved the beam enough for Louis to pull his leg out. He tested the leg and found that he could stand. Blood trickled from a cut on his arm below the shoulder.

"Can you walk?" Clayton asked, as he held Louis' arm. They both winced with each step as they supported each other through heaps of crushed cars, ripped pipelines and destroyed buildings, heading toward Dock Road.

Louis spotted his destroyed warehouse as Mack appeared like a ghost out of the smoke. As they embraced, Mack explained that he had been standing between two rows of loaded pallets when the ship exploded, which saved him from the falling roof and flying shrapnel. As they stood looking at one another, cries for help echoed around them.

As another storage tank ripped apart with a roar and the percussion pulsed through them, flames shot into the air. Louis panicked, turning to limp down the road through twisted metal and smashed cars.

"Let's go. This whole place is going to burn!" Louis yelled above the roar of fires.

Mack grabbed his arm. "We can't leave these men out here!" he shouted, waving his arm in the direction of the cries. "We have to help them!"

Louis pulled away. Mack grabbed him by both shoulders and shook him. "We can't leave them here!" he screamed at Louis. He turned and called to Clayton, who was moving off to find his family.

"We need you, too. There are wounded men that we have to help."

"I have a family. I need to find them."

"Give us some help. Just for a while."

Mack tore the sleeve off of Louis' tattered shirt and made a bandage for the gash on Louis' arm.

"What can we do? We're going to die if we stay here!" Louis pleaded.

The acrid smell of burning oil and acidic chemicals filled his every breath. Heat waves rolled over them with each new tank explosion. "We can't help them!"

"We can't leave them!" Mack pulled Louis with him and moved toward the cries of injured men under piles of debris.

Clayton was about to object and insist on finding his family. But he had to acknowledge the man's bravery. *I don't owe these men anything*, he thought, as he took another step in the direction of the gate. Immediately, the image of a little girl in the back seat of a flaming car flashed through his mind. He had stood in flames and saved that little girl. He knew what that one act had meant to him. Everybody deserves to live, he told himself.

"Oh, hell." he muttered. "God will take care of Momma and Shana for a little while."

Clayton turned around and joined the others. He began lifting metal beams and chunks of concrete, digging deeper into piles of debris to free injured men.

Mack took charge. "We'll get the men out, take them to the gate. Start a triage area. From there they can be transported to the hospital."

Louis followed Mack's orders. Working in tandem with Clayton, they used pieces of lumber or metal to pry away larger chunks of rubble. Clayton lifted huge pieces of stone off of the injured who were pinned down. They pulled a man out of the pile with a broken bone sticking out of his twisted leg. Mack and Louis together carried him to the entrance gate where they laid him on the grass to await help.

They returned, going directly toward the fires. The three of them, now joined by other men, worked beyond belief, fueled by adrenaline and the urgency of the fires. The wind was now pushing smoke to the south and, with it, the direction of the flames. They hurried back as fast as they could to the destroyed docks.

Eruptions continued from the adjacent tank farm. Hot metal whistled past them. Mack made the judgment calls: he left those too injured to be moved and passed by the dead.

Survivors covered in sludge began to emerge from the black smoke. Horror-struck stares guided their way as they sucked hard for air. They struggled to walk through the accumulated debris. Only the whites of their eyes showed from their oil-covered bodies. Some ignored their own injuries to assist in the rescue efforts. Others walked away from the inferno, heading for the gate.

Mack made sleds out of pieces of wood or metal and pulled those who could not walk. They filled a large area with wounded. By now, dozens of vehicles had arrived. They formed a line on the road where the injured could now be loaded and taken to the hospital, as more volunteers joined the procession of makeshift ambulances.

Louis grew inured to the horror. He ignored the blood and the bones, and the dead bodies. Inspired by Clayton's relentless attack on mountains of debris, he and Mack grew stronger. They ignored the threat of death that surrounded them, no longer thinking about themselves. They lived with that grim reality but were able to stay focused on the moment. Get to the wounded before they die.

Somewhere in late morning, Clayton could no longer ignore his anxiety about Shana and his Momma. Without saying a word, he turned away from the fires and headed toward the gate. He needed to find his family. Maybe they lay injured – or dead – in their flimsy house that was so close to the refineries. He fled through the gate and ignored the help offered to him by medical aides in the triage area.

Standing in front of his house, he feared what he would find inside. Houses around him had no roofs. Walls, cracked and splintered, lay akimbo on concrete pilings.

"Momma?" he called out and listened for an answer. His world suddenly and completely went mute.

He entered the broken shell of the house. The ice box had fallen over and smashed the kitchen table. Glass littered their beds. Trembling, he surveyed every room, relieved to find no one at home.

Through his shattered windows, he saw vicious flames dance out of the malignant tower of smoke. Maybe it would spread to the Hallows, he thought.

He laid a sheet on the bed and threw a few of his clothes on it. The calamity outside no longer frightened him. Instead, a curious sense of freedom embraced his body. He knew that his Momma and Shana were all right. God would see to that. They all would be okay. He felt a giddy sense of relief and did not give a damn if the house burned to the ground. The entire Hallows could burn for all he cared.

He tossed in clothes for Shana and a small stuffed dog that she always clutched when she went to bed. He put in his mother's strand of imitation pearls that she wore to church every Sunday. He put in a change of clothes for each of them, gathered up the corners of the sheet and tied it into a bundle.

He left the house. A block away, he suddenly stopped, turned and started running back to the house. He had forgotten his saxophone. It still stood in the corner, untouched by debris that had crashed through the roof.

Clayton crossed Texas Avenue. He dodged speeding cars, not caring that he was a Black man with a white bundle over his shoulder and a saxophone case. Aware that he appeared to be a looter, he also knew that only one thing was on the mind of everyone he passed: Get the hell out of town.

He walked into fields on the west side of town and left the burning morass behind him. He joined an exodus of the Black community as it threaded through waist-high grass, with no destination in mind, only the thought to escape the imminent danger.

Clayton searched for his Momma and Shana as he kept up a hurried pace toward the highway to Dickinson. He crossed over the road that led out of town and passed through a line of cars that was stopped bumper to bumper. Horns blared and panicked drivers scrambled to find passage around the traffic. Some drove on the grassy sides of the ditches in their rush.

Now that he was certain his Momma was not dead in the wreckage of the house, he knew that she would get to the school and take Shana to a safe place before she tried to find him. Pipelines and storage facilities filled with explosive materials thundered and burst into flames behind him.

He could be dead as far as his Momma knew. However, he was anything but dead. He was very keenly aware that he had dodged this maelstrom and a new energy surged through him. He trudged through the fields and pictured the exodus that had followed Moses. His yoke of oppression had lifted and a sense of euphoria propelled him toward freedom. He had no words to describe this euphoria, but sensed that the cataclysmic event had changed all of the rules and had obliterated his fear. Having nothing to lose felt like freedom to Clayton. It gave him options.

Tall grass moved in the wind like waves on a sea. Green fields freshened by spring lay ahead of him while fires raged behind. He knew what he had to do. His old life was burning in the fires.

Twenty-Two

Wednesday, April 16, 1947
10:30 am

Grace stood in the packed waiting room of the small hospital with its too few beds. People with open wounds lay on the floor in the hallways. Blood ran under the soles of the nurses' shoes. Cries of pain echoed off the walls.

Dr. Morgan had organized a triage system. He directed the acutely critical patients to be put into the west hall. Those with less serious injuries went into the east hall. Grace searched the faces of the distressed people lying on the floor of the west hall.

"Are you injured?" the doctor looked up from a kneeling position next to a patient and asked Grace as she approached.

Grace shook her head. "I'm looking for Father Joe or Louis Broussard."

"They haven't been here. Some people are being taken to Galveston. They may be there." Dr. Morgan moved to another patient as he talked. "If you're not injured, we could use some help. Go with her," he nodded to a nurse. "Get her a gown and some gloves," he directed.

"I can't... I don't know about...." Grace tried to reply, knowing her own aversion to blood and how it shocked and appalled her.

"Please. We need you."

The nurse, her scrubs soaked with blood, hastily took Grace to a small supply room and handed her a gown and gloves.

"Just follow me. I'll tell you what to do."

They cleaned wounds, placed tourniquets and pressure packs, and moved rapidly from one person to another. A nurse with a large morphine syringe followed behind them and injected the injured, pausing only to replace the needle as she hurried from one person to the next.

Some suffered quietly and wrung their hands, some prayed aloud, others cried for a doctor. Anxious parents and spouses searched the halls for family members. A chorus of despair sang throughout the building. Sobs echoed from family members when a loved one died, while others were equally overcome when those they searched for were found alive.

The odor of blood wandered through the clinic's corridors. Death's angels roamed the halls and tapped those beyond saving. Many were called as the blood of life drained out of them.

More injured arrived. Grace moved mechanically, closing her eyes when a mangled body overwhelmed her. She had no time to think. She did what the nurse directed, moved with her, tended to broken bodies, studied the next oil-smudged face, and hoped beyond hope to find her men alive. Urgency propelled her. Bedlam continued interminably.

Early in the afternoon, Dr. Morgan sensed that Grace was on the verge of exhaustion and relieved her of duty with the patients. Grace moved to the reception desk where she helped with identification and recorded the movement of patients, some of whom were sent out to facilities in surrounding communities. Very little reliable information came in from the docks. Only anecdotal references from the injured who were able to speak or brief descriptions from drivers who brought in the wounded provided her with a picture of the ever-changing inferno.

Vincent Russo made a statement in the early afternoon that

officials expected no more major explosions. The message circulated through the relief workers. It brought no consolation to those who worked at the clinic with the injured and dying, nor among those who searched to find loved ones.

Sirens continued to shriek and an armada of ambulances transported the injured from the docks. Doctors and nurses from surrounding towns had rushed into Texas City. Patients now overflowed the few hospital beds. Tents with cots set up outside held both the dying and injured. The most critical were being sent to the big hospitals in Galveston and Houston as quickly as possible.

Grace stared intently at each wave of casualties brought through the front doors of the clinic and as she walked among the cots outside. She occasionally recognized parishioners she had encountered in the church office and offered words of encouragement to them.

The number of casualties continued to grow in a constant march now into late afternoon. Tents and cots had also been set up by this time at City Hall where some of the less injured could be attended. The bright sunshine began its shift into evening. Neither Father Joe nor Louis had appeared among the arrivals. Having searched for so many hours through so much misery, her hope had eroded. She now anticipated hearing word of their deaths.

Twenty-Three

As darkness closed over this Hell on earth, Louis and Mack sat on the ground in a tent outside the gates at Dock Road. Generators roared and provided light for National Guardsmen who had set up tents and tables in the triage area. Medical staff attended to the casualties until they could be transported to another facility. A medic stitched the gash in Louis' arm and taped on a clean bandage. A volunteer brought them coffee and sandwiches. In all of this death and destruction, Louis could not eat.

Rescuers covered in oil and blood, with their tattered clothes hanging in strips, took short rests and returned to the docks. Grim-faced men, exhausted by the labor and carnage, refused to give up searching for anyone still alive. Ambulances from surrounding counties now idled in long lines, waiting to be filled with injured survivors. A continuous lament of sirens urged volunteers back into the waiting Hell.

"Did you see Father Joe Irons anywhere out there?" Louis asked men around him. "I know he must have come when the fire started."

Some who did not know him asked what he looked like. But no one had seen him.

"I know he is out here," he said to Mack. "If I could talk to Grace, she would know something about where he was headed. I hope that she is in a safe place."

Bulldozers had arrived by afternoon and began clearing a path through the rubble. The roar of their engines and clanking of the metal treads lifted above the noise of sirens and fire engines. Drivers steered their dozers through demolished cars and mountains of debris. Finally, a route was opened to the docks. Fire engines followed behind them, their headlights reflecting a junkyard of ruin.

Fires continued to erupt, oil storage tanks blazed, and ruptured pipelines spewed showers of flames. Sulfur, cotton and chemicals of all kinds from the destroyed warehouses continued to feed each other in outbursts of combustion.

Louis saw all four of Texas City's fire engines crumpled into heaps, either flattened like empty beer cans or hurled on top of other smashed vehicles. He thought of Steve Nader standing on the deck of the *Grandcamp* and arguing with the French captain before the ship exploded. Nothing would be left of them or anyone else who was on the ship or close to it that morning.

Earlier in the afternoon, Vincent Russo had declared at a press conference on the grounds of City Hall that there would be no other major explosions. The news brought a sense of relief and allowed rescue efforts to become more organized. A new energy infused the many volunteers who had arrived to help.

At the docks, fires continued to burn but fear about the ability to contain them abated. Two ships remained at the docks, the *Wilson B Keene* which was partially sunk at its moorings and the *High Flyer* in a third slip. The *Keene* had loaded mostly flour and somehow did not catch fire. The *High Flyer*, which was farthest from the *Grandcamp*, sat evenly in the water and garnered little attention.

Burning sulfur continued to send yellow smoke into the black night. Firemen wore gas masks and stepped over dead bodies that were illuminated by huge military searchlights, as well as ongoing fires. Firefighters hurried to new eruptions of fire as they occurred. Silhouetted by flames, they created eerie shadows like faceless dancers, leaping and twirling in a desperate battle against a tide of flaming oil and toxic chemicals.

Thursday, April 17, 1947
12:45 am

A stunning discovery occurred late in the night. The *High Flyer's* cargo, thought to be cotton and sulfur, actually contained large amounts of ammonium nitrate. In the chaos, no one had paid any attention to this third vessel, and thick smoke and debris had kept crews away from that slip. They could now see flames creeping out of its forward hatch. Earlier in the afternoon, attempts had been made to move the *High Flyer* from its mooring to prevent further damage to it. Workmen had used torches to cut the anchor loose, but the ship could not be budged by tugs in the turning basin.

Louis, searching rubble close to the two remaining ships, heard a familiar voice over the shouting and engine noises. In the flickering light of flames, he saw the sloped shoulders and bald head of Father Joe. He was kneeling over a body, making the sign of the cross on the man's forehead and speaking words of the Last Rites.

"Father Joe!" Louis shouted. He rushed to his side and wrapped his arms around the priest's shoulders. "Are you alright?"

"I'm okay, Louis. I'm okay. It's so terrible... so terrible. So many dead... so many dying. I've given last rites to everyone because I didn't know who might be dead or alive. I have no holy oil left."

"Are you hurt?" Louis asked again.

"I'm okay. I need to keep going. So many... I need...."

Without finishing his thought, he moved toward another body and began his prayers anew. He did not raise his head when yet another storage tank blew up, shaking the ground beneath them. Louis heard the halting and confused words Father Joe said over the dead man on the ground in front of him. Louis grabbed his arm and forced the exhausted priest to stand. He thought only of getting Father Joe out of danger. At that moment a fireball burst through a hatch on the deck of the *High Flyer*. Flames and sparks flew into the air like a Roman candle.

"EVACUATE! EVACUATE! EVACUATE! EXPLOSION IMMINENT! A loudspeaker mounted atop a truck drove through the area and blared a new warning.

Panic erupted. Firemen dropped their hoses. Shovels and picks flew aside as everyone ran, hearts pounding inside their chests. Memories of the morning's huge explosion catapulted people into wild scrambles toward the main gate as fear stampeded the mass of men: They sought only to survive.

"Come on. Let's go!" Louis pulled at Father Joe.

The priest hesitated. Louis pulled and pushed him toward the gate. He looked around for Mack, suddenly aware that they had separated. The crush of men funneled them along Dock Road. Louis could hear Father Joe praying in Latin. They shuffled arm in arm, trying to outrun the expected explosion.

1:10 am

As they neared the gate, the *High Flyer* disintegrated in an apocalyptic moment. Death and destruction ravaged the docks once again. Another supersonic blast, greater than the one in the morning, wrenched everyone to the ground, twisting, turning, rolling, and skipping their bodies along its surface like tumbleweeds. Louis lurched forward, glimpsing men silhouetted in brilliant illumination like noon on a sunny day, as though the immense explosion had spun Earth on its axis from night into day. The flash revealed a landscape of nameless men viciously assaulted by an invisible giant fist.

Louis saw his entire life in that eternal second. All his known existence passed before him. He knew not whether he lived or died, but thought that he had arrived in Hell itself, as if God had decided that Texas City should be the site of Armageddon and its time had come.

The shock wave pummeled him to the earth. He pushed up onto his hands and knees, shook his head and tried to calm the riotous disruption of his mind. Those who could move scrambled to their feet and stumbled again toward the gate. Louis hunted for Father Joe through the murky smoke-filled light. He found him a few yards away on his back, a thick sheet of steel across his chest. Louis crawled to his side.

Father Joe coughed and blood spewed from his mouth. Louis struggled to lift the steel on its pointed end and, with a great effort, pushed it aside. He slid his arm under the priest's shoulders and held him to his chest. Their faces touched.

"Father Joe. Father Joe. Father, can you hear me?" Louis implored the priest to speak. Father Joe opened his eyes and briefly stared at him.

Louis cradled his friend's body in his arms, stood and carried him toward the gate. People rushed past them, bumped into them and almost knocked them to the ground. Louis screamed in anguish and cursed the men who collided with him. Dazed and on the edge of losing consciousness, Louis knew that Father Joe was terribly wounded and that he needed to protect him. He would hold him until he could get him to David.

"Hang on, Father. Don't die, don't die. I've got you. Please don't die, don't die," Louis mumbled through his dizzy mind and distorted vision.

Once outside the gate, Louis could see darkened figures through the headlights hustling the wounded into vehicles that were idling in line. Havoc prevailed as priority shifted again from rescue to escape. Louis staggered under the weight of Father Joe's limp body. A pickup truck sped toward him, made a U-turn in the middle of the road and slid to a stop next to him. A boy with a crew cut, hardly old enough to drive, jumped out and helped Louis, still carrying Father Joe, onto the back of his truck. The driver wanted to lay the priest onto the flat surface of the truck bed, but Louis refused to release him. He held Father Joe tightly in his grasp.

The boy helped several others into the back of his truck before gunning his way back onto Main Street with his horn blaring. Louis squinted into a line of bright lights that followed behind the truck. Exhausted and in shock, Louis pressed Father Joe against his chest, trying to hold onto any life left inside of his unconscious friend.

"Oh, my God. Oh, my God," Grace cried when Louis carried Father Joe through the entrance of the clinic.

"Oh, Louis." Grace touched his face and threw her arms around both men. She led Louis to a chair where he sat down, still holding the priest. He stared at Grace with no sense of recognition. Father Joe's ashen face lay against Louis' chest.

"Dr. Morgan. Dr. Morgan!" Grace called out.

Dr. Morgan, exhausted by hours of work, turned to the chair with a deep sigh and placed his stethoscope on Father Joe's chest. He felt the spongy release of the crushed rib cage and tried to find a pulse. Louis stared past Dr. Morgan, still conscious, but lacking any lucid awareness of the tragedy around him.

"Louis, I need to take Father Joe," Dr. Morgan said gently. Dr. Morgan and a nearby volunteer took the lifeless body from Louis and carried him out of the room.

Suddenly, it all became more than Grace could manage. She had searched for so many hours and through so many wounded and dying people to find Louis and Father Joe. Finally, they were here.

She knelt on the floor next to Louis, who continued to stare into space, unable to comprehend the turmoil around him. Grace held his hand. She moved closer and held tighter to Louis, afraid he might also die.

Dr. Morgan returned to examine Louis and, after a brief exam, turned to Grace and said, "Louis will be okay. Are you alright?" He felt for her pulse as Grace nodded yes.

"He is exhausted and shows signs of a concussion and traumatic amnesia. He walked in here carrying Father Joe, so I don't think he has any hidden injuries, and he has no signs of internal bleeding. But he needs sleep. Can you take him home?" The doctor paused as he watched Grace for a response, knowing she had suffered much during the day.

"He lives near here, a few blocks up Ninth," he patiently advised her. "It's the first house in the last block before Bay Street. Can you take him? Louis needs someone to watch him for a while. I don't want to send him to Galveston. So, can you take him home and stay with him?" The doctor paused, anxiously watching Grace for her reaction. It would be a short walk, some fresh air, and finally some rest. He hoped she would go.

Grace pulled herself up from the floor. "Yes, I can take him. I know where he lives. I'll stay with him."

They walked out of the hospital and away from the chaos. The cool night air enveloped them and calmed their senses. Grace guided Louis down the sidewalk. He did not notice the flames that danced into the night sky and formed eddies of thick black smoke in their light. She held tightly to him and kept him from falling as he stumbled several times. He glanced at Grace with eyes still devoid of any recognition. A slight smile crossed his face as if he were recalling another place and a different time.

Grace helped Louis to a chair at his kitchen table and found candles in the wooden cupboards to light their way through the house. She took him upstairs and removed his shredded, dirty clothes. Louis followed her directions as she helped him into the bathtub. She washed his hair and scrubbed his body. She also cleaned numerous small cuts in his scalp. Louis responded slowly to every request she made of him. She finally clothed him in pajamas and helped him into bed. He immediately fell asleep.

Grace bathed herself, trying to scrub away what she had seen at the hospital. Images cycled through her mind: Mangled bodies, terrified patients who feared they would die, and families crushed beneath the weight of their own fears.

Images of Father Joe's sheet-white face and his dead body in Louis' lap somehow froze her emotions and enabled her to lose herself in order to take care of Louis. What she did at the hospital and what she did now came from a strength beyond anything she had known.

She understood that this cauldron of tragedy would not leave her, but she had made a passage through it. Horrible memories remained, but with them came a confidence that she was able to function in a crisis. The wounded and dying had clung to her, had wanted her to hold their hand or touch them while she tended to them. She talked to them and told them they would be alright. They held onto life through her.

Their need brought Grace out of herself. She had closed her heart to alleviate her pain for so long. She had suffered from the death of her baby, and heroin had blighted her emotions. She had lived in physical and emotional poverty to protect herself in prison. In this huge tragedy, her heart finally opened. Love given and love received was now expressed in compassion.

She found a white dress shirt in Louis' closet. It fit her like a nightgown almost to her knees. She moved a stuffed chair close to his bed, pulled her legs beneath her and watched Louis. She thought about all the people who had started the morning thinking today would be as the day before. The disastrous turn had blindsided them with a horrendous cruelty that engulfed the entire community in one swift moment. Some prayed that God would let them live. Others stoically, or hysterically, anguished through the pain. Many suffered the tortured suspense of not knowing their loved ones' fate as they searched for some news of them.

The pale light of candles lit the silent room. Away from the torrid pace at the hospital, a sense of composure now flowed into Grace. A new core of strength she had found in the devastation of this day now melted away her old wretchedness. She felt washed clean by the blood of those she had served. The past events of her life paled in the enormity of this human suffering.

Grace fell asleep for short periods but awakened often to see if Louis' chest still rose in a rhythmic cadence. Just before daylight, Louis mumbled incoherently. He shivered with a chill. Afraid he might stop breathing or have a seizure, Grace slid beneath the covers and held him tightly to warm him. He returned to a quiet sleep.

She remained close in the comfort of his warmth, her arm across his chest. It had been so long since her senses had been filled with the scent of a man or she had felt a man's body close to her. Having Louis close by reassured her. All of the feelings that she had buried hovered close to the brim. She had no more will to resist. Slowly she slipped through the thin divide and acknowledged her desire to hold onto him, to allow desire to dispel any lingering fear.

Louis awoke shortly after dawn confused. As his gaze went around the room, he realized where he was and that it was Grace next to him. So happy to see her, he leaned toward her and instinctively kissed her. Grace awakened slowly like coming out of a dream, not totally aware of her surroundings. Seeing Louis alert and recognizing her brought a smile to her face. She stared at him and put her arms around him, grateful to see him awake.

"Are you alright?"

"Yes. I think so." He moved his head from side to side and breathed deeply. Excited by their closeness, grief melted away in their desire for one another. Their bodies silently moved past the boundaries. Grace returned his kisses and whispered his name. She wanted him – needed him – to love her.

As the morning light slipped around the edges of the curtains, Grace lay on her back. She alternately looked at the ceiling then at Louis' face, as if trying to ask a question. She heard no sirens from the streets, no cries for help. Only their breathing sounded in the silence of the room.

For the first time in years, Grace basked in the afterglow of ecstasy. The scent of fragrant candles mingled with the scent of shampoo in their hair. Her mind luxuriated in a space where nothing outside of this room existed. It allowed her to grant amnesty to herself as compassion replaced her shame. The sadness of this tragedy would not soon be over, but she could experience it with a new strength forged out of confronting her fears.

Outside, fires still burned at the docks. Inside, Grace and Louis drifted into a restful sleep.

Grace awoke and went to the kitchen to make coffee. When she returned to the bedroom, Louis was sitting on the edge of the bed. She took his hand.

"How are you feeling?"

"Groggy."

"Do you know where you are?"

Louis looked around the room. He noted the embossed wallpaper, dark brown curtains on the windows, a pastoral picture of a stag standing in the woods on the wall above the bed.

"I'm in my bedroom, in my home."

"Do you remember last night?"

He smiled. "Every moment of it."

Grace smiled, realizing that either he did not fully understand her question, or he understood but desired only to focus on their night together. So she told him how he came to the hospital, but omitted Father Joe from the story. She wanted to tell him but was afraid of the effect such news would have on him. She decided that this could wait until he was feeling stronger.

As she watched him, Grace puzzled over her new freedom. Where would her waking up take her? Was this the beginning of love? Could she start a new life, putting the decadent life she had lived behind her?

By afternoon, utility crews had restored power to much of Texas City. Grace sat in Louis' kitchen with the radio on. Hundreds of people remained missing. Announcers read their lists of names, places of employment and places last seen in an effort to connect families. Grace assumed that Greta and George had fled to Houston to stay with friends. They would want to get Michael far away from the scene. Fires still burned. Some were allowed to burn while guarded to keep them from spreading. The Fourth Army Corps and volunteers from around the nation continued search and rescue operations amid the fires and devastation, hoping to find anyone still alive.

Dr. Morgan, taking a short respite from the chaos at the clinic to shower and nap, had stopped by to see Louis and tell him about Father Joe. Knowing now that Father Joe had died, memories of carrying him returned to Louis. He lamented that he should have tried harder to save him or should have been taken in his place.

"Why wasn't I killed? Why him and not me? We were hurrying toward the gate right next to each other. One step this way or that. One less step. A little hesitation, anything, could have taken my life…. But I'm here and Father Joe is gone. Forever gone."

Louis could not comprehend the finality of it. And he did not want to believe it. Just a few hours ago he had carried Father Joe in his arms. There remained no comfort of faith. To Louis, he was just gone.

Grace and Louis talked about Father Joe. "He had such a goofy laugh," Louis said.

"He was kind to me," Grace replied.

"Bad things happen to good people," he said. "He believed in the goodness of all people. So why did God allow such a thing as this?"

Louis sipped his coffee. A somber voice from the radio recited a list of missing people. "He told me that I still believed in God, that I only carried anger against Him like a petulant child does at times by turning away and ignoring his parents."

"Father Joe didn't concern himself very much with why things happen the way they do," Grace said. "He talked more about our response to what happens."

"He loved mystery," Louis replied. "'Inscrutable,' he would say to me. God's ways are inscrutable."

They continued to talk to slow the wave of grief that they knew would soon arrive. They sat with aching hearts and no words to soften the pain.

Louis' mood turned sullen, resentful of all of the losses that filtered back into his thoughts. "What kind of God would allow this to happen? All those lives. All this suffering."

"Oh, Louis, I am sure that Father Joe would find some meaning in all of this."

"Well, he is not here now, is he? It is too cruel! Why take the man who could help the most?" Louis looked upward. "You are a cruel and punishing God. You have no regard for the suffering of all of these families. You have destroyed this town along with all those lives. It's not the Devil we should fear. It is You! You are the destroyer!"

"Stop it, Louis!"

"Father Joe prayed every day. Look where it got him. A just reward for his faithful service? My mother went to Mass every

Sunday and prayed the rosary. God didn't help her either. He led her into misery and despair, so much so that she hated living."

Louis covered his face with both hands to hide his tears. His shoulders convulsed as he wept. Grace wrapped her arms around him and held tight to him as grief and anger burrowed deep into them both. Grace wept with him, mourning the loss of her beloved priest.

In the Hallows, Clayton returned to his house early Thursday afternoon and stood in his Momma's kitchen, again looking for his family and surveying the damage to the house. Reality had set in as he had raced away from his past, and his euphoria had turned to depression: He had no place to go. Even though fires still burned, he had trudged home after spending the night in a field west of town, weary and worried about his family. He had heard the *High Flyer* explode and felt the earth tremble from its force during the night. He could do nothing but pray for his family.

He had no idea about how to look for his Momma and the knowledge immobilized him. A neighbor stopped by and told him the explosions were over. But Clayton continued to keep a wary eye toward the fires.

Suddenly, Shana ran through the front door and threw herself onto him. Clayton burst into tears at seeing her. His Momma followed close behind and they all hugged in a circle of relief.

"Oh, honey, I thought for sure you wuz dead," Momma spoke through her tears. Shana held tightly to him, afraid to let go. Emotions shifted back and forth from laughter to tears.

"I didn't know what to do, Momma. I wuz scared, but all I could do is come back here. I had some clothes and things for you, but I didn't know where to find you."

"Me, too, son. But I wuz prayin' for you the whole time. And God, He answered my prayers. I went to the school and found Shana, then we walked to the church. There wuz broken glass, but it seemed like a safe place to be. We prayed hard for you. After a while, a couple total strangers took us to their house up on the north side and let us spend the night there. Oh, I'm so happy you alive. Shana wuz sick 'bout you."

"I spent the night in the fields west of town, thinkin' the Hallows would burn down," Clayton replied. "It made me happy to think that this place would be gone. But this mornin' I knew I had to come back. Where did I ever think we could go? Oh, I'm so happy ya'll be safe."

Twenty-Four

Friday, April 18, 1947

The number of fires finally decreased, but constant surveillance around the dock and oil storage tanks continued. Rampant rumors commenced that another explosion was imminent or that toxic gas was leaking from broken pipes and was drifting toward residential areas. Rumors panicked people again and fear resurfaced. Residents climbed into cars packed with their essentials or set out on foot to flee northward again. Fear roamed the streets like a thick coastal fog, just beneath the surface of a fragile confidence that no more horrors lay hidden in the rubble.

After breakfast with Louis, Grace walked back to Greta's house. Noise and uncertainty swirled in the air. The sheer number of volunteers, the media and the curious created turmoil. Grace hurried to see Greta, knowing her sister would be frantic to hear from her.

She found George at the house. He rushed to greet Grace in the opened doorway, happy to see her alive and uninjured.

"Greta has been distraught. We drove to Houston and have been staying with friends there. I tried to come home yesterday but couldn't make it because of all the emergency vehicles. She will be so relieved. And Michael. He's been worried, asking constantly about you."

"Tell me what happened to you," she urged.

"I'm ok. My refinery is far enough west that we did not get too much damage. There were many broken windows and shrapnel whistled all around us, but only a few injuries. A coworker gave me a ride home. It took forever with so much traffic and frantic drivers. Greta and Michael were sitting on the front steps holding each other when I finally made it here. I wanted to find you, but Greta felt that you were okay and we needed to get Michael out of town. We all panicked."

Grace told George her story. "Father Joe was killed when the second ship exploded. I was at the hospital when Louis brought him in. It was awful, I was so afraid. We are lucky to be alive and unharmed."

Grace walked through the house. Steel rivets that had crashed through the roof lay on the floor. A large chunk of steel had ripped a gaping hole in the front of the house. The front door, blown off its hinges, lay on the sofa across the room. A back door lay in the yard. But it was livable for the most part. She then inspected her apartment and found it was also full of broken glass and littered with debris.

George could not say when Greta and Michael would return. "I think the worst is over. As soon as I can get the doors up and windows boarded, we should be able to get back in the house. I'm going to Houston tonight. You should come with me."

Louis had already informed Grace that he did not want her to stay by herself if George and Greta would not be there. He wanted to protect her because he loved her and wanted to be with her. He said she could stay with him forever. Grace experienced so many emotions clashing together in her mind, that she had not sorted through that simple but complex declaration. She needed to concentrate on the moment and take one step at a time.

"I need to go to the church, George. I'm going to stay here to help. Tell Greta that I'm fine. I'll be okay here with Louis. We'll all be together soon."

Grace left George to his repairs. She walked to the church office, anxious about what it would be like without Father Joe. Volunteers had boarded up broken windows. She cleared glass and dust from her desk and picked up papers blown onto the floor. Her heartache pressed into her throat. Whenever a workman walked in, she expected to see Father Joe.

She went into his office to clean and gather his personal belongings. Holding the Buddha statue in her hands, she could see Father Joe's smile in her mind. She did not want to believe he would never come back to this office, never again tell her one of his corny jokes.

Curiosity led Grace into the church and into the choir room. She sat on the piano bench and cleaned away debris. Her fingers moved over the keys and ran the scales as she thought about Clayton, wondering about him and his family. She had no way to contact him. She sat in meditation, reflecting on the magnitude of what had happened as she allowed grief to rush in again. She silently prayed. Please God, let them be okay.

She began playing the 23rd Beethoven Sonata and her sorrow turned to anger. She transposed to the *Presto Agitato*. As her fingers pounded the keys, the music was fueled by emotion. She bowed her head, almost touching her hands with her face. She rocked back and forth, attacking the keyboard, and poured her rage into Beethoven's score.

She played the fast arpeggios. The notes flowed into her fingers, carrying her fury and grief with them. She finished the *Presto* feeling spent, hardly able to move, and stared at the keys. Shifting to the *Adagio*, she played the mournful movement pianissimo. The music carried the anger away until only sorrow remained.

The sorrow that had filled her body now released itself in sobs that groaned out of her. The music lamented all that she could not speak: her baby, Father Joe, the life she had not lived. This disaster catalyzed the sorrows that were embedded in the very cells of her body, bringing them up to be transformed. The regret and shame that had defined her life paid its price and ransomed her spirit.

Strength now began to pass from the music through her hands and surge into her with courage and lucidity. The authenticity of her birth returned and released her from her prison.

Music returned to its place in her soul.

A priest from the diocese arrived at the office and, together, they organized the work ahead. Grace listed the families who would need funeral services and those who would need counseling. She consoled people who came to the office and shared their grief. Others asked her to come into the church with them, to sit quietly and pray. Grace welcomed these weary and broken people. Together they grieved.

Once again in the Hallows, Clayton sat on his bed in a surreal fog. Just being alive was a miracle. Having his family intact with no injuries should have filled him with gratitude. But here he sat in the same rat hole, the elation he felt in the aftermath of the chaos already absent from his mind. The catastrophic events had not lifted him out of the Hallows after all.

Clayton had covered the broken windows and doors and closed shrapnel holes in the roof. These were enough repairs to let them reoccupy the house. Apprehension about what might happen next strangled the family physically and emotionally. The mayor had declared that the danger of more explosions was over, but their nearness to the destroyed docks kept them anxious and inundated with fear of the unknown. Every sudden noise, like a bulldozer cranking up or a siren warbling in the air, initiated a moment of panic in each of them. They each felt the impulse to jump up and run. They stared at each other, seeking reassurance. The uneasiness remained for hours after the recognition that there was no immediate danger.

Shana stayed close to one of them at all times. The fear in her eyes made it easier for Clayton to make his decision. He went into the kitchen to talk with his Momma.

"I ain't goin' back to those docks to work. I won't go back there."

Ella Mae stood stoic with no emotion in her face. "It will be a while before they want you, anyway. Ain't nobody workin' out there now 'cept searchin' for bodies."

Clayton spoke softly. "When that ship exploded, it threw me to the ground. The whole place lit up with a blinding light. I thought I had died and gone to some place for the dead. When I realized I weren't dead, I started runnin'. All I could think of was Shana, that maybe she was dead or hurt. I had to get home.

"But I stopped to help a man. A white man, covered in oil so that he looked like me. For a second, we the same, jes' two men who needed each other. And color didn't matter anymore. I had to help him. Then I heard other men cry for help. And I worked to free them. I wanted to come home to find you and Shana. But I knew those men needed me to help them. They all covered with oil. I couldn't tell who was Black or who was white, unless their shirt pulled up or their pant leg. I helped them all the same. We all the same in that mess."

"What kind of work you gonna find 'round here if you don't

work out there?" Ella Mae responded. She continued to stare out of the window, nodding toward the docks. "You can't jes' run away from the bad."

"I ain't jes' runnin' away from the bad. I'm tryin' to find somethin' good." Clayton straightened his back and puffed out his chest. "We goin' to California. All of us. Maybe things will change here, but someone else will have to fight for it. We goin' to California! You want Shana to stay in that segregated school she goes to, where she can't have what those little white girls up the street have? You wanna live in this shack next to that atomic bomb across the drainage ditch and wait for it to blow up again? You want me to stay in this town where I gonna be a 'boy' all my life, lookin' over my shoulder even when I ain't doin' nothin' wrong? I ain't stayin' here. I can't. I ain't gonna give them another chance to treat me like a dog. I can't walk that tight wire no more. I'll end up in prison or dead."

"We can't jes get up and leave. Go to California."

"We'll go to Long Beach. They got docks in Long Beach. I'll get a job. We got nothin' here we can't leave behind."

Clayton sat at the table feeling defiant. Ella Mae stared at her son. She hid the upheaval that churned inside her. She had been the rock that kept them together. She hated the Hallows, but it provided some stability for them. She knew what to expect here.

"I come to Texas City 30 years ago. It's not the best place, but it's all I know. It's my place. You want me to pull up and go to California? Somewheres on the other side of the world? I got roots here, son."

"You got nothin' here, Momma! I got nothin'. I am invisible in this town. We are nothin' but free slaves. We have no value, no place. Where's your sense of dignity? Please, Momma? For

Shana? I been dreamin' and hopin' that someday we could leave. I don't know how we gonna get to California yet, but I will find a way. Ain't you got a cousin or somebody out there? We won't have to be afraid no more. We can make a new start in a new place.

"I know what I want now. I seen all those pretty houses in Houston. I know we can have that, too. We'll get a sturdy house, painted, with proper screens. We gonna plant flowers. And have real grass, green grass that grows up to a sidewalk that leads to our front door. We'll have pretty houses next to us. The whole block will be neat and cared for. We'll have a sense of place where we belong and feel good about where we live. I know we can do it, Momma. We just have to have the courage to try."

Clayton looked into his bedroom and saw the sax back in its corner. Light glinted off its shiny metal. He drifted into a reverie where he stood on a stage again in front of a big band, the sax hung around his neck. He smiled that big radiant smile at dancers on the floor and snapped his fingers to the beat of the band behind him. He put the mouthpiece to his lips to play. A ball in the middle of the ceiling turned like the big ball of Earth, with spikes of light spraying onto the crowd that jumped and jived to the rhythm. Peace flooded over him.

"Please, Momma. Don't fight with me no more on this. Let's leave this place, find our forever place in California. For Shana. For me. We all deserve better."

Although Ella Mae did not answer, Clayton continued to work out a plan to get them on their way. There would be some preparations to be made, foremost of which would be to find the money.

oTwenty-oFive

Friday, April 18, 1947

After Grace had departed for Greta's house earlier in the morning, Louis went to find out what he could do to help his town. He limped up the concrete steps of City Hall. The triple arches of the building's exterior facade had received widespread damage and the roof, while not totally collapsed, had various-sized holes that were already being repaired. In the area around City Hall, a tent city had been erected by the Army to provide cots and places of rest for firemen and rescuers. The Red Cross and the Salvation Army headquartered on the grounds. There was also a media center where hundreds of journalists and network news representatives pursued stories or sought information. Hundreds of volunteers flooded into the town from around the nation.

Inside City Hall, groups of people huddled in hallways, and men and women rushed in and out of offices. The Mayor's secretary directed Louis to see John Hillman, an engineer by profession, who had inherited the job of chief organizer to bring order into the chaos. Except for a shower and short naps, he had worked over 48 hours straight.

A new sense of ownership had birthed itself in Louis: This was his town that was hemorrhaging. He would do whatever city officials asked. He listened intently as John described the current situation to Louis in a tired, irritable voice now that the threat of more explosions appeared to be over.

"I know we said it before, but there's nothing left out there to explode except maybe a few more oil storage tanks. Fires are burning themselves out. I finally have coordination between the military, Red Cross, Salvation Army, police forces and hospitals. We've formed committees to handle everything from identification of dead bodies to supplying hot coffee and food for all these volunteers. Even the Boy Scouts formed teams to assist us. We were totally unprepared for this. So much of what I have had to do should have been in place a long time ago."

"We had our heads up our asses for sure," Louis replied. "Any news about Steve Nader?"

"No. There are several hundred people unaccounted for. Many, I'm afraid, we will never find."

Louis pictured Steve on the deck of the ship arguing with the captain. He believed that Steve's body had vaporized at the same time the ship disappeared from its slip.

"Steel and flesh returned to molecules by the supersonic force of a 'harmless' fertilizer." John Hillman's wearied face grew darker. "All 24 members of our Volunteer Fire Department remain missing."

Louis thought about Steve's family, now without a father. "How about Mack Hale? He worked for me."

"No, I haven't heard that name mentioned."

John gave Louis several options as to where he could be of help. Louis promised to return the next day. For the moment, he desperately wanted to find Mack.

Louis drove to Mack's duplex. Part of the roof had caved in and sunlight bathed the floor through an open hole. Curtains fluttered in the breeze and waved through shattered windows.

The doorway to the apartment stood ajar. Louis searched the rooms but found no sign of Mack. It appeared that he had not been there since the explosion. Louis drove to the hospital in Texas City, then to the Galveston hospitals. No one had information. There was no trace of Mack Hale.

Louis reluctantly forced himself to search the temporary morgue at the high school gymnasium. He did not want to go there. Louis realized that he was smoking constantly, often lighting one cigarette from the previous. A cloud of smoke now hung over him as he stood in a long line of people waiting to get into the gym.

Hearses idled by the curb on Third Avenue adjacent to the facility. Inside the gym, corpses had been laid next to each other in straight lines, with space to walk between the rows. Those seeking to find loved ones bent close to examine the turgid bodies blanketed with oil. They defied identification with just a casual glance. A few weeks prior, the gym had hosted a high school basketball game and cheering fans had filled it with excited shouting to support their teams. This morning a mélange of mangled bodies, some with no limbs and a few decapitated, awaited those in line. Frightful images assaulted the eyes of the searchers. Stench paralyzed the breath of the somber procession as they walked amid the cold, gray corpses. Louis found no trace of Mack there.

He moved on to an auto repair garage conscripted as the site for embalming. It reeked of chemicals as morticians toiled beyond exhaustion to embalm the dead who had been deposited at the garage. Veteran morticians as well as young students still in embalmer's training suffered physical and mental duress at the immense task. Loouis did not find Mack's body there either.

Louis knew about another morgue that had been set up next door exclusively for body parts. He remembered Mack's tattoo from his time in the Navy and went next door to search this last place. He moved hurriedly along a line of arms and legs, looking for an arm tattoo he would recognize. At the end of a long table, a woman was searching through a washtub of hands. He watched her colorless face as she examined each hand for a ring. On her left hand she wore a gold filigree wedding band. She looked up and saw Louis. He stood speechless, stunned at the understanding of her task.

"I've been to all the other places three times," she said. "I've been to all of the hospitals. I put appeals on the radio. He could be wandering around in shock…. He always came home…. I don't know what else to do. I have to know." She put the last hand back in the tub and reeled toward the door, gasping for fresh air.

Louis knew that Mack could be among those that John Hillman said would never be found. But, for Louis, finding him was imperative. What they had been through together made them brothers. When the first explosion had occurred, Mack had forced him through his panic and saved him from the shame of a coward. It troubled him greatly to think of how many times he had taken Mack for granted. He needed to pay his debt of gratitude.

At the end of the day, a smoggy shroud hung over Texas City. After hours of futility, Louis felt deflated and defeated. He was filled with an unease that was twisting his insides until he wanted to scream. He had refused to assess the impact of the losses in his life but could no longer ignore the emptiness in his heart. His business was totally destroyed. Father Joe was gone. Steve Nader. Mack. What did remain was his life. And Grace.

Twenty-Six

Over the coming days

The mood of Texas City transformed from fear and hysteria to sorrow. The search for hundreds of missing people continued, while rescue crews became recovery teams. With critical decisions under control on the docks, Texas City began to bury its dead.

Lines of ambulances and emergency vehicles were replaced by scores of hearses that transported the dead to cemeteries. Grief pressed its weight over the entire town, as everyone beneath it struggled to breathe. Churches filled with caskets and eulogies. As soon as bearers wheeled out one casket, another rolled its way down the aisle in a marathon of burials that brought a painful closure to the survivors. For people waiting to hear news about those still missing, incessant anxiety and irrational hope remained.

Gradually the time of funerals in Texas City eased and the mood shifted once more. Grief remained but was masked by hard work and attention to the details of recovery. Building materials poured into the town. Steel workers and carpenters came from surrounding towns to rebuild industries and repair damaged homes. Volunteer glaziers replaced shattered glass. Buildings were pieced back together with bricks and mortar. Businesses reopened. Residents filtered back to their homes, with new roofs, doors and windows occupying their minds. Those whose houses were totally destroyed sought temporary shelter.

Grace and Louis met Father Joe's brother who had come to

take his body back to Philadelphia. They expressed the gratitude and love they had for Father Joe in their own ways. They shared tears and said their painful goodbyes.

Funerals and volunteering had filled the days for Grace and Louis. Exhaustion from their recovery tasks kept them from seeing much of each other. Grace was working with the substitute priest, although she still had to rewind every time he walked through the door and she realized once again that he was not Father Joe. She also continued to volunteer at the clinic.

Greta had stayed in Houston to delay Michael's return for as long as possible. Louis spent long hours at City Hall organizing work forces for new recovery projects that were begun every day. Neither Louis nor Grace had time to think about what the future held for them, either separately or together.

Eventually, they felt strong enough to reach out to each other and begin to meet at Louis' kitchen table and talk in the evening. Or they walked along the bay shore at the end of the day. A trust built between them. Whatever guile that had existed had burned away in the tragedy. Their individual needs for support in rebuilding their lives pulled them closer.

Grace reconnected with that part of herself that had been secreted away. She enjoyed the breeze off the bay that fluttered against her face on their evening walks. She noticed the sunrise. Her body and spirit revived from their coma, and she reveled in sensations: the taste of food, a hot shower, a flight of cowbirds in the fields. She learned to laugh again in between the moments of sorrow and grief.

She told Louis about Chicago and her life as a singer. "I wanted to be famous," she admitted. She told him everything: the addiction, the dissipation, the misery that replaced her dream. She told him about her baby and about prison, and about how at times she had wanted to die.

They sat together in the kitchen, as Louis had once sat alone in the shadows of the hall light.

"As a young girl, I loved life. I needed only air to be happy. Playing the piano and singing excited me every day. But I lost that. I lost sight of my values and felt sorry for myself because I was rejected by the big bands. I made bad choices and blamed the world for my actions. I didn't know how important the choices we make are. It's always about choices, though, isn't it, Louis? I didn't understand that."

Louis studied her face. She looked like a beautiful, ceramic doll. "I don't know how you survived. Where did you find the strength to pick up so many pieces and put them back together?"

Grace shrugged. "I think I was too afraid to die, even though I wanted to. And I never did pick up the pieces. I learned to exist in a limited space and walked a thin line. Shame enslaved me."

She took Louis' hand in hers and kissed his palm. She held it to her cheek. Tears filled her eyes. They sat in a close and companionable silence.

Most of the search and rescue teams had departed, leaving recovery teams to search for bodies. Clean-up crews had cleared the docks enough for Louis to return to his destroyed office. The explosion of the *High Flyer* leveled what had remained of the dock area after the *Grandcamp* had begun the destruction.

Beyond the row of destroyed warehouses, lay a mangled mass of boxcars and locomotives, one on top of the other. Oil storage tanks in the field close to Louis' office lay smashed, their sides and tops collapsed into charred scrap metal. The Terminal Railway Company, the docks, and the chemical company adjacent to the port resembled Hiroshima in its total destruction. Only ghostly pilings of wood and twisted steel stood above ground.

Dock Road, which had been white shells, wore a sticky coat of black oil and sludge. The calm, green water of Galveston Bay washed the apron of a waterfront wasteland. Only the refineries to the west remained intact and continued to process oil, albeit at a reduced rate.

Louis sifted through the remains of his office and found, to his amazement, the display case of marlin spikes unscathed. He set the wooden case with its glass top into the trunk of his car. He thought of Alcid and the fact that this collection was the only remaining link to his father's legacy. With his business gone and his town on life support, Louis experienced an icy loneliness so deep he could hardly breathe.

The carnage on the docks ambushed him. It became too much to bear and he turned his thoughts to Grace. She had returned to her apartment and reunited with Greta and Michael. Louis acknowledged how much her presence had carried him through those early dark days and how lost he would be without her.

He walked out of the office and left the docks behind him. The rumble of steam shovels and dozers faded as he drove away. Seeing the office had reminded Louis about Mack. He had not been found and Louis began to accept the inevitable. He could rebuild the warehouse, but Mack could never be replaced.

Outside the gate, he passed Demetrios' Cafe, now a jumble of spiky sticks on the ground. Demetrios had traveled back to New York, grateful to be alive. He did not know when he would return, if ever. Louis smiled as he recalled the night Father Joe had danced with the waiters and sailors, and remembered the pure joy on the priest's face, like nothing else existed in the world.

Many houses on either side of Main Street had been flattened. "Lola's Place" lay in a heap, leveled to its concrete blocks. He wondered what had happened to the women who had worked there. Did they survive?

He thought about the Rice Hotel and how he had often fled there in an effort to find an antithetical world, unreal as it might have been. Grace had changed that. He no longer sought solace in such pretense.

Louis headed home, then impulsively made a U-turn and drove toward Galveston. He needed respite from the broken town. Death filled his awareness and left him discordant, no longer able to abide its assault. He needed relief from the constant images and the painful truth of what had happened.

After crossing the causeway bridge, the new Chrysler, which Louis had hastily bought off the dealer's ravaged showroom floor, rolled along Broadway, across Seawall Boulevard and directly onto the sand of East Beach. At the jetty that formed the entrance to the ship channel, he parked and walked along the water's edge.

Clothed in a new awareness of his world, he saw the columnar clouds that rose like stone monoliths above the Gulf and felt the salty air that hung over the sand on East Beach. He watched ships ply their way up the channel from the Gulf to Houston's port, doing business as usual. Children close by built castles in the sand and frolicked in the waves. Louis knew that people in other towns and cities went to movies, shopped downtown in department stores, or sat in their living rooms listening to radios. Families gathered together for a meal after a day of work or school and engaged in mundane chatter. Or they visited museums, staring in awe at beautiful paintings. They fell in love and rode bicycles. Jackie played baseball with the Dodgers in Brooklyn, New York. Life ventured forth, habitual and normal while Texas City smoldered in ruins.

He thought about how the great Earth revolved on its path around the sun, oblivious to pain and death. The universe, with its planets and galaxies, continued to expand. Texas City commanded headlines across the country, and people responded with compassion and support, but beyond the ravaged town, the story inherent in being human continued.

People outside the bounds of tragedy remained untouched, undiminished by the pain, unaware that they had missed the implacable reaper, and never acknowledged their good fortune.

Louis imagined an imperceptible timer dictating a time to live, a time to die, a time for all things under the sun. Catastrophes like this occurred in isolated zones. Those outside of them remarked about the misfortune but soon looked away, not wanting to be ensnared in the awful agony of the experience.

He walked the beach as his thoughts continued in a solemn direction. Nearby, seagulls took flight and landed with weightless ease further down the sand. The briny Gulf rushed to shore as it had for millions of years. He wished a great flood would come and wash away the ruin that was Texas City, leaving a clean, bright landscape behind it. He needed Noah's flood to wipe away the torment and provide a new beginning.

A flock of pelicans passed above him in their silent glide, peaceful and effortless in their journey. They moved in an undeniable rhythm. Louis saw in their flight that all life, no matter what its experience, holds on fiercely. "Sanctus, sanctus, sanctus," Louis whispered to the pelicans.

"Life produces life," Louis spoke into the wind, repeating Father Joe's favorite aphorism. "All of life is holy, even the sorrow. Life is a drama with a script that is oblivious to the ending."

I can't go back to my old self, he thought. This agony has stripped me bare, exposed me to the reality of my life. What was I thinking, living such a life? Who am I but a cynical drifter blaming the world?

The sound of the tumbling waves brought Louis out of his reverie and a sense of relief spread over him. He questioned how the voracious rage of death that rampaged through the docks had missed him as he stood just on the other side of its invisible boundary. Why did it not reach across and take me, he asked. Maybe I just got lucky. Maybe I was chosen to survive. Whatever the case of my survival, I know that I have another chance to figure things out, to get life right.

He took a deep, cleansing breath. He understood now that he exercised no control over his death. It would come in whatever time, in whatever form, but it *would* come. Every living thing dies. But life! Life presented a different set of options. He could and would determine how to *live*. He was the captain of whatever his fate would be. He would raise it out of the ashes.

He had glimpsed through the thin veil that separated the dead and the living: He had stood so close to Death that the memory of its face would never again allow him to be rudderless. It wrenched open an unconscious part of his mind that he had not known existed.

He stopped and watched another flock of pelicans fly overhead. He addressed them out loud. "Father Joe tried to teach me that I can't live in the past. I can't stand with a pat hand, either. Whatever that vital force that guided Father Joe was, I want it."

Pointing his finger at the birds he continued, "I can tell you, pelicans, I am going to pursue life, not hide from it. I will listen to what is defined in my heart by Father Joe's 'inscrutable' force."

Louis finished his "soliloquy on the beach" and his spirit rose. He looked at the quizzical faces of the children nearby, their task of castle building suspended by this odd man talking to himself on the beach.

"You kids have some fun, now. Life is short," he said as he passed by and headed for his car.

On his way off Galveston Island, Louis stopped by the wharves to buy fresh shrimp and crabs from a fishing trawler. He met Grace at the church office and drove her home with him. The time had come for them to put the explosion and its devastation aside for a while.

"I am going to introduce you to one of the finer things in life – Cajun cooking. We will fatten you up with some great food. I know the town is grieving and that will continue for a long time. But tonight, we are going to celebrate being alive."

He started with gumbo. Bits of onion flew off the chopping block and into the pot to create the holy trinity with celery and green peppers. He started the roux and stirred it until a chocolate brown mixture glistened in the pan. Between sips of bourbon, he mixed herbs for a large pot of jambalaya.

"My mother used to say that jambalaya is not a meal, it is an event!"

He found a radio station playing music and hummed along as Sarah Vaughn sang "That Sunday Afternoon." He stirred the pot of jambalaya to mix the rice, spices, seafood and sausage into an aromatic concoction.

The feast began with gleaming chunks of boiled crab meat from claws cracked open and dipped in a spicy red sauce. They cracked open the claws with mallets, laughed when droplets of crab boil splashed on each other. Next came boiled shrimp dipped into red sauce strong with horseradish, lemon juice and cayenne. Spicy gumbo with New Orleans-style French bread followed. And the jambalaya came last. Cold beer chased it all down. The tabasco and cayenne brought a flush to their faces.

Images of the docks and the hospital left their minds and laughter filled the void. Beer enhanced the rich flavors of the Gulf's bounty. This repast loosened the chokehold of gloom. They relished the hot spices on the backs of their tongues. They ate and laughed. The sadness seemed to cut less deep as healing began to build. They knew in time that they would recover and that happiness and sadness could exist together. They could move on and formulate the future.

They cleared and cleaned the kitchen, sated with the feast. No emergency sirens or dire warnings about calamities interrupted the welcome quiet. The radio played softly in the background while Louis washed and Grace dried the dishes.

As they finished, Louis turned to Grace and kissed her. She kissed him back, put her arms under his and held him tightly to her. In the muted light of the kitchen, Louis began to dance with her in slow easy steps, a little awkward at first. Soon, they melted into a smooth rhythm with the music, swaying and turning, holding tightly to each other.

Louis raised his eyes to the ceiling. "I'm dancing, Demetrios. I'm dancing."

The following week, Louis arrived at Grace's apartment midmorning to accompany her to a memorial service organized for the town by Texas City Ministerial Alliance at the high school football stadium. In spite of the somber anticipation of this event, Louis bounded up the stairs full of energy.

"I have great news!" Louis was ebullient, unable to contain his excitement, as she opened the door to him. "Mack is alive! I received a message from the Red Cross this morning when I went by City Hall. He is in the VA Hospital in Houston. The second explosion almost got him. He was in a coma and had no identification with him, so no one knew who he was."

"How is he now? Is he alright?"

"He is going to be okay. He has a broken leg. Femur, I think the note said. He had a ruptured spleen, a concussion, broken ear drum and lots of cuts and bruises. But he is going to be okay. I am so happy to find him. They said all he asked for when he woke up was to find his motorcycle."

"Oh Louis, what great news! I'm very happy for him, and for you."

Their mood became subdued as they arrived alongside hundreds of other people filling the stadium with cheerless faces. They sought a place of refuge to lay their grief, to grapple with the enormity of the events that had disrupted every facet of their lives. Sadness muted the crowd.

Many men wore suits and fedoras. Others came dressed in jeans, tee shirts or blue denim work shirts. Some women wore cotton dresses, others dressed as they would for Sunday church with high heels and hats in place. Families came together, the children uneasy in the solemnity.

A large cross fashioned from white roses hung from the top tier of the stadium down to the ground. Thousands of floral arrangements with every flower in season surrounded a podium that straddled the 50-yard line. A kaleidoscope of colors greeted mourners as they found seats in dignified quiet. Black, white and brown people gathered next to them - all united as one.

Ministers from seven churches officiated. They struggled to find words of comfort for grief of such magnitude. As the final speaker bowed his head to complete the service with a prayer, Louis felt the Black man next to him take his hand. He turned to see him with his head down. Grace took the hand of a Mexican woman next to her. Greta, George and Michael stood in the row in front of them. A young Black girl about Michael's age stood next to him. They looked at each other a little hesitantly. She smiled a shy smile and took his hand. Michael glanced up at his mother and shrugged his shoulders. He looked back at the girl. "Okay," he said and bowed his head.

Louis recognized Clayton, the man adjacent to the girl, as the one who had lifted the beam from his leg and helped with so many rescues. For a brief moment their eyes met again. Louis hoped all the gratitude that he carried in his heart passed through that glance. He saw strength and confidence in the other man's eyes. Grace nodded at Clayton, smiled and leaned forward to hug him.

Everyone grasped the hand of the person next to them. Black, white and brown people gathered next to them - all united as one. The minister prayed and a palpable spirit of community spread over the stadium. Louis felt it surge through him, knowing at that moment that Texas City would rise from the ashes of this catastrophe. These people, together, held the toughness, the perseverance and the willingness to overcome all obstacles in resurrecting their hometown. They would be the phoenix on behalf of all those who had died.

Louis exchanged glances with Grace and knew that she felt it as well. Hope surged and embraced the entire stadium. It seemed so real as it moved through the crowd that Louis expected to see a majestic angel, with wings spread wide, hovering above them.

Louis squeezed Grace's hand. He would go forward with her, be in her life. He would never leave her behind. They would grow together and build their future. He experienced what he had searched for all of his life. Peace came over him.

Twenty-Seven

Thursday, May 8, 1947

Grace sat at the kitchen table with Greta, talking and finishing their coffee after breakfast. Michael burst in through the back door and ran to his mother's side. He held tightly to her with his head buried in her waist. "What's that siren for?"

Greta held him close and looked around the room. She heard the siren. "It's okay, honey. It must be a small fire somewhere in an old warehouse or something. It's nothing to worry about. We're not going to have any more big booms. Just small fires sometimes. I promise."

Michael had been on the roof with his father when he heard the siren. A small plume of smoke could be seen to the south. He had bolted down the ladder and hurried inside. George came down from the roof and followed him into the kitchen, tousling his son's hair as he held tightly to Greta.

"You okay, buddy? It's just a small fire on the docks. I think they're roasting hot dogs or something down there. We can finish up on the roof tomorrow. No need to go back up there today. Thanks for helping me."

Michael relaxed his grip and turned toward George. "They're not roasting hot dogs."

"You never know what those crazy guys will do." George mocked a serious look and nodded his head affirmatively.

Greta cleared the table and put dishes in the sink. She wore a faded baby doll house dress, which matched her tired face. Michael drifted off to his room.

"Michael doesn't talk about the explosion, but he is nervous about it. I guess we are all still a bit tense. I feel bad for him. They have closed the schools until next fall. He misses his schoolmates."

Grace glanced around the house at the myriad tasks that still awaited attention. Not only repairs, but normal things like a basket of clothes to be washed and ironed, and vegetables in a bowl to be prepared for supper later that day.

"I don't know how you get everything done, Greta. It wears me out to watch it all. Not to mention taking care of Michael and George. How do you think Michael is doing, really?"

"Well, if he were an adult, I would say his nerves are shot. He still gets upset at any loud noises, any sirens. I know he worries all the time. It will take a while for him to let it go."

"I am sure he will be okay," Grace said. "At least you are all safe."

They had not spent much time together since the explosions and not had time to talk. Grace quietly shared, "I've been playing the piano again recently."

"Really? Seriously playing?"

"Yes, seriously. I was amazed at my memory." Grace described her first effort at the piano. "I had not played Beethoven for such a long time. I found it cathartic. Mother would have been happy for me. When I'm not busy, I think about playing more often now."

"Do you think about Chicago, too?"

"I suppose I do. My whole life has been turned upside down, just like everyone else. But for the first time since I came here, I can think about a future without my past dictating my decisions. Seeing all those people fighting for their lives made me realize that I had to fight for mine. I realized that I was the fortunate one to still be alive. Life suddenly became precious, not a thing to apologize for. Seeing patients' lives slowly drain away while they clung to every last breath made me ashamed of how I viewed my own life.

"The time for remorse is over. Father Joe told me that a mistake doesn't carry a life sentence. I know now what he meant. I'm not cavalier about it: Ghosts will always remain, but I feel stronger and more confident in my choices. I can be sad for what happened and happy that I am alive at the same time. What I do now will be filled with gratitude for my life.

"I'm okay for now because there is so much to do. I can't continue to work at the church long term, not without Father Joe. Right now, I have a purpose. I talk to parishioners to find out what they need. They give me information to make funeral arrangements. I scan rosters from the church. Louis gets me a list of the known deceased from City Hall. I'm in charge of arrangements for the funerals and I work with the funeral directors from here as well as those out of town. Not an easy task, but it's rewarding to be able to help people. After all of this is over… I don't know…. That reminds me, I had better get on to work."

"What about Louis? Do you love him?"

Grace stared at Greta, perplexed. She had not spent time sorting and categorizing her emotions toward Louis. Greta made it sound like a step that should have been made, something already decided. The question confused her.

"I don't know the answer to that. Louis and I have supported each other through a very difficult time. I love what he has done for my confidence. He has given me a sense of who I can be again.

I think love paints its own landscape. That picture is not yet complete. I don't know…. Maybe I have just avoided the question."

"Maybe you could just settle down here and raise a family, forget about Chicago altogether."

Grace thought about Greta's life, about Michael and about someday having her own child. "Love? Right now, I don't know. I think I am confused by loyalty and obligation, by love and my own ambition."

She abruptly changed the subject. "I'm sorry, but I have to get to the church. I have to go, Greta. We'll talk about this another time. Thank you for everything you have done for me. No one could ask for a greater sister or friend."

Grace went over her conversation with Greta as she walked to the church. It angered her slightly that Greta had asked the question. But it did force Grace to look at that part of the equation. She wondered if she was being unfair to Louis. Had she taken advantage of the comfort he had offered? It had all happened so quickly. It was true she had not given enough thought to his feelings and his ideas about their future. Their romance had grown suddenly out of a cataclysmic desperation that had changed her almost overnight. Their circumstances held no semblance of a usual courtship. She knew she appreciated Louis. But was this enough to base a future on?

Grace debated the question about love in her mind and acknowledged that she had no idea how she honestly felt about him. The circumstances had not only enabled her feelings for Louis but had also brought acceptance of emotions that she had shelved for a long time out of fear and shame. Could this be sufficient for her to stay in Texas City? To settle down and become a housewife? Raise a family?

She remembered how music had conquered her heart so long ago. Father Joe had told her that day in the office that she had to return to the music where her life had begun. But that music called her back to Chicago. Could she go back there? Should she go back? The risk of being pulled back into the nightlife brought a new apprehension.

Louis could give her the love she needed. He could provide stability, comfort and security. But that would not help her solve the problems she had left in Chicago. It would not take her back to the music where it all began. It would not make peace with that part of her that had drawn her to Chicago in the first place.

In an instant, she knew - in that secret, all-knowing place in her heart - that she could not stay in Texas City. Small-town life complemented Greta, but it did not fit her. In the end, staying would destroy her love for Louis.

Grace thought about Greta's question. Love? Yes, I do love Louis, she thought. But I'm not right for him. Our worlds are too far apart.

Grace realized that she had made her decision. She hated what it would do to Louis. He would be devastated and he deserved better. She knew it would be best for her and – in the long run – best for him. That knowledge did not make her task easier.

Late that afternoon Grace watched Greta cook. She quietly and pensively said to her sister, "I'm going back to Chicago."

Greta stopped and stared down at the counter. "I don't think you should go. I don't want you to go. It is too dangerous for you. Too many bad things happened there."

"I appreciate your feelings, Greta, and I love you because of that. But I am stronger now. My life has been transformed by the tragedy of Texas City. Father Joe. And Louis. And you, Greta. You started it. You made it all possible."

Greta stirred her casserole thoughtfully. "Both choices have risks, I suppose." She turned to look at Grace. "You do have to follow your heart. I know that wanting you to stay here is selfish. But I don't want you to go. We lost each other for so long. We're just getting to the best part. Can't you give it a while longer?"

"No. That is the bitter part of it. Leaving you. And Louis. And Michael. You have been so good to me. I can't explain it. I am excited about music and life again. I have new ideas, a chance to begin a new path, and I know it's right. If I don't go now, I may not be able to go later. I can always come back, Greta. But I will not always have this moment, this time to complete the picture. If Chicago fails this time, I will know that I have tried."

After supper, Grace walked to Louis' house. It gave her time to sort through how to tell him of her feelings. As she walked in the fading light, she heard saws ripping boards and hammers pounding nails. Restoration of the damage to Texas City had escalated to a new level. More people had returned home. Volunteers had arrived in droves, energized to rebuild and contribute to the vibrant new buzz of a town once near death. Part of her felt that same way about the decision to return to her music. Unfortunately, Louis complicated that determination.

Louis met her at the door. "Grace! You will never guess what just happened. I met Frank Sinatra!"

"Frank Sinatra. Really?"

"At City Hall. He and Phil Harris and some other entertainers are in town. They are with the mayor to discuss plans for a fundraiser in Galveston."

Grace remembered meeting Frank Sinatra in Chicago early in her – and his – career. She loved his style and copied some of it in phrasing her lyrics.

"Grace? What are you doing here? Is something wrong?"

"I need to talk to you," she offered, very quietly.

Louis caught the edge in her voice. A mild panic stirred in his stomach. "Come in, sit down."

Grace fumbled with her purse. The image of stepping off the train to meet Greta in Galveston swept over her. Her voice now trembled with the torrent of emotions. "I've made a decision, Louis, to go back to Chicago."

"What! For how long? How long are you talking about?"

Grace did not answer. Rather, she remained stoic, unable to find the right words even though she had thought herself prepared. She resisted the urge to make it easy and assuage his feelings with equivocation.

"If you need to go for a while, I understand. You're coming back though, right? Grace, I love you. We're going to make our future together.... Grace?"

"I love you, too, Louis. It's a beautiful feeling." Grace closed her eyes for a moment before taking a breath and continuing.

"I have lived my entire life so far as a child, Louis, refusing to be an adult. I've been foolish, unaware and oblivious. Really. The result was that I arrived here crushed by my personal tragedy.

"But the horror in Texas City wrenched me awake. I am no longer my beginning, no longer my mother and father's little girl. A new 'me' emerged from this horrible disaster that we have been through. I can no longer be a child. Part of me would love to stay here with you. But I can't."

Louis began to plead. "You can't leave. We have a second

chance. I could be dead, like Father Joe or Steve, or hundreds of others. You're a new person. I am, too. We have all been changed."

"All the more reason for me to leave," she patiently continued. "I would not be good for you. You have had your epiphany and I have had mine. I know what I want and I cannot live in Texas City. If I stayed, I would give up my dream.

"As much as I love Greta, I'm not her. Raising a family, cleaning floors, cooking…. I could not live that life. In time, I would blame you. I'm sorry, Louis. I'm a city girl and my music has become vital to me again. Music will always come first. You deserve better than that."

He was now close to panic. "Do you want to sing again? You can do that right here, in Galveston, at the Balinese Room. Big stars perform there. You could start your career over right here."

"It's not just about singing, Louis. It's about closing the circle on a part of my life. If I don't go, it will always be unfinished. You gave me the courage to make this decision."

"I could go with you," he pleaded.

Grace placed her hand over Louis' mouth. "We have created a beautiful memory here and I will never forget it. I must go back to Chicago. I must do this on my own. Please. Don't make it any harder than it already is for me."

Twenty-Eight

Wednesday, May 14, 1947

In the beginning, Greta and Louis allied with each other in an effort to change Grace's mind about leaving. This morning, he greeted Greta at her house with a hug and a face full of desperation.

Greta, however, now resolved and calm, contradicted her earlier attempts to dissuade Grace from returning to Chicago. She now wanted only to be a positive force, to instill confidence in her sister's decision to leave while hiding her sorrow. Louis had offered to drive Grace to the train station in Galveston, but he was not ready to give up the fight.

Grace and Michael said their goodbyes as tears flowed. She promised Michael that he could visit her soon. He would love the tall buildings and they would take in a baseball game at Wrigley Field.

For Louis, it was his "last dance." His chances narrowed down to slim and none. They drove south down Main Street toward Galveston and the all-too-close destination, the train station.

Leaving Texas City, they passed the Greyhound Bus Station on the corner of Second Avenue. It had once been a tailor's shop where many pieces of clothing had been transformed to start new lives. Greyhound remodeled it with a ticket counter and a waiting room.

If Louis could have peered into its brightly lit interior, he would have seen Ella Mae in her white linen dress and pearls, sitting stoic and serene, Shana in her church dress, her eyes bright with excitement, and Clayton in a coffee-bean brown shirt and Levi's. Clayton sat straight in his chair, restlessly turning a twisted steel rivet from one of the exploded ships that he had found on the floor of his house. He carried it as a reminder of a life they would soon leave behind.

They all sat on a long wooden bench in the Colored section, each with a single suitcase. He stared at the dirty linoleum floor, following the intricate maze of intersecting geometric lines on its surface. Its pattern seemed to be chaotic, but after a long study it presented a sinuous path leading to a coherent center.

A sudden fear came over him. Was he doing the right thing, forcing his Momma and Shana to leave the only home they had known? But the fear lasted only a brief moment. He recalled the sign over their entrance to the bus station that said it all: "Coloreds." That presented his option. He had to trust that they would find "a coherent center" out west. It would take all the courage he could find.

There must be a reason he survived that terrific explosion, he thought. He glanced at Shana, her hair braided, her face shining with excitement and holding her stuffed puppy in her lap. A deep breath exhaled from his chest. He knew they would be alright.

Clayton had their tickets for Long Beach in his shirt pocket. Ella Mae had surrendered her position about not leaving Texas City and now felt excited to go, although she retained her disinterested demeanor. After all, she told herself, what she wanted most was for her children to be happy.

Shana, sad at first to be leaving her school friends, now dreamed of going to Hollywood. Clayton, the most excited, could hardly wait to get to California. He knew this move was right, that it would open up the world for him and Shana. Even his Momma would eventually embrace their new freedom.

They would find a home with green grass growing in the yard, and flowers, too. Shana would go to college. Maybe he could, too. They would all be *somebody* in California. They could dream big. In California, Clayton would no longer be an invisible man.

Leaving Texas City set him free from the oppression he had endured. He was excited for the future. Shana would see a larger world, full of possibilities, where she could express her true self. They would travel as the sun traveled, with it rising behind them on their journey to the west, and in time they would watch it setting on the horizon of the beautiful and powerful Pacific Ocean.

Clayton harbored only one regret. In order to get enough money for tickets all the way to Los Angeles, he had pawned his beloved saxophone in Galveston. The horn fortunately brought an appreciable sum since it was a Selmer Balanced Action saxophone – a top-of-the-line brand – made in Paris, France. When Shana saw they were leaving the house without his saxophone, she reminded him not to forget it. When Clayton told her what he had done, she cried. He hugged her and told her not to worry. "I will get another one in California. I never really owned that one anyway."

Louis took no notice of the Greyhound office as he drove past the white brick front with its newly installed plate-glass window. With Main Street in his rear-view mirror, Louis thought only of Grace's leaving.

He steered the car over the causeway where sunlight reflected off the wave tips and sparkled like diamonds in the choppy bay, just as Grace had seen them seven months ago on her arrival in Galveston. He wore his best dark suit with a sky-blue silk tie, thinking it might entice Grace to change her mind. But his heart felt heavy in his chest as he acknowledged there was little likelihood of that. No words came to either of them to break the silence.

He no longer tried to convince Grace to stay. She sat quietly, more beautiful than ever in her trim gray suit and white blouse. Tension and fear were no longer discernible around her mouth and eyes as it had been when they first met.

She stared into the water. They exchanged glances but neither knew how to breach the melancholic air between them. Grace knew her decision to be correct, but it did not lessen the sadness. For a brief moment, she wanted to tell Louis to pass the train station, to just take her to the beach and let her run barefoot through the surf.

Part of her yearned for Louis' touch and wanted to give in to her desire for him. The awakening of her body remained a wonderful gift from Louis. It had greatly influenced her move back to center and had empowered the woman in her. Those intimate times tugged at her heart and softened her decision. But she had the clarity to know that she did not love Louis as he did her. And he deserved more than she could give him.

It was complicated, she told herself. Her music would always come first. She calmed her mind with the thought that Louis would be alright, that he would find another woman more suitable for him, and that he would not be alone for long.

They passed through the tall station doors, purchased her ticket at a booth in the main concourse, and proceeded to the crowded platforms outside of the main building.

Grace held Louis' arm for the somber walk under the long canopies to her rail car. People hurried past them carrying suitcases and shopping bags. Well-dressed men in suits and ties, and ladies with stylish hats on their heads, hurried toward their trains. Porters pushed carts loaded with leather luggage and brocaded bags. A familiar mixture of steam and briny air swirled around them. Grace lingered close to Louis. He could see the longing in her eyes. For a moment, he thought she would change her mind and announce that she would not leave.

"Don't go."

"I must go."

"Are you coming back?"

"I don't know," Grace hesitated. "Someone once told me that life produces life. Right now, we have this moment."

A porter in a deep bass voice shouted, "ALL ABOARD!"

Louis, in a mangled imitation of Humphrey Bogart replied, "Well, here's looking at you, kid."

They kissed briefly and Grace hastened toward the Pullman.

"You have to come back!" he yelled at her, over the noise of the idling train engine. "You could still use a few pounds and some sunshine!"

Looking out of the large Super Chief window, she forced a small smile to acknowledge his attempt at humor, as the Pullman rolled onto the open track. He stood in the crowd, feeling alone, as her train gathered speed and became smaller and smaller, until he could no longer see it.

But he saw her face – that beautiful, haunting face – etched in his mind. Sadness for himself and happiness for Grace's recovery flowed together. Unable or unwilling to move, he fought the urge to cry and just stared at the speck that had once been a train, that had once been Grace, that had once been his hope.

He left the station and stood on the curb, train whistles echoing in his ears. Cars sped past in the street. Two elderly ladies stepped out of a cab, tenuous as they waited for the driver to hand their bags to a porter. They cautiously moved toward the station.

The earth continued to rotate around the sun. The Milky Way still flowed. Stars still gleamed in the heavens. The Universe continued its sprint into the void.

Twenty-Nine

Sunday, April 16, 1967

When Grace returned to Chicago, she began the habit of keeping a diary. Initially, it was a large part of the process of reconciliation of all she had experienced since she had first come to Chicago. Later, it allowed her to organize her thoughts and mull through the frequent variation in emotions that occupied her mind.

Through the past 20 years, her writing had undergone many changes, from diary to journal and, ultimately, to a sort of memoir. Today marked the 20th anniversary of the Texas City explosion that began her new life's journey. She awoke in a pensive mood and immediately opened her diary when she realized the date.

Dear Diary,

I read recently, I can't remember where, that the earth moves 1,000 miles an hour at the equator as it rotates. That seems impossible to believe. I don't feel any movement. But when I awoke this morning, I could believe it because it seems like my life has flown by that fast. Today is the 20th anniversary of that awful explosion. I am sure that Greta and George will be at the memorial service. They go every year and I'm glad they do.

So much has changed in my life since that day. "Life, Love and All That Jazz," the one-woman show that I wrote, came out of my experiences before and after that disaster. Was it 10 or 12 years ago that I wrote the dialogue – as well as the music – for the show? That show eventually brought me to New York. I loved being on Broadway, although the difficulties of doing a one-woman show exhausted me. I had never thought that I would pack my bags and move to the Big Apple, much less stay here. But here I stayed. Now the papers call me a "cabaret singer." So many memories.

As strange as it may seem, April 16th is like a birthday to me, a date I will never forget. It is bittersweet that I found my redemption through so much destruction, pain and loss. I never forget the day or those people close to me at that time. Memories of that trauma will never be erased. But I have moved on, even while carrying the scars of my past.

So much has changed over the years. Poor Louis. I received letters from him for a while. He told me that the tragedy of that day had changed him, too. The counseling sessions he had shared with Father Joe held fast, and his confidence in making his own decisions kept growing stronger. Over time, the shadow of his father hovering over his shoulder had almost disappeared. It's just a little ghost now, like Casper, he joked in one letter.

His close brush with death strengthened him. I think he almost felt invincible after that. After finding Mack Hale alive, he brought him in as a partner and together they rebuilt Tiger Ship Chandlers. Partnership with Mack, whom he trusted implicitly, allowed him to relax and have more time for himself. He bought a big sailboat, 40 feet long, I think. He said he could sail it around the world if he wanted. He named it Grace, *written in large letters across the stern. He said, bragging just a little I think, that he sailed her in competitions and often won. It seems that he was able to achieve his dream of being the captain of his own ship after all.*

It still makes me sad to think of him possibly carrying a torch for me. I prayed that he would have moved on from that time. Maybe he had because his letters sounded confident and upbeat. He worked hard on changing the safety regulations at the docks and led the committee to annex the industrial complex. He was able to accomplish a great deal to protect the people who work and live near the port.

His life appeared to be blooming. And then a letter from Greta a few years ago told me of his untimely death from a massive heart attack. Perhaps struggling against his invisible father for so many years took its toll after all. Too young, too young. I think of him often.

My sweet Father Joe. Such a tragedy that he died in that explosion of the High Flyer. I owed him so much. He truly saved my life. He told me early on that I had to return to the music. I rejected that at the time, but he was right. He was so wise and could see the future for me much better than I could. He knew that music contained all of the experiences that needed to be revisited and acknowledged in order for me to heal. I had to say "yes" to the music. I guess I could say I had to "face the music." He was a blessing to all who knew and loved him.

Returning to Chicago opened the door for me and, with a lot of hard work, my previous shame and doubt receded and my courage grew. No longer shuttered in shame, I slowly regained confidence. Eventually, I found my long-dormant creativity and it led to new songs and stories. From the core of that material, I was able to write the show that brought me to Broadway. I guess I could say that now I am "a star." But that star has been forged with enough pain to keep it well grounded. And I know that Father Joe was the beginning of my success. He led me back to my core, to the things that I love.

I am also thinking of my friendship with Clayton Malveaux on this day. I was so happy to get his letter a couple of years ago. I still don't know how he found me. It must have been through one of those trade magazines. It was a wonderful long and newsy letter. A love story really, and a good one.

Clayton had initially found work on the docks in Long Beach, as he had hoped. He also found more equality because most of the discrimination in California targeted the Chinese. "Mongolians," they were called. He left the onerous Jim Crow laws of the South behind.

Because he was smart and hardworking, he became a foreman and soon went to work for the longshoremen's union. After a few years, he enrolled at Long Beach State College and earned a degree in Management. He now works as a negotiator for labor and management disputes. People listen to him and respect him. It is all he ever really wanted. I am so very happy for him.

Arnett Cobb is still his hero, but he says he no longer needs "to be" Arnett Cobb. He still plays the saxophone, occasionally joining in on jam sessions at a local club. He bought a house and his Momma lived long enough to see the bright green lawn growing right up to the sidewalk. Together they planted flowers in neat beds fronting the house.

I could almost feel the pride seeping through the pages of his letter as he told me about his little sister Shana. Not so little anymore. She began to attend an integrated school immediately on their arrival in California. That in itself opened new worlds to her. Clayton said that in high school she came to him and thanked him for all of those private tutoring lessons he made her endure.

She graduated from college and then law school and now works for a firm in San Francisco that specializes in immigration law. Many of her clients are recipients of discrimination because of their skin color. She definitely has a clear understanding of that problem. Wow.

Yes, moving to California was a good decision for Clayton. He told me that the founder of the law firm had great praise for Shana. "She is smart and afraid of nothing. She is a high-profile member of our firm." Clayton is so happy for her.

He also had a P.S. at the end of his letter. It read: "P.S. There is racism everywhere, even in California. After seeing the persecution of the Mongolians, I no longer believe it is just about me. And maybe I *understand it a little."*

I am still grateful to Arnett Cobb. He gave Clayton a sense of worth as a man that has stayed with him and grown through the years. Clayton's experiences in California validated it. That may be all he needs to know.

Fortunately, this anniversary comes around in springtime. Seeing the blossoms and leaves bursting forth always reminds me of renewal. I appreciate having the opportunity and ability to start over. I often think of seeing the pelicans flying along the beach in Galveston. They are a great symbol to me of the freedom I have found. In spite of their awkward appearance, their flight appears to be effortless. They innately know they are beautiful. I am also grateful that something inside of me made me afraid to die. I could not have articulated it, but in a tiny corner of my soul I knew that the best was yet to come. Father Joe knew it. What he had, he gave to me, and I am forever grateful.

Well, the dogs are sitting next to me and staring with those question-mark faces that I love to see. It is time for their walk. And it is a beautiful spring day. So, I'll talk to you tomorrow, Dear Diary.

Grace stood up to leave the room, but decided to sit at her piano for a moment's memory. She ran a few quiet chords and then began to sing.

"Swing low sweet chariot, coming for to carry me home.
I looked over Jordan and what did I see?
A band of angels coming after me, coming for to carry me home."

Epilogue

The Day My Bicycle Died
by Carl Trepagnier

As a nine-year-old boy, my proudest possession was my bicycle, with its mock gas tank and built-in horn, a second-hand Schwinn that Dad had painted silver and blue. I loved that bike because it allowed me to roam all over town. Whether delivering papers, running errands or just exploring, it carried me on countless adventures.

I could ride from Third Avenue in Texas City where we lived, follow the seawall on Bay Street all the way to Nineteenth Avenue, the northern boundary of our town, cross over to Sixth Street, the main street through the town, and sail back to Third Avenue. This route encompassed about three-fourths of the town – and it was a great ride!

But I did not ride my bicycle on April 16, 1947.

That day began like any other at our small frame house, which was built on concrete blocks. Mother roused me out of bed and I prepared myself for school, oblivious to anything out of the ordinary. A mild cold front had passed during the night and created the perfect spring day.

The clock showed almost 8:00 am as I walked out the front door and caught my first glimpse of the smoke rolling into the sky down at the docks. I could see the smoke behind the Davis Mansion across the street, a three-story Victorian (Mother said) house. We called it the Davis Mansion because it was owned by Mr. Davis, and it was the biggest house we had ever seen. It was different from the clapboard wood-frame houses up and down both sides of Third Avenue, with its turreted third-floor room and its quirky architecture. It looked out of place, marking it as a point of constant curiosity. The kids in the neighborhood spoke of it in whispers and, of course, it gave birth to many tales of horrors and hauntings.

This morning, the Davis Mansion was the perfect centerpiece to the scene, silhouetted by a massive plume of smoke that rose half a mile behind its green presence. The smoke glowed a beautiful orange as it billowed up into a cloudless and brilliant blue sky. My older sisters, Phyllis and Gerry, already stood in the street watching the chaotic swirl of orange smoke rise as I joined them from the house.

A few neighbors had also gathered to gawk at the spectacle. We knew it was a fire down on the docks, but people were more curious than worried, as seeing smoke rise from the industrial area occasionally created no cause for alarm. However, this fire brought a special curiosity with it because of the vibrant and strange color. We all knew that, when a fire occurred, such as a lightning strike to an oil storage tank, it produced black smoke. This vibrant orange was different. It mesmerized us all.

I stood in the street and watched the fire, lingering a while before starting toward school. From the house behind us across the alley, Joel Watkins came and joined us. He and my sister Phyllis were both 14 years old and would not be going to school until that afternoon.

At the time, the growing industrial base of Texas City was expanding faster than the town could adapt. Consequently, schools suffered from a shortage of classroom space and we went to school in shifts. First through sixth grades attended in the morning, and junior high students in the afternoon. Phyllis and Joel, eighth graders, did not start until after lunch.

Dad, a shift worker, had not yet come home from his "graveyard shift," the midnight to 8:00 am work time that he thoroughly disliked. Mother worked taking care of us children and the home. This morning, she was in the kitchen getting breakfast for my sister Diane, just four years old.

I only had three blocks to walk to my school, Danforth Elementary, which was straight up Third Avenue to Fourth Street. Shortly after 8:00 am, Gerry, I and others who lived on the street, began our walk to school. I looked back over my shoulder at the flames that began from inside the roiling smoke. I turned both my body and my mind toward school.

Mostly I was looking for my fourth-grade teacher, Miss Jones, who rented a room in the Davis Mansion and who also often walked to school. She was my first love and anytime I could walk alongside her, it became a special day. But I did not see her this morning. I quickly arrived at the school and played on the tilt-a-whirl until the bell rang for class.

The fire continued to burn and I could hear the wail of sirens from the playground, but I ignored the commotion and thought little about it.

However, Phyllis and Joel were curious and decided to get a closer look at the fire. I am sure they did not tell Mother. If they did, they probably told her they would only be going down two blocks to the seawall at Bay Street. They grabbed my bicycle because it sat conveniently close. With Phyllis on the handlebars and Joel pumping the pedals, they went toward the docks and the fire. This distance only required a six-block ride to put Phyllis and Joel in the parking lot.

Very soon this naive pair of teenagers, enchanted by the fire and activity of the firefighters, made their way to within 200 yards of the burning ship. Phyllis still sat on the handlebars and Joel on the seat as he held the bike steady to watch. I am sure they were excited by the sirens and the men running back and forth, shouting and pointing at the fire on a ship at the docks, the *SS Grandcamp*.

I knew nothing of this until later, and innocently twirled on the tilt-a-whirl with my classmates on the school ground. At home, Mother puttered in the kitchen, caring for Diane and cleaning up from the breakfast she had prepared for Dad, who had arrived home at 8:30. Normally he would go to bed around 9:00 am. It was his routine to sleep for about five hours during the day. Today he delayed his rest to work on a leaky faucet in the bathroom.

The bell rang for class. I went to my second-floor schoolroom and began my day. By now, Mother had begun cooking for the noontime meal. Diane was playing with her dolls in the bedroom. Dad was working to replace the leaky sink washer. Gerry sat in a classroom like mine at the other end of the rectangular school building. Phyllis and Joel continued to stare mesmerized by the flames coming from the ship.

Our classroom was typical for the time. On the east side, facing toward the docks, metal-framed windows lined the wall. As we gathered in the room before the second bell, we moved to the windows to watch the smoke and fire. The south and west sides of the room were covered with blackboards. Over the blackboards on the west wall, small windows called transoms opened onto the hallway. Transoms are rectangular framed glass about two feet by three feet; they swivel and are set close to the ceiling. When open, they allow a flow of air through the room. Our building had no air conditioning, so we relied on the transoms in warm weather. On the other side of that wall our lockers lined the hallway.

The second bell marked the beginning of class. Miss Jones called us to our desks so she could start health class. For the most part, this consisted of lessons about good grooming. We needed to have our hair combed and faces washed. Our hands would be inspected for cleanliness, especially our fingernails. As Miss Jones walked slowly down the aisle checking each child, I held my hands out before me just off the top of my desk, happily waiting for her to reach me. The clock on the wall showed 9:12. I looked to my left toward the windows on the east side just before she reached my desk.

I'm not sure why I looked toward the windows. I don't recall hearing a sound or feeling percussion. But when I looked towards the windows, I saw a whiteness coming toward me. It came in slow motion and appeared to be water thrown violently from a bucket, separating into long droplets and flying horizontally just above the desktops. I saw the other children sitting at their desks, looking like human sculptures frozen in time. The whiteness cruelly became thousands of shards of glass racing toward us like rain riding on a hurricane wind. I instinctively turned away. I would later find the back of my head peppered with small fragments of glass.

Suddenly I was under my desk. Maybe I fell when I jerked away from the flying glass. Maybe a second blast threw me down. Then I heard the screaming. I looked up to see a frightening scene.

Miss Jones was pulling frantically at our classroom door to

get it open. Swirling dust filled the room and broken glass covered the floors. Behind Miss Jones, a mob of nine-year-olds was pushing against her, crying and screaming for their mothers. But the door had jammed shut from the force of the explosion and could not be opened. We were trapped in this box, not knowing what had happened, or whether it would happen again. I don't remember being scared, just kind of confused. At the same time, my family was experiencing the blast.

When the ship blew up, it threw my sister Phyllis and her friend Joel for some distance and rendered Joel unconscious. A large piece of metal from the ship sliced through my bicycle frame shortly after they had been tossed aside.

I don't know what kept Phyllis from panicking and running for home. She was 14 years old and dazed by the supersonic blast, which ruptured her eardrums. Fire and chaos roamed just beyond her and Joel. Thick black smoke surrounded them. People lay sprawled on the ground, some dead, some horribly mangled, but she would not leave Joel lying there. She dragged him to a nearby road. Moments later an old school bus that took men to work at one of the refineries came by and the driver helped them both inside. He then drove across town to Danforth Hospital on Ninth Avenue. Joel remained unconscious and barefoot, his high-top Converse tennis shoes blown off of his feet.

Mother rushed out of the kitchen looking for Diane. All of the windows of our house were imploded. The front door had been thrown across the living room and lay on the sofa bed where I slept at night. Our refrigerator had fallen on its side and now blocked the swinging door between the dining room and the kitchen. Rivets and large chunks of metal were raining down through the roof like hailstones. My Dad's bed was littered with jagged remains of two bedroom windows that could have done him great harm had he followed his usual routine of going to bed when he returned from his shift.

I suppose my Dad, being a refinery worker, had an idea of what had happened. His refinery trained its men for fires and mishaps. But nothing of this magnitude had ever confronted them. Both Mother and Dad panicked. They feared the refrigerator had fallen on Diane, but they found her in the living room. They stood bewildered and afraid, not knowing what to do next, whether to leave the house and look for their other children or to wait for us to come home. They had three children somewhere in the midst of whatever had just occurred.

Gerry ran out of her classroom and attempted to come down the hall to find me, but debris blocked her passage. She was able to leave the school building and headed for home. I remained trapped in my classroom with my classmates' screams and a haze of dust and debris hanging in the air.

When Gerry arrived at home, my parents were still there, and she told them that she couldn't find me. They had no idea where Phyllis could be and feared that she might be dead. They fled out the back door to the car and came looking for me. They could only anguish over Phyllis at that time, with no idea about where to search for her.

In my classroom of shrieking fourth graders and choking air, I could see that the door was not coming open. I grabbed a desk at the back of the room and pushed it against the wall lined with blackboards. Then I stacked another desk on top of that, leaning it against the blackboard. I climbed up on top of them to the nearest transom. I squirmed through the small window, knelt on the top of the lockers in the hallway and looked back into the room. My friend, Don Keegan, was climbing on the desks, too, so I reached back and extended my hand to him as he pulled his way through the transom. When I turned to look at the hallway from atop the lockers – where I perched like a bird – I could see crumbled walls and children and teachers scrambling in every direction.

Directly across from me was the split-level stairwell going down to the first floor. One series of stairs went halfway down then U-turned, and the next level ended at the first floor. Portions of the north wall above the stairs had fallen over the upper level of stairs. A teacher stood at the U-turn imploring the panicked students to go to the other end of the building to get downstairs.

I looked down that long hall, saw the mass of screaming confusion and decided I was taking the shortest route. I jumped down from the lockers, ran to the flat, broad banister of the staircase and slid down to the U-turn, ran past the frantic teacher yelling to go back, then down the next level of stairs and out of the building. I don't know how long it took for me to escape, but Gerry had gotten home before I left the school.

Outside, plumes of thick black smoke dominated the sky; the billowing smoke cradled flames that floated high into the air. Parents bolted out of cars, left the engines running with doors open, and wildly searched for the faces of their children. It was like looking at a disturbed anthill with parents, children and people from the neighborhood all dashing around in a frantic dance. I headed for home in a daze - in retrospect, I would call it shock. I walked like a zombie while the world exploded and burned around me.

At the corner of the school, I encountered Margo Vines, another fourth grader. She just stood there quietly crying, then turned toward me. She asked me with a bewildered voice, "Is my face bloody?" And it was. She was covered with blood running down from her scalp. I looked at her, pushed on past heading down Third Avenue to my house, and said over my shoulder, "Yes, it is," casually, like it was a normal occurrence.

Oil storage tanks were now exploding with loud thumps and with each explosion I could feel the heat on my face from the rising fireball. My whole body felt the percussion of the explosions.

I kept my eyes on the smoke and fire, which extended the entire length of the south edge of town, and I thought that my house, as well as the whole town, would be burned away.

As I walked up the sidewalk to our house, I could see the windows blown out and curtains hanging in disarray. A hole had been blown in a front wall, and the front door had been wrenched from its hinges and now lay on top of the sofa bed across the living room. I walked toward the kitchen.

In between explosions, it was quiet. I pushed against the kitchen door, but it would not budge, and my heart raced with the first recognition of fear. I pictured in my mind the door being blocked by the bodies of my family. I imagined my Dad lying dead behind the door and became aware of my deep fear. I turned back to the hallway and entered the kitchen through my parents' bedroom. The refrigerator had been knocked over and lay against the kitchen door, holding it shut. I searched each room and found no one in the house. I went into the back yard and looked up. All of the southern sky held the roiling, black smoke and leaping spurts of jittery flames. The storage tanks kept exploding and each time the fire swept upward more fiercely, more intensely. I felt the heat and again feared the whole town would burn to the earth, and it felt very close to me.

We had a small garage behind our house, adjacent to the alley that ran between the two rows of houses. As I walked toward the alley, moving instinctively away from the flames, I believed that the fire would get everything and decided that I should save something. With an action that showed my state of mind, I grabbed the garden hose and started dragging it down the alley on my way to the only place I knew to go, my friend Butch Chauvin's house. A large piece of steel stood embedded in the middle of the alley. I kicked it, thinking I could knock it over. It did not budge and the pain felt like it had broken my toe. I stopped dragging the hose.

Butch, my best friend and constant playmate, lived half a block away on the corner of Third Avenue and Second Street. During the summers, we spent every day together. His father worked at the Monsanto facility, which was at the heart of the explosion. He was a safety engineer and Butch knew his dad would be around the fire. As I came into his yard, Butch ran out the back door. He was crying and telling me that he thought his dad was dead. For the first time, I started crying, too.

Mrs. Chauvin and her brother rushed out of the house. They were frantic and sure that Mr. Chauvin could not have survived but hoped desperately that they were wrong. Butch and I stood in the middle of the yard, bawling and suddenly very aware of the possibility of real tragedy.

At that moment, I heard someone calling my name. I turned toward the street and there was my family, with my Mother screaming for me to hurry up and get into the car. I ran to the road, not saying a word, never looking back at Butch, and climbed in the back seat. I am not sure that Dad had completely stopped the car and I see myself now jumping through the open door with the car still rolling.

Mother, Dad, Gerry and Diane were in the car. Gerry had scurried home from school and, when I did not quickly arrive, they all came looking for me.

"Where is Phyllis," I asked.

"We don't know," Mom responded.

At some point, my parents had made the decision to get Gerry, Diane and me out of danger because they had no idea where Phyllis might be. I can now only imagine the difficulty of the decision to leave a child behind in order to get the rest of us out of harm's way.

The magnitude of the explosion and the resulting fires gave them great fear about where and when it might end. They acted first to save us, deciding to take us to Mother's Aunt Louisa Seale's house in La Marque, about ten miles west of Texas City.

Dad turned the car toward Ninth Avenue to leave town. In 1947, prairie filled the land west of Twenty-First Street. As our car crawled through the traffic jam on the two-lane road, I watched the flood of people, mostly Blacks, walking through that prairie with the fire in the background, now spreading from the docks along the industrial corridor.

I wondered where all those people would go. Would they walk to Houston, 60 miles away? I am sure now that most of them had no idea where they would go. They were fleeing the fire the only way they could and getting as far away as possible.

Aunt Louisa's home had not been damaged. She and Mother quickly made pallets of blankets on the floor and laid us down, trying to calm us. After a brief stay, Mother and Dad, sick with worry that Phyllis might be dead, prepared to return to Texas

City to search for her. When they started toward the front door, I had a meltdown and grabbed my mother, begging her not to go. Aunt Louisa held me and they hurriedly left. I was terrified and did not want them to go back into that fire.

In retrospect, it was an incredibly courageous act on their part. They had no idea what to expect. Fire raged out of control as it spread from one refinery to another. Of course, they had no choice and any parent would have done the same. Still, it was an act of heroism.

In a cruel bit of irony, as they stepped into the car to leave, a truck with a loudspeaker on top passed in front of Aunt Louisa's house. It blared the warning, "Open your windows and move away from them. We are expecting another explosion at any moment." I was sure my parents would be killed in the next explosion. This was my first instance of debilitating fear. I think I went into shock because I don't remember anything else about what happened until the following morning, April 17.

Because of the traffic and intermittent jams caused by the panic, it was close to noon when Mother and Dad drove back into Texas City. Ablaze with oil and chemical fires, many more small explosions continued to have their way with the entire complex.

Mother and Dad drove to our house first but did not find Phyllis. They may have gone inside to get any money or important papers that had been left, but they did not tarry long. They drove to Danforth Hospital and discovered that Phyllis and Joel had been there. Joel had been transferred to John Sealy Hospital in Galveston. Phyllis was ambulatory with no visible wounds, so the hospital personnel had told her to go home. It is incredible that they would just turn her loose, an obviously dazed 14-year-old, with the instruction to just go home in the middle of a continuing disaster. But the staff at this tiny hospital struggled with an enormous task and was totally inadequate and unprepared to handle the influx of serious injuries.

Phyllis had started home, walking down Main (aka Sixth Street). This meant that she walked directly toward the fire south of town. Sidewalks were covered with the shattered pieces of storefront windows along her path. She had no shoes and later we noted that she miraculously did not have any cuts on her feet.

Phyllis had, in fact, walked from the hospital to home and then back to the hospital. She was on her way home the second time when – through a miracle, my Mother would say – they saw Phyllis walking like a sleepwalker down Main Street. She was dazed and dirty, her hair tousled and sprayed with oil, and oblivious to the wailing sirens and frantic traffic whirling past her. She must have passed dozens of people, but they were too shocked to offer assistance.

Mother and Dad had been to the hospital twice and had not found her either time, and they had decided to travel to Galveston and search at John Sealy Hospital. On their drive to get out of town, they discovered Phyllis between Third and Fourth avenues, in front of the high school gymnasium, on her way home.

Dad screeched to a stop. My parents jumped out, wrapped their arms around her and swept her into the car. Fifty years later, Phyllis would tell me that that moment was the only time she ever saw our Dad cry.

They drove immediately to La Marque, gathered us from Aunt Louisa's, and drove us all 15 miles further up the road to my Dad's sister's house in Dickinson. I slept through that night, feeling secure that my family was all together and that we were far away from the fires and the dying that continued along the waterfront. The next morning, Mother told me that another ship, the *S.S. High Flyer* had exploded with an even more terrifying and devastating blast shortly after midnight.

Two weeks later, we drove back to Texas City and found the destruction unbelievable. The force of the blast had collapsed houses, smashed cars and splintered probably every piece of glass in town. Nothing remained of the buildings at the docks except charred wood and steel I-beams. Skeletons of burnt cars further littered the desolate landscape. Huge chunks of steel from the hulls of the ships had been rocketed all over town, in some instances miles away from the docks.

We returned to our house and found that the town had not burned to the ground as I had imagined it would. I also learned that, shortly after the explosion occurred that morning, Joel's mother had stood in the alley watching the fires and explosions, terrified about her son - and her husband, who worked at Monsanto. She didn't know what to do. A short time later, her husband came walking down the alley, but she did not recognize him. He had fought his way through the fire and debris and walked home, but he was unrecognizable, covered from head to toe with a thick layer of black oil.

They gathered their young daughter Jo Ann and began the anguished search for Joel. They found him at John Sealy Hospital in Galveston after two days of frantic searching. He had suffered a concussion and remained unconscious for a while, so no one had known who he was. Phyllis had cuts and bruises and burst ear drums. Both recovered. Butch's dad, Henry Chauvin, finally walked into his yard that afternoon, not seriously hurt. (He would live to be 100).

Our neighborhood had all of its people safe and, for the most part, sound. We were fortunate that none of our neighbors were among the 576 people who died. The collective consciousness of the town came under tremendous pressure. Individual families talked of moving because of the ongoing danger presented by the industrial complex. Some industries talked of closing rather than rebuilding the devastated infrastructure. And, although others made immediate plans for rebuilding, a huge psychological scar remained.

For a time afterward, whenever I heard a siren, I rushed inside, more often than not crying and expecting the worst. During reconstruction of the Terminal Railway and repair to the refineries, small fires would flare up. On several occasions, the same eerie orange smoke arose as small pockets of the remaining fertilizer caught fire. The fear started all over again.

For most of my adult life, I have carried a non-specific angst and I have often wondered if it could be a result of my experiences with the explosion, similar to what we now call PTSD.

In Greek theater, tragedy either ennobles or leads to despair. Texas City recovered its strength and became ennobled. The town buried its dead and paid tribute to those who gave valiant effort in countless ways. Then the people gritted their teeth and began the healing and rebuilding, a triumph for the human spirit. Texas City grew out of the ashes of disaster and prospered.

Dad repaired the damage to our house. There were many holes in the roof, and we found the steel rivets that had made the holes laying on our floors. He patched holes in the exterior walls and replaced windowpanes. Slowly, we returned to normal.

Note: Because some of the plant workers normally rode

bicycles to their jobs rather than driving cars, during cleanup of the wreckage around the refineries, these bicycles were gathered and stored behind City Hall so that they could be claimed by their owners. Weeks after the explosions, I found my bicycle in this pile of unclaimed bikes. However, the frame between the handlebars and the seat had been cleaved by a piece of shrapnel, rendering it useless. Dad and I scavenged the storage area for parts. Eventually I had another bicycle so that I could join Butch in exploring our world. A boy could not live in Texas City without a bicycle.

    -- Carl Trepagnier

Praise for RISE UP
from other survivors of
the 1947 Texas City tragedy

I was a small boy in April 1947, just as Carl Trepanier was, and reading *RISE UP* has recreated vivid images in my mind of the disaster that we both experienced. Carl Trepagnier brings a fresh new element in this account of the disaster that occurred in Texas City, Texas, in 1947. Other books that have been written are either based on first-person accounts or are statistical in nature, i.e., including mortality counts, physical and financial damage that resulted.

Carl has imbued his characters with feelings and emotions set in the ambiance of the time. He has told this heart-rending story of something that we thought could never happen to us, our families or our town, and placed an emphasis on individual victory over the unthinkable.

This is a book that will be bittersweet nostalgic reading for those of us who were there and an emotional experience for those readers lucky enough not to have been there!

-- Thomas Linton, *TAMU Professor Emeritus (Ret.)*
A 1947 Texas City Disaster Survivor

Carl's novel based around the 1947 Texas City Disaster, certainly stirred up emotions in me that I have not experienced in many years. The sadness and sense of loss within the survivors was almost overwhelming. Carl has captured the heartbreak – as well as the perseverance and sense of rebirth within Texas City's people – with his wonderful narrative.

-- Joseph A. Hoover, *Architect*
A 1947 Texas City Disaster Survivor

CPSIA information can be obtained
at www.ICGtesting.com
Printed in the USA
LVHW111620070422
714962LV00001BA/5